SURVIVING LOVE

SAINTS PROTECTION & INVESTIGATIONS

MARYANN JORDAN

Cover design: Cosmic Letterz

ISBN ebook: 978-0-9984832-6-9

ISBN print: 978-0-9984832-8-3

When I was a child, my parents took my brother and I camping...not in a big, modern recreational vehicle, but in a tent. In the 1960's and 1970's, most campgrounds were filled with families camping in tents or pop-up campers and I loved it.

We also went for hikes in the Great Smokey Mountains and some of my fondest childhood memories are of standing on a rock overhang and stare out onto the unsullied wilderness.

I dedicate this book to my parents, who wanted their children to appreciate the simple things in life and the beauty of God's world.

"Papaw, look!"

Thomas Jenkins grinned at his grandson fondly, appreciating the boy's enthusiasm. "I know, Marc. I see it."

The small Boeing Stearman PT-17, used as the family farm's crop duster, flew low as Marc looked out at the fields below. As long as he could remember, he had watched his grandfather go up in the plane. Begging his parents to let him fly too, they had made him wait until he was six years old. And now, finally, he scanned the fields below from the passenger seat, fascinated by the patchwork quilt view of the different crops with narrow lines of asphalt road cutting through them —he recognized the various roads and neighbor's farms as they circled over the county several times.

"When can I learn to fly?" he asked, watching his grandfather's hands on the controls.

Chuckling, Thomas glanced at Marc, the eager child bouncing in his seat, his denim overalls matching his own. "Soon as you're big enough and your daddy says it's okay." He added, "But no reason why you can't be learning some stuff when the plane is on the ground."

The idea of being able to learn the controls as soon as possible had Marc even more excited. Turning back to look out the window, he shouted once more. "Papaw! Deer!"

A herd of deer came running out of the edge of the woods and across the field below, fascinating the young boy. Turning back to his grandfather, a snaggle-tooth grin plastered on his face, he shouted, "This is the best thing in the whole world!"

Thomas agreed, "Well, I started flying out of necessity. I could dust my own crops and, since I could hire myself out, it was a way to bring in more money. Then I taught your dad so he could bring in the dusting money while I didn't lose any time on the farm."

"And I can do it too?"

"Sure thing, boy," he replied.

Circling around again, he brought the plane lower and lower as they approached the long, flat, dirt road he used for his landing field. Bumping along as they touched down, Marc clapped his hands and laughed out loud, completely unafraid.

Coasting toward the barn, Marc began to unbuckle but was stopped by his grandfather. "No, no, boy. Not until we've stopped. Safety first."

As soon as they came to a halt, Marc popped out of his seat and threw his arms around his grandfather's neck. "Thank you," he enthused. "That was the bestest!"

At eighteen years old, Marc was well over six feet tall. Working on the farm, as well as playing football in school, had noticeably honed his muscles. He filled out his worn t-shirt and jeans, having no problem catching the eyes of the girls at school. With a sly grin on his face, he remembered a few of the ladies in town checking him out as well.

Walking out to the field, he approached the bright yellow 1980 Piper Brave his father had bought. With his pilot's license, Marc took over the dusting part of the farm's business, earning money while doing what he loved.

Climbing into the cockpit, he grinned as he ran through the safety checks, thinking of his friends who were working as grocery bagboys or restaurant busboys for minimum wage. As he coasted down the runway and the plane lifted off the ground the rush of adrenaline hit him and he grinned wider. *Hell, yeah. Best job in the world!* As he viewed the world below, a surge of awe mixed with power filled his mind.

Looking down, he saw Misty Parsons on her daddy's tractor and he waved his wings as he flew over. He watched her wave and his cock jumped at the memory of her in the bed of his pickup truck. *Hell, nothin' better than a country girl who could drive a tractor and didn't mind gettin' her hands dirty in the great outdoors!*

He sobered as he thought of their last few conversations where she pleaded for him to stay on the farm, but he knew his future was not in agriculture. The first time his grandfather had taken him up in his plane, Marc knew he was destined to fly and travel as far as he could go. Her tears only served to annoy him, but he knew his mother would have liked for him to stay as well.

His grandfather understood. Had always understood. Marc thought back to his grandfather's last days two years before, when his cancer was finally winning. Marc had sat in his grandfather's bedroom, watching as the hospice workers came and went. Before slipping into unconsciousness the last time, his papaw regaled Marc with tales of his travels.

"I never had a college degree, but back in 'Nam, we was on a plane taking us away from a hellhole to back where we were gonna get a break from fighting. I swear, the pilot got shot soon after we took off and I crawled up in the cockpit and looked over at the co-pilot. I told him that I'd been flying planes for a long time and he could do what he needed to do and I could get us landed."

Papaw fell into a coughing fit and I jumped up to assist. As he lay back on the pillow, he said, "Hated the war, but gotta say, boy, I loved seeing other lands. Was glad to get home to your mamaw so we could get married, but..." his voice died away as he took several raspy breaths. "I loved flying to other places."

"I know, papaw," I agreed. "I do, too. I can't wait to travel the world."

My grandfather's weak eyes focused on me and he smiled gently. "You still got that St. Mark medal that your mamaw gave you when you turned thirteen?"

I reached around my neck and pulled on the sturdy chain, withdrawing the silver pendant from underneath my shirt.

Papaw smiled and said, "That symbol is a winged-lion. I remember when your grandmother was buying it, she said that anything with wings on it must be right for you. But then I looked at the lion and thought of the power. You're a big boy, Marc, and will be a big man. Use your strength wisely, but follow your heart. Travel the world...fly wherever you can."

"Do you think that mamaw was thinking of that when she gave it to me?" I asked.

Trying to laugh without coughing, papaw shook his head. "Hell, naw. She just saw it in a catalog and thought it was purdy. I was the one that figured it matched you real well. Nothin' wrong with having something to live up to." He stopped and coughed again before adding in a rough whisper, "But look for a good place to land when you're ready. Your mamaw was that place for me. Someday, find yourself a good woman and you'll have that place to land."

It was the last conversation he had with his grandfather and as Marc landed the small plane, taxiing back to the barn where his father waited, he knew he would soon be living the life his papaw imagined for him.

————

(Twelve Years Later)

The morning mist rose slowly over the Blue Ridge Mountains, casting the sunrise in a smoky haze. The woods in late winter were stark, bare trees mixed in with the evergreens. The quiet was broken only by the sounds of birds chirping and the rustling of leaves on the ground by whatever woodland creatures had woken and began their foraging.

Marc stretched his large, muscular frame as sleep slowly let go of his body and he worked the kinks out. Hearing a slight noise from the side he turned his head, smiling at the rumpled hair of his tent companion. Well, at least, companion for the night.

Hiking the previous day, he had run across another hiker as he turned up the path behind her. The view had been spectacular. Long, tan legs. Long, blonde hair. Great ass. As he walked alongside of her, he noticed her dark brown eyes and luscious rack. By the time he was ready to set up his campsite, she was ready to share his tent for the night.

And one night was just fine with him. One night was all he ever wanted. Still, he did not consider himself a player—his hookups were not very frequent. Sitting up, he rested his forearms on his bent knees and viewed the morning from the slit in the tent flap. Pulling the cool air into his lungs, he twisted his head to the side a couple of times, cracking his neck. Stifling a groan, he realized his thirty-year-old body was no longer as resilient as a teen's and sleeping on the ground now added a few joint aches.

His companion rolled over, her face still slack with sleep. He sat observing her for a moment, wondering

6

why he felt nothing more than just physical satisfaction. Bar hookups were sometimes necessary, but the heavily made up, high maintenance women he occasionally found never appealed for more than a night. But then, so far, the women he met while camping, who seemed to understand his way of life, had not stirred any interest either. *I just haven't found the right one yet.* That thought never used to bother him, but glancing back to the sleeping woman, he now wished he had kept this trip solo.

Rubbing his hand over his face, he sighed louder than he intended and watched as her eyes blinked before closing again. Slipping quietly out of the tent, he walked through the trees to take care of business before moving back to the embers of the campfire.

Stirring them to life and adding some wood, he built the fire up before setting a pot of water on the metal grate he had placed on the fire last night. A few split bagels and pre-cooked sausage patties were added to the thick aluminum foil to heat. After a few minutes, he stirred the hot water into mugs with instant coffee.

Sitting on a large, flat rock near the fire, he settled back with his coffee, watching the ever-changing vista in front of him. The sun slowly rose over the top of the trees, painting the winter mountainside in various shades of brown, bare trees and green pines and cedars. He could see his breath in the cold air before closing his eyes for a moment in peaceful reverie. His grandfather had taught him to appreciate each new day as a fresh start on life.

He knew miles below was his boss' acreage and

smiled thinking about the Saints' compound. Jack Bryant, while still in the Army Special Forces, had worked with a team of highly trained members, making up a multi-task force consisting of SEALs, SF, CIA, explosive experts, and others. Finding the team worked well together Jack re-created the idea of an exclusive multi-task force once he was a civilian. He recruited from SEALs, FBI, SF, ATF, DEA, and CIA for his new team. Top of the line equipment, weapons, security systems, vehicles, and computers—everything the Saints Protection & Investigations could need was at their disposal. For Marc, that meant his own equipped plane, ready and waiting at the local airfield.

The nine other Saints used to fill the local bar with him, looking for the night's entertainment, but now they were all in committed relationships. Somehow, they had each found their perfect mate...their place to land. Looking back toward the tent, he grimaced. *Not me...not yet. Maybe not ever.*

Soon the tent flap opened and the woman crawled out, sniffing the air. "Oh, my God, you've got coffee!"

"Instant, but yeah, it's coffee," he replied, handing her a steaming cup. "It's black," he added, then grinned as she wrinkled her nose.

Taking a sip, she nodded toward his backpack. "No sugar or sweetener in there?"

"Do I look like a sweetener kind of guy?"

"Hmmm, no I guess not," she admitted, taking small sips. Taking the sausage bagel from him, she ate heartily. Standing, she stretched her arms over her head exposing a band of tanned skin above her jeans. She bent down to tie her boots before moving back to the tent to grab her backpack. Throwing it over her shoulder, she grinned as he stood and walked over.

"Are you breaking camp today?" she asked, barely waiting for him to answer before standing on her toes to offer a quick kiss before stepping back toward the trail.

Observing her distracted body language, Marc was aware her mind was already on her day, no more interested in spending extra time with him than he was with her. *Shouldn't this make me happy? This is easy, so why do I feel...unfulfilled?* In theory, she should be perfect—loves to hike and camp, is able to cook outdoors, and has no compunction with getting naked out in the wilderness.

As he watched her walk away with a wave and a wink, he turned and stared out over the valley laid out before him, the sun rising a little higher in the sky. He broke camp earlier than he normally would, the sense of dissatisfaction taking precedence over the beautiful vista.

Remembering the words of his papaw, he wondered when he would find a good place to land. *But what does that mean? Maybe I need a woman who needs me also...but would be able to take care of herself as well. Does that woman exist? And if so...where the hell would I meet her?*

2

Marc stood in the modern kitchen of his log cabin, pouring a cup of coffee. Leaning his hip against the L-shaped counter, he sipped the hot brew as his eyes roamed around his home in appreciation.

He had built the home with the help of a log-cabin company. He had the company set the log frame on the foundation and then insisted he do the rest. *Well, me and some friends.* He grinned at the memory of quite a few weekends with the Saints all pitching in to add the roof and some of the heavier interior construction. *But then it was all me.*

Thick logs lined the walls of the open floor plan. The living room, with its stone fireplace, was separated from the kitchen and dining areas by a counter. Not much of a cook, he nonetheless made sure the kitchen appliances were good, though not top of the line. Heavy, masculine furniture filled the space.

Glancing at the clock on the oven, he knew Blaise would soon be there. Right on cue, his security alerted him to a vehicle in his driveway. Checking his monitor, he saw his fellow Saint's SUV pulling up to the house. Opening the door, he waved Blaise, Luke, and Charlie inside, all three heading straight to his coffee machine after greeting him.

"How's your ulcer?" Marc asked Luke.

Luke grinned at his fiancé, Charlotte—known to everyone as Charlie—as she rolled her eyes. "She's got me down to just one cup a day, and not my strong brew."

Charlie patted Marc as she passed him and said, "I told him he could have a cup of yours. Thank goodness Blaise was driving or I think Luke would have broken the sound barrier just to get here for his caffeine fix!"

Laughing, Marc reset his security as the four piled into Blaise's SUV, heading to work. The three men had often shared rides, living close to each other, and now Charlie had joined the Saints. As they drove the short distance to Jack's compound, the conversation was comfortable amongst the friends.

Pulling up to the security gate, Blaise quickly punched in the code and the gates swung open. The long, wooded drive opened to Jack's massive, luxury log cabin. Marc appreciated not only the view, but the structure itself, having built his own log cabin from the ground up—much smaller than Jack's house, but he loved his home.

The four walked up the steps to the wide front porch and entered through the front door. One thing Marc appreciated was that Jack and his wife, Bethany, considered the Saints to be friends and not just employees.

Greeted by the striking blonde, he bent to kiss Bethany's flushed cheek.

"Sorry, everyone," she gushed. "I've got to get to the cabins. Got a big wedding today and just heard the flowers haven't come yet." She ran over to Jack, quickly kissing him goodbye before running out of the house.

"Well, it looks like her decision to run a wedding business from her Mountville Cabins was a good one," Blaise noted.

"Yeah, she's busier than ever," Jack agreed, walking into the kitchen and setting out the cinnamon buns Bethany had prepared earlier. "Monty, Patrick, and Chad are already downstairs."

Jude and Bart walked in next. Both former SEALs, the two large men immediately headed toward the kitchen counter, grabbing plates and coffee before heading downstairs.

Cam, still yawning, came through the front door, scowling as the others laughed.

"Damn, that baby keeping you up all night?" Charlie asked, taking in his clearly exhausted face.

Blinking, he shook his head and replied, "We've almost got him sleeping all night. Thank God!"

Together, they all headed downstairs to join the others in the hub of the compound. Once settled around the table, Jack nodded to Luke, who had fired up his and Charlie's bank of computers, and now projected a photograph on the projection screen.

"This is our new assignment, which will fall mostly under Marc. I've already briefed him on what will be needed but, as always, in case he needs assistance, we all need to be aware of the specifics."

The group studied the photograph of an older man on the screen as Luke began. "This is Dr. Kenneth Rhodes. To the public, he works as a professor at Louisiana State University with the National Center for Biomedical Research and Training. NCBRT provides training and research to emergency responders throughout the United States and its territories under the Department of Homeland Security Training Program. In addition, he is an expert in micro-organisms used in terrorism and is currently the head of a discrete government think-tank."

Jack took over, saying, "There's an international bio-terrorism symposium going on right now in Fairbanks, Alaska. We've been asked to provide secure transportation for Dr. Rhodes from Alaska to D.C. The FBI and CIA have their eyes on the symposium and security is tight there, but they want to make sure he gets to D.C. to report to them safely...and under the radar."

"Sounds fairly routine," Chad commented, looking over to Jack. "Is there something special going on?"

Marc replied, "From what we've been told, the symposium group has been discussing antidotes for many of the micro-organisms that terrorists can currently get their hands on. But in the process, Dr. Rhodes is an expert in the antidotes for the micro-organisms that could be used for nefarious purposes, which makes him a target for terrorists, who'd like to interrupt his work."

"In the past, most terrorists used biochemical means

to simply strike terror, not necessarily to kill a lot of people," Charlie explained. "The intent was to interrupt business, trade, and bring governments to a halt trying to deal with the terror of possible threats."

"And now?" Bart prompted. The large blond leaned forward, resting his forearms on the table in front of him, his blue eyes scanning the group.

"Now, the possibility may exist that with only a few micro-organisms, large groups of people could be wiped out," Luke replied.

"Think of the plague back in the middle ages," Patrick said, shaking his head, looking over and noticing the grimace on the face of his brother-in-law, Monty.

"Who's going with Marc?" Cam asked.

"No one," Jack replied, immediately bringing the Saints to attention.

Why nots and *What the hells* resounded from everyone around the table, but Jack silenced them with a raised hand.

"The CIA and FBI have security at the conference taken care of, but they want Dr. Rhodes taken to D.C. privately by a secure plane. And," he emphasized, "they want it done unobtrusively. No official plane. Once Dr. Rhodes is there they'll escort him."

The others focused on Marc, whose slight smile was the only indication of any emotion on his impassive face. He looked around the table and shook his head slightly, saying, "Nothing new about the cloak and dagger from my CIA days."

The other Saints knew Marc was more than just a

pilot for the CIA in his former career, but now had a little insight into what his role really entailed. It was clear he must have completed many such bait and switch missions.

"It should be no problem," Marc confirmed, his forearms resting on the table.

"Nick Stone, our newest FBI contact, is finalizing the proceedings with Marc this afternoon," Jack added.

Monty chuckled and gained the others' attention. "Sorry," he said, still grinning. "Just wondering how long Nick'll be able to stand staying with the FBI. At some point, it'll drive him as crazy as it did me."

Jack leaned back in his chair, and replied, "He'll be welcome here if he decides to make the jump."

"Not sure the straight-laced agent would be able to adapt to our…uh…particular way of doing things," Blaise added, his smile matching the others'.

"What? You all aren't straight-laced?" Charlie asked in mock indignation.

The others laughed, appreciating Luke's fiancé fitting right in with their mentality.

"So what are the rest of us working on while Marc is taking a scenic tour of Alaska," Cam joked, still yawning.

"We've got some security details to work on. I've just settled a contract for the security system for the ammunitions plant Dani and Evie work at."

Chad's wife, Danielle, and Patrick's fiancé, Evelyn, both worked at a munitions factory north of Charlestown. Several breaches in security had brought the company owners to the Saint's door, asking for more thorough security.

"Luke and Charlie will work on the computer end while several of you will be assigned to the installations. It's a big job and will take over a month to complete, so we'll be busy."

The Saints began their planning session as Marc and Bart moved to the equipment room to choose what weapons and supplies Marc might need on his trip.

Marc, Jack, Luke, and Charlie were now alone in the compound, the other Saints having left to work on their own assignments. Luke connected Nick Stone up on the screen for their video-conference.

"Good to see you all again," Nick said nodding curtly. His dark hair, neatly trimmed, along with his brusque manner gave him a military countenance.

"What's the latest?" Jack asked, getting down to business.

"I don't see that much has changed since I sent you the brief. The symposium has world leaders in bioterrorism, as well as government officials, DEA, NSA, CIA, and what the hell other alphabet soups you can throw out there, all in attendance. Seems the threat of bioterrorism has increased and countries are scrambling to get the latest information on how to protect themselves, as well as ensuring they have antidotes on hand in case something happens."

"Anything special happening on the horizon?" Marc asked.

Nodding, Nick, grim faced replied, "Just found out that members of the Olympic security team are there as well. The next three Olympics are in the Orient—Korea, then Tokyo, and then Beijing. We dodged a bullet with the last Olympics, but there are rumblings that the next one may be a huge target. This makes Dr. Rhodes' research invaluable."

Rubbing his hand over the back of his neck, Marc asked, "Can you send the latest itinerary to us so I can finish getting my supplies ready?"

"Absolutely," Nick agreed. "In fact, I've got it right here. I'll send it to Luke and then you can let me know if you have any questions." Looking straight into the camera, he added, "And Marc? I'll be your point of contact for this mission. The agents in charge of the flight arrangements will let me know what's happening and I'll be in constant contact with you."

Nodding, Marc smiled. "Thanks, Nick. It'll be good to work with you again."

The screen went blank and Luke began sending the latest itinerary to Marc's tablet. Bart came out of the equipment room and looked over Marc's shoulder. "You let me know what you need and we'll get it packed into your plane."

Looking over the itinerary, Marc said, "Looks pretty straightforward. I'll fly up in two days, spend one day in Fairbanks at the same hotel as the symposium, rest, refuel, and then meet with Dr. Rhodes the next morning at the airfield. The FBI agent there will provide escort for Dr. Rhodes, so I won't be doing that security. We'll need to have a refuel break and the flight itself is about thirteen hours. I can do that, but they've also built in a break to be taken at my discretion." He looked up and added, "They don't specify where for security purposes, so I'll choose and be on guard during that night."

Jack signed off on the paperwork and Marc stood and headed back to the equipment room with Bart. Pulling the basic emergency equipment from the shelves, he and Bart packed two duffle bags with flares, lighters, thermal blankets, MREs, along with several weapons. He looked over the cold weather gear. "Better grab some of that as well, since I'm heading north."

"Take the Kevlar since you will be doing some security outside of the plane," Bart advised.

Marc nodded and continued to pack two duffle bags. Picking them up, slinging one over each shoulder, he smiled and said, "Think I'm ready for anything."

3

Flying over the western mountains of Canada, Marc viewed a valley surrounding a lake. Thick, lush forests as far as the eye could see, separated by rivers but no roads. Thinking ahead, with the knowledge that he could fly a water-landing plane to land on the lake, he smiled in appreciation of the untouched nature. *God, what would I give to be able to hike and camp there?* Deciding he would consider this as a possible vacation spot for next summer, he checked on his flight controls. The trip so far had been easy. He'd flown from Virginia to Washington the previous day and now was flying north on the last leg of his journey to Alaska.

A snow storm was predicted within a few days, but he and Dr. Rhodes would leave ahead of it and should be well away by the time the snow arrived.

Several hours later he landed at Fairbanks International Airport, taxiing to the hangar he had been directed to. Knowing the FBI had cleared one for him, he pulled inside, with the doors to the large hangar closing behind him. Climbing from the cockpit, he observed as a man walked from an office to greet him.

The tall man, with trimmed salt and pepper hair, stepped forward with his hand out as Marc's feet landed on the concrete floor.

"Marc Jenkins? I'm Kevin Pierce, FBI contact here in Fairbanks. Good to have you arrive safely."

Kevin's handshake was firm but, Marc noted, was not used as a power play, something he had often faced in his days in the CIA when someone wanted to show whose dick was bigger. Nodding in appreciation, he replied, "Nice to be here too."

Walking alongside Kevin, Marc listened as the FBI agent ran through the details for the Fairbanks portion of the mission. "We've got you booked in the same hotel as the symposium, though you won't be meeting Dr. Rhodes until tomorrow morning when you're back here. But you can rest, relax, have dinner, just enjoy yourself tonight."

Marc turned toward his Cessna and began, "I'll need—"

"We'll have you refueled by the time you get here tomorrow."

Nodding, Marc added, "I've got my own supplies and emergency equipment."

"Good, good," Kevin smiled, "but we'll have some things for you as well."

By this time, they had made their way to the dark-windowed SUV that screamed FBI, and Marc grinned as they climbed aboard. *So much for not being noticed.*

The drive to the hotel was uneventful, affording

Kevin the opportunity to keep up a running dialog about the area. "Fairbanks is the largest city in the interior of Alaska, but" he chuckled, "we've only got a population of about thirty-five thousand people. Not all that large compared to most major cities." He perked up, adding, "But we are known as the coldest city in America!"

Pulling to the front of the large hotel and conference center, Kevin let Marc off at the door and, as he turned to grab his overnight bag, Kevin called out, "I'll pick you up tomorrow morning at eight o'clock."

With a mock salute, Marc headed through the massive glass doors, the blast of heat a welcome relief from the frigid air outside. At the registration counter, he checked in, receiving his room card.

"We hope you'll be very happy during your stay," the efficient receptionist said. Her perky smile was firmly in place as she leaned conspiratorially over the counter toward him, lowering her voice to a whisper, "We have a conference going on and if I were you, I'd get your dinner a little early so that you can eat before all the others come into the restaurant."

Smiling, he thanked her and made his way to the elevators. Stepping out onto the eleventh floor, he walked quietly down the carpeted hallway to his room. Entering, he was pleased to see a king bed suite. Walking over to the windows, he looked out over the Fairbanks skyline. The sun had already dropped low into the sky even though the evening was still several hours away.

Turning around, he grinned when his eyes landed on

the plush robe lying across the thick comforter on the bed. *No way that'll fit me...even if I was a robe-kind-of-a-guy.*

Making a security sweep of the room, he found it clean before opening his bag, pulling out fresh clothes. Moving into the large bathroom, he stepped into the shower. The hot water sluiced over his body as he washed off the sweat, the travel fatigue flowing down the drain as well.

Refreshed, he dressed for dinner in dark slacks and a pale blue dress shirt. Securing his room, he made his way back down to the hotel's restaurant and lounge. His eyes traveled to the bar running along the wall and he noticed a woman sitting alone, her gaze raking over him. She was a beauty with blonde hair curling down her back and heavy makeup emphasizing her blue eyes and pouty lips. Her tight black dress had a slit up the side that bared her thigh, showing off a toned leg. She turned toward him, allowing the deep V of her dress to expose her impressive cleavage. She lifted her drink in a salute and her wink gave little doubt to her invitation. But the high maintenance look she sported did not appeal to him—not even for a night's fun. Turning away, he heard a slight gasp from her, causing a smile to slip across his face. *I guess she's not used to someone turning away.*

Moving to a table near the opposite wall, offering a view of the whole restaurant as well as a bank of windows at the back, he settled into his seat. After the waitress served his drink and took his dinner order, a large group of people came in, all talking at the same time. Looking over, he observed the eclectic ensemble, sure he was seeing many of the symposium attendees.

"Dr. Rhodes—"

Marc's head jerked around to see who was being spoken to, but a group of older men in suits, all with grey hair, were standing at the hostess station waiting to be seated, making identification difficult. As they walked past his table, he recognized Kenneth Rhodes. Silver hair. Goatee. Wire-framed glasses. Tweed jacket.

Glad to have laid eyes on his mission, he turned back to his steak, now that the waitress had delivered it. The food was surprisingly good and as he finished he gazed out the window overlooking a park. The dark night now created a mirror effect with the glass and he noticed a woman sitting alone at a table nearby, her head in her hand. Glancing over his shoulder to see if anyone else had noticed her distress, he observed as the waitress approached.

"Are you all right, ma'am?"

The woman lifted her head and offered a wan smile. "Yes, I just have a slight headache."

"The reception desk will have some aspirin, if that will help."

The woman's pained smile focused on the attentive server. "Thank you, but I have some medication in my room. I'll take some as soon as I finish my soup."

The server nodded sympathetically and walked away. Marc, concerned, continued to keep an eye on the woman. She finished her light meal and stood, wavering slightly as she held onto the back of the chair. He rose to assist but she gathered her strength and moved past him, leaving the restaurant.

Sitting back down he called the waitress over and nodded toward the now empty table, saying, "I believe the young woman was too ill to stay any longer and left. I'll take care of her meal as well as mine."

"Oh, thank you," the young server gushed. "I didn't even notice she was finished. That's very kind of you, but don't worry about it. She gave us her room number to add it to her stay when she came in."

"Really, I insist." Unwilling to look too closely at why he wanted to help the woman so much, he quickly settled the bills and walked back to the elevators, seeing the door just about to close. Throwing his hand out, he stopped the doors and stepped in quickly. To his surprise, the woman was in the elevator. She had a wet napkin from the bathroom in her hand and stepped aside so he could press his floor button.

"Are you all right?" he asked, seeing the pain evident in her eyes.

"I will be," she replied softly as though it hurt to speak. "This will help." She held up the napkin and pressed it to her head. "I get these a lot, but this one came on so suddenly, and my medicine is upstairs."

"Nothin' worse than feeling sick on a trip," he commiserated, then immediately wondered why he felt the need to continue talking to her when she clearly wasn't feeling well.

She was a head shorter than he was, neither short nor tall. Her brown hair was pulled severely back from her face and twisted into a bun. Black rimmed glasses were perched on her nose and a wisp of lipstick appeared to be her only makeup. Her unadorned white blouse was tucked into navy slacks, paired with a matching navy blazer. Completely different from the woman sitting at the bar, but she pulled his attention. Maybe it was how fragile she appeared, as though a stiff wind would blow her over. Sighing, he turned his gaze to the lighted numbers over the elevator doors.

Marc noticed they were both traveling to the eleventh floor. As the doors opened, he held the door as she passed through. Walking side by side, she twisted her head, her eyes wide as she looked up at him. He noticed and quickly said, "I'm not following you, I promise." Stopping at his door, he held up his room card between his fingers. "This is me. I hope you feel better."

She stopped at the door across the hall from him and offered a slight smile. "Thank you," she murmured before turning back to her door.

He watched her enter before walking into his own room. Later, falling into bed, his mind was on the woman across the hall. She was pretty, but compared to the dolled-up or athletic women he usually noticed, there was something vulnerable that called to him. Rolling over, he punched his pillow, willing sleep to come, as he tried to plan for his mission tomorrow. But his sleep was filled with the woman across the hall as they were both chased by demons in his dreams.

"So, have you met any Alaskan hotties?"

Rolling her eyes, Kendall held her phone between her ear and shoulder while slipping on her flannel pajama bottoms. After that, she pulled on her thick socks. With her research assistant convinced that the streets of Alaska were teeming with handsome mountain-men, she replied, "I hardly think that a bioterrorism symposium full of scientists and researchers is the place to find one!"

"But everyone knows that there are more men than women in Alaska. In fact, it ranks as the number one state in the imbalance between the sexes!"

"Karen, I flew in the day before the symposium, have done nothing but sit in one meeting after another, my head is splitting, and I fly back to Louisiana tomorrow. Just when was I supposed to get out and discover this inequity?"

Unable to come up with an answer, the phone line was silent for a moment. Finally, Karen prompted, "Well, at least tell me you met someone interesting in the hotel bar! I mean, seriously Kendall, you need to get out more. Life should be an adventure!"

A flash of the man from the elevator, who was this very moment across the hall, flew through her mind as a smile spread across her face. Tall, broad-shouldered, handsome in a rugged way. Sighing, she responded, "Nope, sorry. No adventures on this trip. Listen, enough about men...or my lack of finding one. I emailed you the notes from the last meeting. Did you get them?"

"Yes and I'll start working on them tomorrow."

Sitting on the bed, she let out a sigh, thinking of all that she would need to do once back in the lab.

"I hear that sigh, Kendall. You're already making lists!"

"Lists keep me organized—you know that!"

"Stop worrying about the research. There'll be plenty of time to get everything done when you get back. You said you had a headache? Are you warm enough? I know you hate the cold."

"Yes—I've taken some pills for the headache. And I'm trying to get warm. I took a hot bath, I've got my socks on, and I'm getting into bed under the thick covers. I'll be asleep soon."

"Okay," Karen sighed. "It's too bad though that you didn't meet some big, macho, Alaskan man at the hotel's bar."

Kendall laughed as she disconnected, her mind drifting to the man across the hall. Curling up, she jerked the covers to her chin, relishing the soft, warm bed. As she relaxed, she tried to keep up with the lists of things she needed to do, but a tall, dark-haired man filled her dreams.

The two dark-cloaked figures slipped around the large brick building on the edge of the campus of Louisiana State University. Stopping at the corner, hidden by tall bushes, they shifted their gazes around, carefully scanning the area.

"Do you think the security is still intact or has it been disabled as promised?"

Shrugging, the second person replied, "Don't know, but our instructions were to get in and get out quickly, no matter what."

Slipping through a window, strategically left unlocked, they padded down a long hall, coming to stairs near the back. The Do Not Enter sign on the door was no hindrance to them, knowing it led to the Biomedical Research Center. Immediately an alarm sounded and the two jolted as they looked at each other.

"Shit!" one cried as they tripped over each other in their effort to run back down the hall. Diving through the still open window, one landed on the other in the bushes. With furtive glances around, they ran to the nearest building, allowing its deep shadows to hide them as they continued across campus until coming to their van.

Climbing inside, they sat panting for a few minutes, neither saying anything as they watched police cars race down the main street toward the NCBRT.

"Was that supposed to happen?"

Nodding, the one in charge said, "I think so. We weren't instructed to take anything...just to cause a ruckus."

As more sirens filled the night air, one replied, "Looks like we were successful, then."

With a grin, the driver started the van and pulled slowly out onto the road in the opposite direction.

Rising early, Marc showered before throwing his toiletries into his overnight bag. Zipping it closed, he scanned the room as he walked to the door. Once in the hall, he stared at the door opposite his and thought about the woman inside. *I hope she feels better.* As soon as that crossed his mind, he wondered what it was about her that brought out a sense of protectiveness. *Maybe it's because she looked delicate. But not my type at all!* Deciding he needed coffee to get thoughts of her out of his mind, he made his way to the elevators. As the doors closed, he glanced back to her door once more, a strange sense of regret hit him, knowing he would never see her again.

In the lobby, it was obvious the symposium had ended as many guests crowded around the desk to check out with full luggage carriers and multiple calls for taxis being made. Towering over the others, Marc leaned forward and dropped his room card off at the desk before making his way through the throng. Seeing a coffee kiosk at the side of the lobby, he made his way over, smiling at the harried woman behind the counter.

"You're in luck," she said, returning his smile. "Just got a new pot so it's fresh."

"I appreciate it," he replied, reaching for the proffered cup. Taking a quick slurp of the hot brew, he closed his eyes, willing the caffeine to kick in quickly. Turning, he scanned the crowd to see if Dr. Kenneth Rhodes was in the lobby, but saw no one he recognized. Especially not the woman from across the hall. Shaking his head, he figured she was still in bed, probably with an eye mask over her face.

Moving through the crowded lobby once more, he stepped outside and saw the dark windowed SUV. With a wave, it weaved through the taxis and stopped in front of him. A bright-eyed young man was behind the wheel.

"Mr. Jenkins?"

Nodding, Marc threw his bag in the back and climbed into the front seat.

"I'm Henry...Henry Tomlin. But everyone calls me Hank. I'll be your driver to the airport this morning. How was your night? Did you sleep well? I know you've got a long flight today, so..."

Marc took another sip of coffee as Henry droned on, seemingly willing to talk and not wait for answers. After a moment he noted the silence and glanced to the side, observing the blush traveling over Hank's face. "Uh...I'm sorry, what did you say?"

Ducking his head, Hank replied, "No, no, Mr. Jenkins. It's me...I tend to babble too much when I meet someone. I've only been with the agency for a short while and this is the first time I've gotten to do anything by myself."

Chuckling, Marc tried to think back to when he had been that enthusiastic and recalled when he first began working for the CIA he had felt very similar. "It's okay, Hank. That kind of enthusiasm is good. Hang on to it during the times when the job gets to be more than you can handle."

The rest of the ride to the airport was filled with conversation as Marc listened to Hank talk about Alaska, the local FBI office, and his desire to begin investigating cases. As they pulled up to the security gate on the side of the airport, Hank showed his badge and began driving through. Looking out his window, Marc saw the large airport terminal to the right as Hank made a left and drove down a side road, hangars on either side. In a moment they came to the same large hangar where Marc left his plane the day before.

Driving inside and waiting until the metal doors slid closed behind them, both men alighted from the SUV. Marc grabbed his bag from the back and moved to the front to shake Hank's hand, assuming he was leaving.

"It was nice meeting you, Mr. Jenkins, but I'm staying until you lift off." Hank's eyes cut over to the Cessna and he said, "Is there anything I can do to help you get ready before Dr. Rhodes gets here?"

"No thanks," Marc replied. "I've got my own checks to do." He turned and walked over to his plane, walking around it carefully, beginning his checks. He looked at the fuselage and empennage, the right and left wings, the right and left wing trailing edges, and the nose. Climbing into the cabin, he carefully completed his pre-flight checks. Moving to the back of the small cabin he saw his duffle bags and made his way over to unzip the closest one, taking stock of what he and Bart had packed.

Just as he was about to check the second bag he heard a commotion outside and, leaning back, noticed a vehicle entering the hangar. Hank called out, "Dr. Rhodes is here," and the young agent walked to the back passenger door of a SUV that appeared identical to his. Kevin jumped down from the driver's seat and was walking around as Hank opened the door and assisted...*Who the fuck is that?* As a woman alighted and turned around, Marc stared into the face of the woman he met last night in the elevator.

Her business attire was exchanged for a light blue, turtleneck sweater and slim jeans. Wearing flat shoes, she appeared even shorter than she had in the elevator. She carried a coat in her arms, along with a purse and large tote bag.

Jumping down from the wing Marc stalked toward the SUV, catching the exact second the woman looked up and recognized him. Her head cocked to the side in question but, before she could speak, Marc got there first.

He stopped directly in front of her, forcing her to lean her head way back to keep her eyes on his. "Who the hell are you and where is Dr. Rhodes?" Marc bit out, noting her wide-eyed expression.

"Um..." she glanced to the side, her eyes searching Kevin's for a second, before turning back to Marc. "I'm Dr. Rhodes."

"You are definitely *not* Dr. Kenneth Rhodes!" Marc growled.

She straightened her back as she looked him directly in the eyes. "No...Dr. Kenneth Rhodes is my father. I'm Dr. Kendall Rhodes."

4

Kendall stared up into the face of the very handsome—and exceedingly angry—man who was glaring down at her. Swallowing audibly, she turned to look at the FBI agent who had driven her to the airport to see what his reaction was.

Marc swung his gaze from the wide-eyed, stunned-silent woman in front of him to Kevin, whose hands shot up in front of him in a placating stance. "My mission was to escort Dr. Kenneth Rhodes back to D.C. Who made the switch and why weren't the Saints informed?"

"For absolute secrecy, we had to make a change," Kevin said. "It was decided at the last minute that Kenneth Rhodes would go back to Louisiana early this morning and we would have you take Kendall to D.C."

Kendall watched in part fascination and part fear as the pilot turned sideways, to face the agent. As large as he was, becoming enraged sent power pouring off him. *All male...completely male.* As fast as the thought flew through her mind, she forced it out. *Ugh! He might be totally unlike the academics I'm around all day, but someone like him would never be my type...and I would never be his.* Irritated that that thought bothered her, she lifted her hand to her head, rubbing her aching brow. The headache from the night before had abated but was now threatening to reappear.

Marc dropped his gaze back to Kendall, observing her slight motion and pinched brow. As concern overtook his anger he softened his voice as he asked, "Do you still have a headache?"

Feeling the sudden change in his demeanor, she lifted her eyes and lied, "I'm fine."

Placing his hand on her shoulder, he turned her gently toward the office at the side of the hangar, moving next to her as he guided her along. Looking over his shoulder, he pierced Kevin with a glare and jerked his head, indicating the agent needed to follow. Entering the office, Marc ushered Kendall to a chair before moving to a water cooler. Allowing herself to be shepherded, she watched as he filled a paper cup with water before he walked back over to kneel in front of her. "Here," he said, his voice soft and low. "Take your pills."

Not sure what else to do—and besides, they would help—Kendall obeyed, her eyes still jumping between the other occupants in the room. She missed his comforting touch when he stood, letting go of her arm.

Marc turned back around to face the agents in the room. "Agent Pierce. My company was hired to fly Kenneth Rhodes. All the information given to us by the

FBI supported this. I want to know why there was a change and why my company wasn't informed."

Kevin, his hands still up in defense, replied, "Calm down and I'll tell you. We got word that there was a breach at the NCBRT in Louisiana. Department of Homeland Security still wants to talk to him but he flew back in the middle of the night. In his place, this Dr. Rhodes is the one DHS wants in D.C. pronto."

Marc swung his eyes back down to the pale woman still sitting in the chair, and rubbed his hand over his face. She looked up at him, uncertainty written plainly on hers. Looking back, he said, "Agent Pierce, I have a Cessna Skylane. It's a great aircraft but it isn't built for luxury. Dr. Rhodes is obviously not well and this is a long two days of travel. Wouldn't she be more comfortable with other accommodations?"

"We need to get her out of here and do it in the most unobtrusive way. With the breach of security in Louisiana, we snuck her out of the hotel this morning."

With his hands on his hips Marc opened his mouth to protest, when a soft touch on his arm halted his words. Jerking his gaze back to her, he saw strength in the determined set of her jaw, but was still conflicted with how to make the long trip more comfortable for her.

"I'll be fine," Kendall said, her hand quickly snatching back from the warmth of his arm. Standing, she plastered a small smile on her face. "I'm not used to luxury and will be fine, I'm sure."

Marc dropped his chin to his chest, a bad feeling in his gut about the change of plans. Sighing heavily, he pinned Kevin with his glare and said, "I've got to talk to my boss and to the agent that gave us this mission. Then, and only then, will I let you know if we will agree to the change in plans." Stalking out of the office, he left Kevin and Kendall behind.

"I'm pissed as hell, Jack—fucking FBI made a decision last night and didn't inform us. Does Nick know anything about this situation?"

"Hang on, Marc, Luke's getting hold of Nick right now."

Marc glanced back over his shoulder, able to see into the office through the large plate-glass window. Kendall was again sitting in the chair, her eyes closed as she leaned her head back against the wall. *Fucking hell! Taking a sick woman, unused to traveling in a small plane, on a long-ass flight—*

"Marc, I've got Nick on the line. He's pissed as well. No one told him about the change. In fact, he didn't even know about Dr. Rhodes' daughter. But he's just verified that Kenneth Rhodes was flown out by the FBI to Louisiana in the middle of the night. His boss says the contract has now changed to escorting Kendall Rhodes."

"Jack, I'm in a goddamn Cessna, not a private jet. She's not well and this could be disastrous."

"Marc, do what you've got to do. The mission is the same, with the exception of the passenger, which I agree, is a huge fucking change. But I'll inform Nick that she's not well and you'll take longer to get to D.C. I'd advise taking a couple of breaks...more than what you had planned."

"Got it," Marc replied, thinking that the increased number of landings and takeoffs would make her feel worse. "I just wanted the change confirmed. We'll leave in less than thirty minutes and I'll be in contact to let you know where we are." He looked back at Kevin pacing the room and added, "And Jack...I'll only be contacting you. Not the FBI. You can filter what you want through Nick. But I'm not sure I trust the agents here."

"Agreed," Jack said before disconnecting, leaving Marc standing with his hands on his hips once more, staring at his plane. Heaving a sigh, he turned to go back into the office.

Kendall watched in fascination as the large man stalked toward the office, his face now a mask. Unable to read any emotion, she bit her bottom lip as she waited to see what he would say now. He entered the office and closed the door behind him. Ignoring the other agent in the room, he walked straight to her, kneeling once more so that they were face to face.

"Dr. Rhodes, I'm Marc Jenkins of Saints Protection & Investigations." He reached out his hand toward her and she took it tentatively, immediately feeling the gentle strength in his handshake. She often categorized men by their handshakes and working in a male-dominated field, she had the opportunity to study her theory a lot. Some men would not shake a woman's hand and she knew they thought she was beneath them. Some men would grip painfully and she labeled them as men who needed to show superiority. Some men had limp handshakes and those she categorized as weak. But Marc Jenkins—his was warm, strong, but gentle. And she wondered if her fuzzy-headedness was from the headache medicine or from his touch.

Blinking, she realized he was watching her carefully and she jumped as a smile crossed his lips. "Kendall... you don't need to call me Dr. Rhodes. Kendall will do."

Standing while still holding her hand, he assisted her up. "All right, Kendall, I have a few more checks to make on the plane and I suggest you use the restroom. We'll get going in about fifteen minutes."

Turning to Kevin, he barked, "Make sure she has what she needs to be as comfortable as possible." With those parting instructions, he walked back to his plane, noting Hank standing near the rear of the Cessna.

"I'm sorry, Marc," Hank said quietly as Marc approached. "I had no idea about any changes."

Marc stared at the young man, wondering if he was telling the truth since he was not high up on the FBI chain and wouldn't be privy to all the details but, at this moment, he was not in the mood to have continued discussions with the Fairbanks agents.

Nodding, he climbed into the cockpit, redoing the pre-flight checks once more. About ten minutes later Marc watched as Kendall walked from the office toward the aircraft. Hank walked next to her, carrying her luggage and she held on to a large tote bag and smaller purse. Climbing down from the plane, Marc met her at the wing.

"Are you ready, Kendall?" he asked, observing her face carefully for signs of a continued headache. She appeared to have more color in her cheeks and her eyes lifted to meet his. Her gaze pierced his and he registered that they held trust. Reaching out his hand, he watched as she placed her much smaller one in his without hesitation.

"Yes, thank you," she replied, a small smile crossing her face before she let go. Her gaze jumped to the plane behind him and she confessed, "I've never flown in this type of plane before, so I'm afraid you'll have to show me what to do."

"No worries," Marc smiled, noting her gentle voice and pleased at her lack of demands. "Come with me." Opening the door, he said, "You'll be more comfortable in the back seats. Once we're in the air, you can stretch out and lay down if you like, as long as you stay strapped in. I can't guarantee you'll be comfortable, but I'll do my best to make the flight as smooth as possible."

"Oh!" she exclaimed, peering inside. "It looks just like a car!" Turning back to him, her smile more firmly in place, she added, "And please don't worry about me. I'm not needy and I'm sure I'll be fine."

Taking her tote bag from her, he leaned in and placed it on the floor before assisting her into the seat. "I'll have you sit on the right side, if you don't mind, since it'll be easier for me to see you there in case you need anything."

Kendall scooted to the side indicated and quickly buckled in. Marc turned back to see Hank and Kevin standing nearby. Kevin walked over, sticking out his hand for a conciliatory handshake.

"Really sorry, Marc, about the switch. I hope you two have a safe flight. Stay in touch, so we know where you are and what's happening."

Cocking his head, Marc replied, "Shouldn't be a need to. Flight is straightforward...unless you think there's a reason to be concerned?"

Eyes wide, Kevin blurted, "No, no. It should go like clockwork."

Nodding, Marc then turned to Hank and offered his hand, smiling when the young agent took it quickly, pumping it up and down.

"It was really nice to meet you, Marc," Hank gushed. "I hope everything goes well for you."

"Nice to meet you too, Hank. And keep that enthusiasm." With a curt nod, he turned and climbed into the cockpit, securing the door behind him.

With a glance into the back seat, he asked, "Ready?"

Kendall pushed her glasses up on her nose and nodded. "As ready as I'll ever be." She watched in fascination as Marc sat in front of a bank of instruments, calmly starting the aircraft.

With the front propeller whirling, they began to taxi. With a last look to the side, Marc noticed Hank and Kevin in a huddle, their heads bent in conversation.

Moving out of the hangar and along the pavement toward the runways, Kendall blinked hard. "I thought this looked like a car, but now I can see it looks like a spaceship up there," she tried to joke but heard her voice quiver with nerves.

Marc, headphones in place, glanced back at her, noting her fingers clutching the armrests. "Don't worry, Kendall. I've got this." She threw him a grateful smile, but he once more wondered how long this trip would feel with a possibly ill and definitely nervous passenger.

The tower radioed and he responded as they made their way to the runway. Getting his instructions and cleared for departure, he continued to the curve at the end. Lining up the craft they began racing down the straight runway.

Kendall watched out the window as they lifted off and the ground slowly fell below them. Unclenching her white-knuckled fingers from the armrest, she sighed in relief.

Concentrating on the take-off, Marc forgot about Kendall for a few minutes until they were at the altitude he planned on flying. Once they were on their way, he glanced back and, seeing her peering out of the window, he let out a breath. *Good...now if we can just do this for two days, we'll be homefree.*

5

Airborne, Marc settled back in his seat, keeping his watchful eyes on the instruments and occasionally glancing to the back. Kendall's forehead pressed against the glass as she peered out the window at the landscape below, her eyes wide behind the plain glasses.

The view of Fairbanks from the sky was beautiful and Kendall noted how the mountains in the background framed the city. The blue-green vista below was much more calming than she anticipated the flight would be. A river snaked through the trees and she finally felt her body relaxing.

Marc noticed her face was less tense and her eyes met his, another smile crossing her lips.

"How are you doing?" he asked. Her hair was pulled back from her face with a headband, but he noticed it hung down her back in a shiny sheet. It gave her a softer appearance than the severe bun she sported last night.

She pushed her glasses up again and said, "I'm fine.

The headache medicine makes me a little woozy, but I'm not in pain."

"Do you get them often?"

Lifting her delicate shoulders in a little shrug, she said, "Sometimes. Usually when I'm under stress or just really tired. I think the symposium was overly long at times, so I was ready to leave."

"Do you work on the same research projects that your father does?" Marc asked, desiring to learn more about her.

Her face brightened as she responded, "We work on many of the same projects, although he is more of a pure bio-chemist. My specialty is micro-biology."

Chuckling, Marc said, "I'm afraid basic college chemistry and biology was as far as I went with those subjects."

"What was your major?" she asked, leaning forward so she could view more of his face.

"Aviation Science and Aeronautical Technology," he replied.

"Have you always wanted to fly?" she asked.

"Long as I can remember. And did you always want to follow in your father's footsteps?"

She was quiet for a moment before answering. "I was good at science in school and, having spent a lot of time in the laboratories when I was younger, well, it just seemed to be a good major."

"That's not exactly a rousing endorsement," he observed.

Chuckling, she agreed. "I guess you're right. I can't honestly tell you that it's my passion, although I do love the research, just not the politics that go along with it."

"You hate the politics and yet I'm delivering you to D.C.," he chuckled.

"Ugh, don't remind me!" They settled into a peaceful silence for a moment while she looked through the window again, the breathtaking view passing beneath the plane's wings. "This area is so pretty. When I flew in, I was on a large commercial flight and had an aisle seat so I didn't get to see anything."

"Well, this'll give you the scenic view for sure," he said, relaxing more now that he accepted she was not going to be a diva passenger in such a small plane—he'd had enough of those to be a little gun-shy when taking a woman on board.

"We're so close to the ground I can see the landscape. This is much better than a window seat in the big airliner anyway," she proclaimed.

"We're flying at 13,500 feet so you're able to see much more." He smiled at her and added, "I'm glad you've relaxed."

"I'm sure I looked like a nervous-nellie when we first took off, but I'm really not afraid of flying. It was just a strange turn of events."

"Did you know about your father leaving early?" he asked, wondering where she fell in the FBI's need-to-know regulations.

Shaking her head, she answered, "No. I even checked my phone to see if Dad sent me a message, but he didn't."

"Is that unusual?"

Nodding, she realized he could not see her head when he was facing forward. "Yeah, it is. Dad and I are pretty close, and not just professionally."

Marc pondered that tidbit of information for a moment, determined to check on her father when he had a chance. *Maybe they took his phone from him or told him not to contact her until she was in D.C.* Wanting to know more, he asked, "So what were you told this morning?"

"About Dad?" Seeing Marc's head nod, she said, "I had set my alarm for about five a.m. because they said I needed to leave the hotel at six. I got up, got ready, and then Agent Pierce came to my room. He told me that our flight plans had changed. He said that our building in Louisiana had had a break-in and security had been breached. Then he told me that they flew dad out in the middle of the night to get back there to check on the status of our research labs."

"And for you?"

"He said that they had the private plane that was supposed to take Dad still ready to go, but that I'd be on it, since I was going to take Dad's place in reporting to Homeland Security."

Nodding silently, Marc tried to find a hole in Kevin's reasoning, but had to admit it seemed legit. Looking down, he said, "We're crossing into Canadian airspace now. You can see the western mountains below."

Grumbling, she slid her glasses off her face and put them in her purse. Seeing him twist to look at her, she explained, "I have contacts but they bother me when I have a headache. So, I've got this old pair of glasses, but they really don't fit well."

"Hopefully the flight will be easy and you can just rest your eyes," he replied.

"Are we allowed to fly here?" she asked, looking out the window.

"Let's just say that the Saints have permission granted by more than just the U.S. Government, in order to take care of business."

Laughing, she replied, "Wow, that sounds so clandestine! I feel like I'm in a James Bond movie!" She turned from the window and stared at the back of his head for a moment, considering what he just said about the Saints, and wondered how far off the mark she was with her James Bond comment.

Just as she was about to ask more, he began speaking into the mouthpiece connected to his headphones, codes and numbers that were all gibberish to her. With his attention in front of him, she stared unabashedly. He had shucked his jacket before climbing aboard and his black t-shirt strained at his arms, allowing her a peek at a tattoo on his bicep. His dark hair was neatly trimmed, not like the slightly long hair of many of her academic counterparts. His skin was tanned and, with the crinkles at the corners of his eyes, he appeared to spend a lot of time in the sun. Everything about him bespoke of power and control and yet, with her, he had been gentle and kind.

Looking down at her hands, she noted how pale she was. *I need to get outside more!* Her mind rolled to work and she wondered what was happening at the lab.

Pulling out her phone she checked again to see if she had received a text, but no messages had come through. She decided not to wait on her father and sent a message to her lab assistant, Karen.

Dad flew home – what is status at lab? Break-in? Please let me know as soon as you can.

A moment later, a quick reply pinged on her phone. **I have no idea what's happening. I'll check in and then give you a call.**

Rubbing her head, she was grateful for the pain reliever Marc had insisted she take before they left. Looking back down at her phone, the lack of communication from the lab was frustrating. Closing her eyes for a moment, she realized worrying about the situation would not help, so she began to think about the interview with the Homeland Security agents when she arrived at D.C. *Dad was supposed to handle this!* The symposium had been interesting from a research standpoint, but the International Olympic Committee representatives had hounded her and her father about possible terrorist activities. She readily accepted that the threat was real, but preferred her work in the lab to dealing with the politics of biological terrorist activity.

Grimacing, she wondered once more how her father was handling the situation. Chewing on her bottom lip, she calculated the things she would need to do as soon as she got back to the labs.

Marc glanced over his shoulder as he heard a heavy sigh coming from behind him. He saw her pained expression and said, "You should just lean back and rest."

She turned, seeing him staring back at her. Assuming he did not desire any more conversation, she nodded. Snapping a few pictures out of the window, she tucked her phone into her purse before leaning her head against the headrest. Following his suggestion, she closed her eyes, willing the gentle movement of the plane to ease her into a nap.

Marc occasionally looked into the back seat, checking on Kendall. Her head lolled to the side, but she was asleep and he did not want to disturb her. Having a chance to study her in secret, he noticed she was prettier than he first thought, but every bit as fragile as she had originally appeared. Giving a mental shake, he chastised himself for even looking at her as anything other than a client. *Sure as hell not like the women I go for.* The woman from the last camping trip ran through his mind, but he had to admit he could not pull her face... or name...up in his mind. *Guess that's what happens when it's nothing but physical.*

Calling in his coordinates, he focused on the flight and not the woman sleeping in the back seat. *Gonna be a long flight... with way too much time to think about things I shouldn't be.*

An hour later with Kendall still sleeping, Marc talked to Jack. "What did Nick find out about the security breach at the NCBRT?"

"That's why I called," Jack said. "Nick's been on the phone all morning and is still pissed as hell. It seems that it was a false alarm. The NCBRT wasn't actually broken into. Alarms did go off and security tapes showed a couple of dark-clothed figures in the campus building, but no one actually made it inside the research center."

"What does Nick think?"

"Not sure. He's doing a lot of checking and raising questions, but we've got few answers right now."

Marc's mind raced as he looked back, checking on his passenger. "Jack, it sounds like Nick's going on the assumption that there's something up with Kenneth Rhodes. What if it's the daughter that someone is interested in?"

"I thought about that and it's another reason I wanted to make contact. I know you can't get here any faster than you already are, but I don't like what I'm hearing."

"We're over the western mountains of Canada right now and she's sleeping. I'm going to let her sleep and we'll land for a break in a few hours."

"Stay in contact. I've got Luke watching your progress."

Disconnecting, Marc checked his gauges as he looked out at the vista below. The beautiful scenery, which normally reinforced his love of flying, had him thinking of the vast wilderness laid out in front of him. Sighing heavily, he willed the plane to go faster.

Another hour passed as Marc stared at the instrument panel in front of him, unwilling to admit what he was seeing: his fuel gauge was dropping rapidly. Double checking, he realized he must be leaking gasoline. *Fuck! How the hell did this happen?* Instantly his mind jumped to the only conclusion—*sabotage. And we're nowhere near an airport. Hell, it was as though whoever did this knew exactly how far he would get when the fuel ran out!* Mountains rose below him and, beyond that, thick forests of trees straight to the horizon.

"Kendall!" he shouted.

Jerking awake, she roused forward sleepily, blinking rapidly. "Huh? What?"

"I need you to make sure you're strapped in tightly. Pull on the shoulder harness and lap belt firmly until you can't move."

Hearing the alarm in his voice, she immediately swept the sleep from her eyes and grabbed the seat belt. "What's happening?"

Not answering her, she listened as he began speaking into his radio again.

"Luke! Got a problem! I'm fucking sure someone has sabotaged my plane. I'm leaking fuel but the fuel gage has been tampered with so I wouldn't notice the loss. No. No. I'm not sending an alarm 'cause I'm betting someone is going to be listening to see where we go down. You call it in to the official channels that you trust."

Hearing the situation from the back seat, Kendall looked out the window but the ground seemed to be as far away as before. Swinging her head back to the front, her chest heaved with each breath as she listened.

"No, no. Got no fuckin' idea. Get a lock on us and stay with us. There's nothing but forest below and no fuckin' road. It's like someone knew our flight route and fuckin' planned where we'd have to go down. Get hold of Nick and our Canadian contact. Yeah, I'll let you know."

Kendall's mind finally caught up to the situation she was hearing. *We're going down! Oh, my God!* Unbuckling quickly, she pulled out of her seat and moved forward.

"What the hell are you doing?" Marc yelled as her head popped up beside his.

"I want to come up here and sit with you," she explained.

"No, get back and get buckled in!"

"But—"

"No buts! Get back. I've got to concentrate and can't be worrying about you right now," he barked.

"Can I help?" she pleaded.

"No…I need you to be buckled tightly in the back where you'll be more protected."

Nodding, she moved back into her seat, re-buckling the seatbelt and harness. Breathing rapidly, she felt lightheaded as she grabbed the armrests, holding on as her eyes turned back to the window.

Marc's focus alternated between the instrument panels and intensely searching the horizon.

"Marc?"

He did not look around but heard her call his name. "Kendall, I don't—"

"I know, I know. I don't want to bother you, but please tell me what's happening. I need to know."

Her shaky words hit him and he recognized from the back seat, she truly felt more out of control than he did at this moment. Nodding sharply, he replied, "I'm flying lower so that as we lose power we can just skim down, even if it's over trees. Going in at that angle will be a much safer emergency landing. Now, I need you to stay calm and let me do my job. Can you do that for me?"

She nodded, then realized that he could not see her head. "Yes, yes...I can." Sucking in a deep breath through her nose, she let it out slowly, unsuccessfully willing her pounding heart to slow.

Nerves taut, Marc gripped the steering column of the aircraft, determined to land...*crash*...as safely as possible. He tried to wipe the fury of someone tampering with his plane from his mind, but was unsuccessful. *They fucked with it while it was in a secure FBI hangar.*

He eagle-eyed the treetops as he skimmed over them, determined to glide down as best he could. Hearing the engine sputtering, he knew time was running out and no strip of land large enough to land on was visible.

Luke came back on, saying, "I've got your location pinned. Charlie's working with Nick to find out what the fuck happened in Alaska."

"Tell 'em not to trust any of the agents in the FBI's office up there!" Marc commanded. "Someone on the inside must have been working against us." The sputtering increased and Marc cursed, "Fuck, we're going down."

With one last command to Kendall to put her head down in her lap, he lowered the plane into the treetops. The sounds of crashing filled her ears as the aircraft slammed against trees and her body jerked against her seatbelt, forcing the breath out of her lungs. With her head in her lap, whipping side to side, her forehead slammed against the arm of the seat. She threw her hands out to find something to hold on to, but the plane bounced all around before flipping over just as her screams pierced the air.

6

The plane came to a bone-jolting stop, tilting precariously to the left side, dangling above the ground as it rested amidst large tree trunks and branches. Marc jerked around in his seat, barking, "Kendall? Kendall?"

His breath left him in a rush as she lifted her head, brushing her hair from her eyes with a shaking hand. Her eyes sought his as she gasped, "We're alive?"

In spite of their precarious situation, Marc felt a grin tug at his lips with her question. "Yeah…we're alive." Sobering, he scanned her quickly, noting her wide-eyes and pale lips. *No bleeding…still strapped into the seat.* "Kendall, are you hurt?" He repeated the question as she gazed blankly at him.

Blinking, she finally replied, "No, I don't think so. I hit my head, but I think I'm okay." She gasped as the plane settled a few more inches and he ordered, "Don't move at all. Let me assess our situation and then we'll get out of here."

Marc's high-tech wilderness phone rang and he

grabbed it quickly. "Luke? We're alive. Landed but not fully assessed yet. Both appear okay for now. You got our location?"

"Yes, and all the Saints are here. Jack's got Nick on conference right now."

"Pull up the security videos from the hangar. I know either you or Charlie can bypass the FBI. I want to know who the hell fucked with my plane!"

"Charlie's on it already," Luke confirmed.

"We'll call when we're on the ground and I get my supplies." Disconnecting, he turned back to Kendall. "I'm going to see how to get us out and then I'll get my equipment. I need you to stay still until I can get you to the ground safely."

Nodding, she silently agreed, unsure her voice would be steady enough to speak. She watched as he unbuckled himself and carefully moved from the pilot's seat. She looked out of the left window, seeing the ground below. Thankful not to be too high in the trees, she tried to loosen her tight grip from the armrests, but her fingers appeared unable to obey.

The craft shifted slightly again as Marc maneuvered his way to opening the door on the passenger side. Sticking his head through he knew this was the best way to get Kendall to safety, as they were firmly pressed into a tight fit between three large trees. A blast of Artic wind hit him and he cursed once more. *Jesus, she's not dressed for this! If it was just me...*

Admitting his thoughts were not helping, he focused on the task at hand. One of the wings was sheered off but the side of the plane rested firmly against a tall tree with branches that could be used as a ladder to get to the ground. *Now, to get her out safely.*

Carefully squatting back down through the door, he looked toward the rear seats seeing the frightened, but perfectly still, woman and said, "Okay, you're doing great. Now, I need you to unbuckle and then take my hand and I'll get you out." She did not move a muscle. Instead, her gaze jumped from the window to him and back to the window and he recognized shock. "Kendall," he said softly, and then repeated firmly, "Kendall!"

Her eyes jumped to his and he said, "Unbuckle your harness."

A quick shake of her head was the only movement she made. Squatting lower, he reached between the seats and laid his hand on hers, gently pulling her fingers from their tight grasp of the seat. With one hand now free, he leaned back further and grabbed the harness buckle and unsnapped it. She fell forward and he caught her with his hand on her chest.

"Kendall...I need you to work with me. I'll tell you what to do one step at a time." Gaining a jerky nod, he said, "Take my hand."

His voice, both gentle and commanding, slid over her. Lifting her hand ever so slightly, she found it engulfed in his firm grasp. He pulled and her body moved forward toward him. The plane shifted again with her movement and she froze as a whimpering gasp escaped her lips.

"Eyes on me, Kendall. Don't look anywhere else but right at me." Marc saw the instant panic hit her face and worked to maintain her attention. "That's it," he crooned, gaining her attention. "Stay with me."

It was not easy to maneuver her between the front seats, but her small frame made it possible for her to step one leg next to his and then pull herself to where she was standing on the console next to him. As her face was now close to his, she whispered, "What do I do now?"

"I'm going to help you climb out the door above and I want you to grab anything you can hold on to until I get out as well."

"I...I can't," she said, hating the words but knowing they were true.

"If I go first and then help you out, can we do that?"

A sharp nod was her response and she prayed it was right. She watched as he hefted his body out the door and onto the side of the plane that was facing up. As he leaned back in, she slowly lifted her arms and allowed him to pull as her feet fought for purchase on the seat to help boost herself up. With her top half out of the plane, she could see the thick evergreen trees all around. A blast of cold wind slapped her face, causing her to gasp at the shock of it. Blinking rapidly, her gaze sought Marc's.

"I'm afraid..." she whispered, too fearful to speak loudly in case even a slight noise would shake the plane. Terror of plunging to the ground clawed at her throat as she watched, wide-eyed, at his movements.

"I've got you, Kendall," he reassured, his face close to hers. His warm breath hit her cold cheeks and she wished she were in his embrace with their feet already on the ground, not dangling from the treetops.

Marc continued to pull her gently until her whole body was laying flat on the plane near where the wing was sheared off. "We're going to slide to the big limbs over here and then we'll climb down, okay?"

She heard him ask but knew no response was needed. Scooting an inch at a time, the wind slamming her constantly, she held her breath until her hands clasped around a thick limb. Thankful another sturdy branch was in her sight just a few feet below, she slid first one foot and then the other onto it, while still clutching the top branch with her hands.

Marc shifted to where his large body covered her as he stood on the same limb. "Okay, we're going to climb down together, just like you would have done when you climbed trees as a kid."

"I…didn't," she breathed, her voice catching in her throat.

"You never climbed trees?"

Barely shaking her head, she breathed, "I didn't play outside very much."

Knowing she was out of her element, he nodded, glad she was staying calm. "Okay, just like getting out of the plane, we'll do this one step at a time."

With his body cradling hers, his hands on her hands, he shifted them down to the next limb. He could feel her heart pounding and her arms beginning to shake violently. "Okay, let's do this another way. I'm going to turn you around so that you're facing me. You'll wrap your arms around my neck and your legs around my waist...kinda like a backwards piggyback."

Before he gave her a chance to worry about the movement, he shifted her arms so that her body slid against his and she was now peering up at his face, eyes wide in fear. He smiled encouragingly as her hands locked around his neck and he used one hand to lift her right leg upward.

She immediately latched her leg around his waist and they repeated the process on the other side. Kendall was now completely at his mercy to get her to safety. Swallowing deeply, she closed her eyes tightly as he moved them down another limb.

"We've only got about twenty feet to go," he said.

She was not encouraged, instead clinging tighter, plastering herself against his chest. Jiggled every time he climbed down one more limb, she shook with fear.

"You should open your eyes," he said, worried about her pale complexion, no color in her lips despite the cold. "You would see how close to the ground we are."

Prying one eye open, all she could see was his face right in front of hers, his eyes holding her attention. Sucking in her lips, she watched as he offered a small smile as he said, "Almost there." With two more downward steps, his hands settled on her waist. "You're safe now."

She slowly unhooked her legs from his waist and lowered them to the ground. He kept his hands on her, holding her closely as she gained strength. This close, he could see her dark brown eyes held flecks of gold and green as they stared unabashedly up at him. Her pale skin was smooth and where she had been biting her lips, they had regained their color.

She shivered—from cold or his perusal she did not know—but welcomed his closeness nonetheless.

He took her hand and led her away from the tree they just climbed. "We don't want to be standing under the plane if it decides to fall to the ground," he explained. He wrapped his arm around her, hoping to offer some warmth until he could take care of her properly. Lowering her to the ground near a clump of evergreen bushes offering a wind break, he knelt beside her. Checking her eyes, he gently said, "Kendall, I'm going to lift your sweater to check your chest and abdomen for bruises from the harness. Is that okay?"

She nodded wordlessly before he quickly lifted the turtleneck and confirmed there were indeed red streaks across her chest and collarbones. Feeling her bones and running his hands along her ribs, he ascertained none were broken. Lowering her sweater, he noted the color in her cheeks as she averted her eyes.

"You'll have some bruising and soreness, but thankfully, nothing appears broken. What concerns me most is the bruise on your forehead from where you hit it. Lucky for us you already have that handy headache medicine, because I'm pretty sure you're gonna need it. You'll tell me if it gets too bad—we need to monitor for a concussion." With a mumbled yes and slight nod of her head as confirmation, he moved closer to capture her gaze. "I'm going back up to get our equipment."

As though the reality of their situation suddenly hit, she gasped, "Oh, my God." Jerking her head around, all she could see was thick forest. "What are we going to do?"

"Shhh, it's okay," Marc assured. "I always pack for every contingency. I've got two large duffle bags with emergency rations of food, weapons, and cold-weather gear. I'm used to camping, hiking—surviving outdoors. We'll be fine." Seeing her shiver, he pulled her back in and wrapped his arms around her, rubbing her back. "You stay here and I'll be back with everything."

"Who'll find us?" she whispered into his shirt, her face pressed against his chest.

"The people I work with will have us out of here in no time," he said. "Kendall, look at me." He waited until she leaned back and lifted her chin. "I'll take care of you. We'll be fine," he promised.

"Gooddamn, son of a bitch!"

Her legs having given out, Kendall had slumped to the ground, her back resting against the rough bark of a tree trunk. She had watched, amazed at the agility of such a large man, as Marc had climbed back up to the plane and was now screaming obscenities. Jumping up, she started to run over but remembered his rules. Number one was to do exactly what he said to do and the second one was to stay where he told her to stay.

Inside the plane, Marc seethed, unable to believe what his eyes were seeing. Having opened the first bag, the one he had started to check this morning before he was interrupted by the changes in the plan, he quickly zipped it back up and moved it to the pilot's seat so he would be able to toss it to the ground. Only half his supplies were there, including a sleeping bag, one of his guns and half his ammunition, some food, and a change of socks and underwear.

Turning back, he lifted the second bag but noticed it, too, was much lighter. Setting it back down, he unzipped it and roared as he realized someone had pilfered the contents. "Goddamnit!" As he took an accountability of what was left, he noted the second sleeping bag was missing, along with his other weapon and food. *Who the hell was there this morning? Hank! The little shit!*

Zipping the bag back up, he maneuvered it to the front seat as well. He looked to see what Kendall had with her and, grabbing her purse and tote bag, along with her coat, he moved them to the front as well.

Climbing back out, he hauled one bag after the other to the top of the plane before letting them drop to the ground.

"Marc? Are you okay? What's wrong?"

"Stand back!" he shouted, but then looked down to see she was still by the tree where he left her.

She watched as the large bags fell to the ground and then her bag and purse followed. Fighting the desire to scramble over, she was still afraid enough of being underneath the plane to stay still. It appeared steady, lodged in its tree hammock, even with Marc moving around inside, but she was not about to take a chance. *Besides, he seems furious and he told me to stay here!*

Marc disappeared back inside the plane to see what

else he could salvage. He pulled out all the identification papers, an extra coat he kept inside, a tarp and some rope he had hidden in the back for emergencies—thank goodness-- and another hidden gun. Tucking what he could inside the coat pockets, he put everything else in one of the bags and took one last look around. His anger, having already risen to the surface, was about to erupt. He knew the plane was insured and could be replaced, but the modifications he and the Saints had made for its security had made it the perfect craft for the missions they took. Now, he would have to start over.

Climbing out, he made his way to the tree and repeated the climb down. As he jumped the last few feet to the ground, he turned and looked at the pale woman still leaning heavily against the dark tree trunk, her arms crossed around her waist as though holding herself up. His job became exponentially more difficult with the knowledge that Kendall was completely unused to being outdoors in this cold weather, much less hiking or camping. And snow was coming. *No problem...I keep her safe right here for the evening until the Saints can get us picked up.* Sucking in a deep breath, his protective instincts in full force, he stalked toward her, not stopping until he was directly in front of her.

Opening the front of his coat, he pulled her forward before wrapping his arms around her, tucking her tightly against his body with the jacket covering both of them. "Let's get you warm and then I'll take care of what needs to be done so we'll be safe for the night."

"Night?" she squeaked, her voice buried against his

shirt. His body was warm as his size blocked most of the wind.

"No one will be able to get to us before tomorrow," he said against her hair, noticing the light floral scent of her shampoo.

"But what about the Canadian police? Or the Mounties? Or...or...someone who knows we went down?"

Wondering how much to tell her, he decided honesty in moderation was best. "Kendall, my plane was sabotaged...while it was in the custody of the FBI. The reason I lost my cool up there was because someone also stole some of my equipment, knowing that when we went down, if we survived the crash, we'd have less of a chance with fewer supplies. I'm guessing they either didn't have time to take it all, or figured I'd notice if they did. Either way, having half the supplies gives us a chance out here."

He watched her swallow deeply, her large eyes staying on his. "I don't understand," she said, her brow crinkled. "Why...why?"

Marc lowered her to the ground, slipping his coat off and wrapping it around her, glad that it swallowed her body. "I don't know. But right now, I need you to stay here while I make a call and talk to my people, okay?" He reached behind him and grabbed her purse and tote bag. "Here's your things in case you need them. I'll be right back."

She watched him walk about twenty feet away to make his call before her gaze drifted back to what was left of the plane dangling in the trees. *Sabotage...stealing supplies...someone wanted them dead.* Her breath came in pants as she tried to understand what had happened, but her vision blurred as she hyperventilated. Falling to the side, she curled up in his large coat, trying to keep from fainting as the fleeting adrenaline left her body weak.

7

Luke picked up on the first ring, jumping in immediately. "Got everyone here. What's your status?"

"We're fine…she's a little bruised, nasty bump on her head I'm keeping my eye on, but otherwise, unharmed. Brace yourselves for this though—someone fucked with not only my plane, but my equipment. Stole almost half my emergency supplies. And that's while my plane was sitting in a goddamn secured FBI hangar." Ignoring the freezing wind, it was barely able to cool his fury.

"Fuck!" was heard in the background from every Saint back in the conference room. Rubbing his hand over the back of his neck, Marc continued, "I've got some food, one sleeping bag, and I still have two guns. If the thief took the stuff last night, I've got a feeling that whoever did the stealing figured I'd check things this morning and knew I'd notice if everything was gone. If it was someone this morning, which narrows down the suspects significantly, then they probably didn't have time to take it all after I checked it."

Jack spoke, "Marc, I've got Nick on the line. He's already incensed about the entire mission changing and him not knowing anything about it, but this is upping the stakes. So now we have to go off the assumption someone is after Dr. Rhodes."

"Do you think they were after her father or is she the target?" Marc wondered aloud.

"No way of knowing right now. When you talk to her, see if you can find out what she thinks. How's she doing?"

"Mostly just cold and scared right now. Being stuck in the wild for a night is not her forte, but I'll make sure she's taken care of. We'll make camp here and wait for you to get a rescue to us tomorrow."

Jack agreed. "We're all on it and Bart's working with a contact—someone he trusts completely."

"Gotta tell you that I'm worried about someone looking for the plane...someone who might just want to make sure we're dead," Marc confessed. "I'm going to make a shelter away from here for us to stay the night. Let me know what you work out."

"The low will be about 15 degrees tonight," Luke cautioned. "And the wind chill will make it worse."

"Got it," Marc said. "We'll be okay." Hearing the hesitation from Luke, he asked, "Is there something you're not telling me?"

"You know snow was predicted but, what you may not have heard, is that the storm has been upgraded to blizzard conditions."

"Fucking hell, can this get any worse?" Marc growled. "Okay, I'll build a really strong shelter," he deadpanned. "You let me know when we can get picked up. It may be harder to get someone to agree to fly in here."

"I've got Bart and Jude on it," Jack said. "They're working with one of Bart's old commanders who flies. They'll coordinate as soon as they get the information. Tough to say this, but we might have difficulties communicating once the weather hits hard. We'll keep trying, but if we don't hear from you, or you from us... keep a level head."

"I always do," Marc assured him.

After a few more details were discussed, Marc disconnected and turned around, the biting wind forcing his mind to building a shelter, when he noticed Kendall on the ground.

"Fuck!" he yelled, jogging to her. Kneeling next to her, he checked her pulse as her eyes flew open. "Kendall," he said, gaining her attention. "What hurts? Your head?"

Sitting up, blushing furiously, she ducked her head. "I'm sorry. I just felt...overwhelmed and then faint. I'm sorry...I'm really fine." She tried to push up, but he blocked her way.

"Just stay there for a minute until I make sure you're okay." He looked over at her purse and asked, "Do you have anything sweet in there?"

"Yeah, some candy bars. Do you want one?" she offered.

Shaking his head, he said, "No, no. I want you to eat it to get your blood sugar level back up." He grabbed her purse and handed it to her. "I'll let you get it out."

Nodding gratefully, she reached inside and pulled out two Payday candy bars. "They've got peanuts in them," she stated proudly. "Full of protein. Here." She held one out to him.

"You eat one and keep one," he said.

"No," she protested. "I won't eat if you don't." Unwrapping one she broke it in half and handed a piece to him. "Here."

"I'm supposed to be taking care of you," he argued.

Ducking her head, her lips curved in a little smile. "I'm afraid sharing a candy bar is about the most helpful thing I can do. Please take it. I need you to be all right too." Looking back up into his handsome face, her smile faltered as she continued to hold the candy bar out toward him.

Taking the candy and popping it in his mouth, he chewed the sweet, salty goodness. "Hey," he said, "don't worry. We'll be fine. I'm going to find us a place to camp tonight and tomorrow we'll make our pick up arrangements."

"Camp?" she said, her eyes wide. "What about the plane?"

Rocking back on his heels, Marc tilted his head to the side. "The plane? Kendall...we can't...it's not usable any more." *Surely she understands that!*

A bubble of hysterical laughter burst out as she admitted. "I know that! It's missing its wings!"

He watched as her mirth slowly left but had to admit, he missed her smile as her face settled once more into fear. Reaching out, he tucked her hair behind her ear and said, "The reason we need to move away from the plane is because it's still very unstable and we don't want to be nearby if it falls closer to the ground."

He hesitated, wondering how much to caution, but decided she needed to know a little more of what the Saints were thinking. "Listen, there are other things that I have to be concerned about and I need you to under-stand as well." Gaining her attention, he said, "To be blunt, someone didn't want us to make it. Someone tampered with the plane and stole half of my gear. I have stayed off all traceable channels so, hopefully, they think we're dead."

She gasped at his words, so he took her hands in his, rubbing her cold fingers. "I have to consider that whoever they are, they may try to find the crash site. So, we'll go a little distance and I'll find a good place to build a warm campsite."

Her eyes shot to the side, seeing nothing but thick woods. "Do you know how to do that? Have you ever camped outdoors?"

Chuckling, he nodded. "Yeah…I've got this."

Wincing, she said, "Oh. You probably do this all the time, don't you?"

"I've camped quite a bit, you could say," he confirmed.

"I'll try to help," she offered, her eyes darting around, "although I don't know what to do. I'm not very…um… outdoorsy, but I'm good at following directions."

"No worries. This is my job. Your job," he paused, holding her attention, "is to try to think who might want you dead."

At that, Kendall's eyes jerked open wide in shock. "Me? Me dead?" she squeaked.

"I think we have to face the reality that someone wanted either you or your father gone. He was my original mission, so there's the possibility that he was the target. Or...," he held her gaze as he continued, "whoever did this knew about the switch."

Standing, he walked over to his two duffle bags and slung one over each shoulder before picking up her small suitcase and coming back to stand in front of her. "Get your purse and tote and follow me. We won't go far."

She quickly scrambled up to obey, but found her legs wobbly as she walked behind him, her mind grappling with the notion that someone might want her dead.

Marc slowed his stride, allowing Kendall to keep up. He noticed her shoes were unsuited for the outdoors, but was grateful she had dressed casually and was not trying to teeter in high heels. Her simple flats would keep her from turning her ankle. *Thank God we don't have to walk far.*

Moving to just out of sight of the plane crash, he discovered a natural shelter where a few downed trees created a covering that resembled a teepee. Dropping his bags, he quickly kicked the twigs out of the way and cleared an area where they could sit out of the wind. Retrieving the tarp from one of his bags, he threw it around the lean-to and secured it with some of the rope.

He pulled the one sleeping bag out next and laid it on the ground inside before putting the duffle bags in as well. Turning back to her, he saw her dubious expression. Trying to lift the mood, he swept his hand out in a grand gesture. "May I show you to your table, madam?"

Her pinched lips relaxed as a smile slipped out. She stepped forward and sat underneath the canopy, making sure to scoot to the side, knowing Marc would require a lot of room. He settled next to her, stretching his long legs out after arranging the bags nearby.

"Marc?"

He turned toward her, seeing the concern in her eyes.

"I'm having trouble wrapping my mind around all of this," she confessed, her breath coming in faster spurts.

"Whoa, whoa, slow down," he warned. "You're going to hyperventilate again." Twisting to face her, he placed his hand on the middle of her chest and pressed slightly. "Inhale…exhale with my hand. Push against my hand."

She worked to control her breathing so that she felt her chest expand against his hand, the pants coming slower and slower. He could not help but notice the curve of her breast underneath his palm. Inwardly chastising himself, he re-focused on her breathing.

"Better?" he asked, watching her carefully. She nodded and he moved his hand away.

"I'm so sorry," she said, tears filling her eyes. "I'm not usually like this. I don't know what's wrong with me."

"Hey," he said softly, taking her hand in his. "Look,

this isn't everyday life for me either, you know? I'm not used to emergency landings over the Canadian wilds."

She felt his fingers squeeze hers and the warmth spread up her arm. For one ridiculous moment, she wondered what it would be like to have a man like Marc holding her hand because she was an interesting woman...*and not a mess like me.* "So you don't usually crash land your plane?" she attempted to joke.

"No," he chuckled. "This is a first for me too."

Looking up at their tree accommodations, she said, "But you're used to being outdoors?"

Nodding, he answered, "Hiking is what I do to relax. I guess I've always liked being outside. This is not much different than what I usually do when I go camping." Glancing at their still connected hands, he realized he had no desire to let go. "Kendall, don't be too hard on yourself. You're doing really well." Hearing her give a derisive snort, he squeezed her fingers again. "No, I'm serious. You're not used to flying...you've just lived through a crash...you've held it together and not fallen apart on me. You're sitting here in a tree shack and not having a fit. Honestly...I'm impressed as hell!" As the words left his mouth, Marc realized they were true. *She might not be the typical woman I find while camping, but she's a lot stronger than she realizes.*

Her large brown eyes held his gaze and another small smile crept across her face. "I'm glad you're the one with me out here," she said. "You seem like the type of person who can handle anything." Looking around, she asked, "So, what's first with Survival 101?"

Reluctantly letting go of her hand he pulled one of

the bags over to him. "Okay, first you have to think about a water source. Then the weather, shelter, and food. Not everything was taken, so we've got some supplies and I have a half-gallon of drinking water. So that's taken care of. The temperature is going to drop severely in another hour or two, so we need to be prepared for that. I have one sleeping bag and clothing we can use to help stay warm. I'd build a fire but the winds will be too high, so the bag and clothes will have to do. Now, as far as shelter, we have this for tonight. We are almost surrounded by branches and fallen tree trunks. There's snow in the forecast, but we'll be long gone before that. Food? We've got that also. Always come prepared."

"Sounds like you've got it all taken care of," she said, admiration in her voice.

"Don't worry," he assured once more. "We'll be fine tonight."

"Uh...what about...well...uh..."

Seeing her blush as she stammered, he caught on quickly. "Toilet facilities, right?"

"Yeah."

"The best we can do out here is just give each other some privacy, while not going too far. And I would advise going while it's still daylight before we try to get some sleep so you don't have to go in the dark after getting warm."

Sucking in a deep breath, Kendall nodded. "Okay, I can do that."

He looked down at the one sleeping bag, sighing heavily. "Here's where it gets tricky. Normally when in a sleeping bag, you don't need many clothes. You don't want to sweat and have your clothes end up holding moisture. But," he sighed again, "we only have the one sleeping bag and therefore won't be as wrapped up as we would if we each had our own."

She started to speak and then thought better of it, deciding to let him work the problem out on his own. *It's not like I have a clue what to do in this case!*

"You'd better go through your clothes in your suitcase and put on something warm but not too constricting."

"Like just pants but no tights underneath?"

"Absolutely. I'm going to give you a chance to change." Crawling out of the shelter, Marc walked away for her privacy and quickly donned thermal long underwear and then two pairs of socks. Looking around, he found a place to relieve himself and noted a place to provide for Kendall. A few minutes later, he approached the camp. "Are you decent?" he called out.

A muffled laugh answered him, which he took to be a positive. The wind had kicked up and blew her hair about her face as she tried unsuccessfully to hold it back.

"Here," he said, as he pulled her cap off her head and twisted her hair all together before sliding the knit cap back on. Her cheeks were rosy with the cold air and the exertion of pulling on extra clothes. "Follow me and I'll show you where you can have some privacy to take care of your needs."

Crawling out, she trotted along until they came to a clump of bushes along a dense copse of trees. "You can go behind there and I'll...um...wait over here." Seeing her blush again as she hurried out of sight, he turned his back to give her more privacy.

Squatting behind a clump of trees, she fumbled with shaky fingers to get her pants down. Searching the ground to make sure she did not see any critters or snakes, she squatted. Quickly finishing, she fumbled getting her pants back up. *God, I hope he couldn't hear me peeing!* Trying to force her mind back to rational thoughts...*peeing is a bodily function just like sneezing.* Dropping her chin to her chest, she shook her head. *Nope, can't make this any better than it is. I so hope he couldn't hear me pee!*

Marc thought of the women he usually picked up on the trail who had no compunction about getting naked outdoors, taking care of business, or just getting down and dirty in the tent. Shaking his head at the direction his mind had wandered, he watched as Kendall came walking from behind the bushes, her shyness unexpectedly refreshing.

Stepping up to him, she lifted her eyes, forcing her gaze to hold his. "I'm ready to go back," she said, hating the way her face continued to flame with embarrassment.

Determined to make her feel more comfortable, he smiled and said, "Come on, let's get something to eat," as he guided her back to the camp. The sun had dropped beyond the line of the trees, casting their world into deep shadows. Marc held the tarp, allowing her to enter before he crawled inside and said, "It may seem kind of early, but let's get settled for the night so we can get warm."

Sharing a bottle of water, he handed her a high energy bar. Watching her sit cross-legged, nibbling the food, he hated to make the situation worse but knew questions had to be asked.

"Have you thought of anyone who'd want you or your father killed?"

Swallowing wrong, she began to cough and sputter. Quickly handing her the water bottle, he apologized.

"Damn, I'm sorry."

Eyes watering as she coughed a few more times, she looked up, saying, "No, I'm sorry. I was just surprised by your question, although I know you told me to think about it." Clearing her throat once more, she held his gaze. "It just makes no sense to me at all. Marc, I know we work on ways to identify possible biological terrorism, but we are certainly not the only researchers. We presented at the symposium, but there were many others there as well."

"Is there any particular group or issue that came out of the symposium that involved you or your dad directly?"

"The IOC...uh...International Olympic Committee met with Dad and me separately for a while and then Dad got the call that he was supposed to meet with a contingency at Homeland Security. During the symposium, we started discussing micro-organisms that haven't been used in terrorism before, but may become a threat in the future. The IOC wanted to learn more about that, considering all the countries present in one location for the Olympics."

"If I was to take your dad to D.C. then how were you getting home?"

"I was flying back commercial—the same way I got to Alaska." Seeing him tilt his head to the side, she explained, "We were originally going to fly together back to Louisiana, but then Dad was supposed to meet with Homeland Security along with the International Olympic Committee in D.C. and they wanted him to get back early. Then the agent came to my room this morning and told me plans had changed since Dad needed to leave in the middle of the night."

"Did that seem unusual?"

A slight chuckle escaped and she responded, "For the FBI? No. Every time we discover something new, they want in on all the information, even though Homeland Security is in charge of our labs. I sometimes think there is competition between the two."

"I'm sure there is," Marc nodded, thinking back to his days with the CIA. "There's always cooperation but each agency loves to pull some kind of rank and file shit." He watched her eyelids droop with fatigue and decided to question her more tomorrow. "I think it's time we turned in," he said, noticing her grateful smile. Reluctant to lose it, he had to continue anyway. "Sucks, but I'm gonna have to wake you every couple of hours to check on your head. Can't mess around with injuries like that."

Kendall sighed, wanting nothing more than to sleep, but nodded her agreement. Settling in, the smaller thermal blanket that had not been stolen was placed on the ground as he instructed, "Since we only have one sleeping bag, we'll lay on the ground with it over us." He hesitated before adding the next part, hoping she would have no objections. "Kendall," he began, "we need to sleep together so our combined body heat will keep us warm underneath the shell of the bag."

Nodding, she said, "Okay," hoping her voice did not sound as breathless to him as it did to her. Glad for his presence, she threw up a thankful prayer that they both survived the crash, knowing if she were out on her own, she would probably die this first night. "I'll do whatever we need to do to stay alive," she promised.

Smiling his appreciation, he lay down after making a pillow out of her bag. Opening his arms, she accepted the invitation and lay down next to him. She squeaked as he wrapped his arm around her waist and pulled her tightly into him before covering them with the thermal sleeping bag. She pulled off her glasses and lay them to the side before resting her head on his arm.

Stiff at first, she began to relax as the warmth settled over her. Exhaustion pulled at her body as she allowed the feel of safety to overtake her. *Crashed in the wilds of a Canadian forest and sleeping with a true outdoorsman... never in my wildest nightmares could I have even thought this would happen.* But as her eyes began to close, she knew if it had to happen, Marc was the person she would want to be with.

Marc felt her slip into sleep as her breathing slowed and evened. Thoughts of the enigmatic woman in his arms made sleep difficult. With her glasses off, he had noticed once more the colors in her eyes, making them so much more expressive than just the dark brown he originally saw. The floral scent of her shampoo, mixed with the earthy smells of the forest around them created a memorable perfume. Her body tucked in perfectly to his large frame...

His mind wandered to the women he had camped with...and slept with...and he knew Kendall was not like any of them. And yet, at this very moment...*why does she feel so right?* Dismissing it as nothing more than his protective instincts for a woman who needed him, he joined her in sleep.

8

Kenneth Rhodes stalked along the hall of the NCBRT, his shoes clicking on the tile floor. Karen Moore, Kendall's research assistant, hustled to keep up, her hands full of papers. Rounding the corner, they ran into Dr. Cliff Wallace.

"Any news from the police or FBI?" Cliff asked Kenneth.

Shaking his head, Kenneth said, stifling a yawn after being up all night, "I've searched the entire lab and gone over the security tapes with the FBI, but there's no evidence the labs were breached at all."

"So it was just some college kids acting stupid?" Karen asked, smoothing her black hair back from her face as she gazed admiringly at Cliff.

Ignoring the graduate assistant, Cliff turned his attention to Kenneth. "Does this delay your trip to D.C.? I was hoping you could brief us on the symposium first."

"Our plans changed and Kendall was sent to D.C. instead."

Cliff's eyes lit for a second before he hid it behind an impassive expression. "I see," he stated.

"And the attempted break-in here?"

Shrugging, Kenneth stroked his grey goatee as he replied, "The FBI hasn't told me if they have any suspects as of yet. And we don't know what their motives were."

"Dr. Rhodes!" a voice called from one of the labs down the hall. Dr. Hassem poked his head out from a doorway, signaling to Kenneth. "Can you come review these results before you go home?"

"Excuse me," Kenneth said to Cliff and Karen, as he continued toward the lab.

Karen looked up at Cliff and smiled. "Since Kendall is out of the way, is there anything you could use some help with?"

Cliff, his scowl now in full force, lifted an eyebrow as he stared at the over-eager graduate assistant. "Out of the way? Interesting way to put her trip to D.C."

Blinking rapidly, Karen said, "Oh, I just mean she's not here right now." Shrugging slightly, she added, "I know this will give you a chance to work on some tests that were important to you."

Before Cliff replied, Dr. Kowtowski came from one of the labs and saw the two talking. "Hey, guys. Any news about the break-in?"

"Will," Cliff acknowledged.

"Dr. Kowtowski," Karen greeted. "We were just

talking to Dr. Rhodes but it seems as though the break-in didn't affect the NCBRT."

Will nodded, "Good, good. So is Kenneth heading to D.C.?"

Grunting, Cliff said, "I've got to get back to the lab," and turned, heading down the hall.

"What's eating him?" Will asked, his attention moving from the retreating back of his co-worker to Karen.

Leaning forward conspiratorially, she said, "I think Dr. Wallace is irritated that Kendall is being sent to D.C. instead of her dad."

"Why should he care?" Will wondered aloud.

"I heard Kendall say that her dad would be one of the main speakers at the Department of Homeland Security and now she'll get the honor."

"Nothing wrong with that," Will said, looking back down the hall where Cliff disappeared in a huff. "She's probably more qualified than her father when it comes to certain biological terrorist activities."

Karen nodded, her attention now riveted on Will. "Since Kendall is gone, can I help you with anything?"

Smiling at the pretty graduate student, he said, "Sure! If you're caught up with Kendall's work, I could always use your help. I might even be able to persuade you to move to my section."

With a grin, she followed him down the hall to another group of labs.

Marc woke suddenly, his mind instantly alert. Glancing at Kendall, seeing her still sound asleep next to him, he carefully slid his arm from underneath her head. She mumbled, her eyes fluttering, and he whispered, "I'll be right back." His words sent her back to sleep as she rolled onto her side.

Slipping his weapon into his coat pocket, he crawled out of the shelter, the cold wind hitting him in the face. He slipped through the woods toward the sound of a helicopter hovering above in the pre-dawn light. A spotlight from the bird was sweeping the area and he hid behind the thick branches as he observed it circling around. Knowing it was not from Nick or the Saints, he wondered who was looking for them. *Canadian government?* He had been flying below their radars but knew there was the slight possibility they might have been spotted.

Placing a quick call, he knew Luke would pick it up immediately, sure that he was spending the night at the compound.

"Yeah?" Luke answered.

"Got a bird circling overhead. Who's searching?"

"Shit, not us and not anyone from the area," Luke confirmed.

"They can't land here but they've probably seen the plane. We can't stay here. I'm getting Kendall but need you to tell me which direction is best. From what I can see, there's a town about fifty miles southeast. Too risky?"

"Start that way and I'll let you know what we dig up as soon as I can, before the weather wrecks our communication. Gotta tell you that more snow is coming your way and it's going to make travel for you difficult as well as for us to get to you. Stay safe and we'll be in touch."

Disconnecting, Marc turned and hustled back to the camp, cursing that he didn't try to camouflage the plane more but, then, maybe the snowstorm coming would do the trick. Releasing a pent up breath, he knew he could easily take out anyone on their tail, but what about Kendall? *Fuck, this just keeps getting more complicated!*

Crawling inside the small shelter, he leaned over her sleeping form. Her face in slumber was at ease, her dark lashes resting against her pale cheek. Her mouth was slightly open and he noticed her breath forming a mist as she exhaled.

Shaking her gently, he said, "Kendall? Kendall? You gotta wake up."

Her eyes immediately shot open as she blinked a couple of times before focusing on him. Sitting up, she blurted, "What? What is it?"

"We need to get packed up and leave—"

"They're here? Our rescuers are here?" she interrupted with a smile.

"No, I'm sorry, but no. Someone else is out there looking for us and I doubt it's friendly."

Her smile slowly morphed into a confused expression as her brow furrowed. "Not friendly?" With a sudden gasp, she asked, "Like the people who tried to sabotage us to begin with are still after us?"

Her voice rose with each word and he shushed her with his hand on her mouth. "You have to stay quiet and work with me, okay?" He observed her eyes, wide with fright before they seemed to focus once more as she nodded. Protectiveness shot through him as he recognized her fragile state. Head injury, unused to outdoor-living, much less cloak and dagger, he knew she would have to rely on him completely.

"What do you need me to do?" she whispered against his palm.

Nodding appreciatively, he said, "Good girl." He began to roll the sleeping bag. "I can pack everything into one duffle and it can be carried on my back. I need you to choose only essentials and pack them into your tote. We'll have to travel as light as possible."

He looked down to her shoes and said, "What other shoes do you have?"

"Um…I have some boots with low heels. They're not for hiking but they're comfortable to walk in."

"That'll have to do. Get your boots on and quickly pack everything you can carry. We'll have to leave your suitcase hidden in here."

Swallowing deeply, she nodded, her mind racing to the task at hand. Crawling on her knees, she slid her glasses on her face and began packing.

Fifteen minutes later, she looked over her shoulder at the small shelter she had slept in, curled up with a lumber-jack of a man, sleeping peacefully after what had been a harrowing day. Sucking in the cold air, she hefted her tote on her shoulders as she turned forward, hustling to keep up with his long legs as he began the trek through the woods.

After only ten minutes, Kendall was winded. The

cold air hurt her lungs and the layers of clothing she wore made her feel like the Stay-Puft-Marshmallow Man attempting to hike. The forest was thick with trees but, being winter, the only greenery was from the evergreens. She was sure Marc was keeping his stride closer to hers but he was still slightly ahead. Wanting to keep up, she wondered how she was ever going to make it for an hour, much less for longer.

Grateful for the lack of underbrush, she trudged along, dodging low hanging limbs. She smiled as he held back some branches for her to pass through safely. The terrain began to change, becoming rockier with each step. The trees thinned some, but the rough path was difficult to traverse. Tripping several times, she blushed as she saw Marc turn back, his face full of concern as he observed her.

"I'm fine," she hurried to say, glad he kept going. *I don't want to be the one to make us stop.*

Coming to the edge of a steep cliff, he waited until she stepped right beside him. The morning sun had risen, throwing a bit of warmth, as well as light, their way. She looked up expectantly, waiting to see what directions he would give.

He took his time, allowing her to catch her breath, as they viewed the magnificent vista in front of them. The craggy mountains rose in the background with a crystal blue lake at the base.

"This is beautiful," she said, her eyes pinned on the scene. "It's like something out of a picture book of Canada."

Nodding appreciatively, Marc agreed. "I wish it were

under different circumstances, but yeah…this is beautiful. When I flew into Alaska, I thought about coming back here to hike sometime."

Snorting, Kendall looked up, a smile on her lips. "Well, you're kind of getting your wish, only I'll bet you hadn't counted on having to drag a lab-rat along with you!"

Sharing her smile, he looked down at the woman beside him, wisps of shiny brunette hair slipping from her cap, framing her face. Her cheeks were rosy and eyes bright. "I wouldn't exactly call you a lab-rat," he responded. "I'm pretty damn impressed with you so far." As he looked over the mountains to the west, he saw the dark clouds rolling in. *Snow is definitely on its way.* "This place is too open and we need to stay near the tree line in case another helicopter comes by."

They hurried down the rocky slope, moving to the forest bordering the west of the lake. After another hour of walking, Marc turned and looked at Kendall as she quietly struggled to keep up. Slowing his pace, he allowed her to come alongside of him. "How're you doing? Your head feel all right?" he asked, searching her face. Her cheeks were red and her chest heaved with each breath.

Offering a slight nod, she replied, "I'm okay."

Stopping, he stared at her, knowing she was lying but was stubborn about letting him know how she really felt. "You need to be honest with me so I'll know how hard to push us before taking a break."

Huffing, she looked away, her mouth pinched in a grimace. Finally looking back up at him, she replied,

"I've never been much for exercise so I can't lie and say this is easy. But I'm willing to do whatever we need to do."

He held her gaze for a long minute before smiling. "Okay…but you've got to tell me when you need a rest break."

She stared into his face and saw true concern as she sucked in a deep breath before letting it out slowly. "Okay…I promise."

"Good," he smiled. Looking back at his handheld GPS, he said, "In about five more miles, we'll run into an area that is rockier, but less forested. The problem with that is, while there's no place to land a plane, a helicopter could land…and could see us."

"Okay," she said slowly, not knowing what response was needed. "Um…you'll have to tell me what to do."

"It'll be longer, but we'll stay at the edge of the forest until we absolutely have to cross the open area."

"Why do I get the feeling there's something you're not telling me?" she asked.

Rubbing his hand over his face, he said, "The guys I work with…some are ex Special Forces and SEALs. Normally they could just come in and get us, but the forecast is blizzard conditions coming soon. We're probably going to have to find a place to stay for a couple of days until it passes."

"Okay," she said, her voice less sure.

"You keep saying 'okay,'" he stated, unsure how she really felt, but could see the uncertainty turning to concern.

"I don't know what else to say. This keeps getting

worse and worse, but we've just got to do what we have to until we can get rescued."

"I know this is hard," he agreed, his voice warm, "so here's what we're going to do. We'll keep going for a little bit longer and then find a good place to make a camp near the edge of the forest. It'll be better than what we had last night so we can get prepared to wait out the storm. Once it's over, I'll be able to get a signal to my group and they'll pick us up as soon as possible."

With no alternative, Kendall nodded, hoping her expression did not show her dismay. *I guess if I have to be wandering in a snowstorm in the wilderness, he's the best person I could be with!* In spite of their dire circumstances, it did not escape her notice that he was also the most virile man she had ever been around. Tall, broad, honed-muscles, capable. And those eyes...they seemed to pierce straight into her.

"Are you all right?"

His words jolted her from her thoughts and she quickly said, "Yes!" Clearing her throat, she repeated, "Uh, yes. Sorry."

As he patted her shoulder before turning to walk again, she rolled her eyes behind him. *I'm such a dork!* Hustling to catch up, she followed in step behind him, glad the thick forest floor was easy to walk through. With each step as she crunched along, she longed for a warm bed and hoped their rescue would come soon.

9

"Jack Bryant?"

Jack reached out to take the hand of the woman standing in front of the main building of the NCBRT. She was tall, her dark blonde hair pulled severely back from her face, which he noticed was unsmiling.

"Estelle Barnaby. Homeland Security liaison here at NCBRT," she announced, her words clipped as she shook his hand.

"Ms. Barnaby," Jack greeted. "This is Patrick Cartwright, one of my team. My security company was originally responsible for transporting Dr. Kendall Rhodes to Washington, D.C."

Patrick shook Estelle's hand, noting the firm grip and steely glint in her eye.

Sucking in a quick breath, she said, "I assure you the FBI has already been over the security measures with the head of the NCBRT. I can't imagine what you hope to accomplish here, now that we have determined there is no breach of the lab."

Not rising to her bait, Jack said, "Is there somewhere private we can talk?"

Bristling, she nodded once before turning on her heels and leading them inside, to an office down the hall. Entering, she moved to sit behind the institutional desk, motioning for Jack and Patrick to sit it the available chairs.

"I've been in touch with the agents that were here last night. I was assigned to coordinate Dr. Kenneth Rhodes' secure transportation to D.C. and without my knowledge a switch was made and he came back here—"

"I had nothing to do with that decision," Estelle protested.

Ignoring her interruption, Jack continued. "We're here because of new developments and need to speak to Dr. Rhodes, as well as other members of his team who may have information we're seeking."

Narrowing her eyes, she countered, "And what information are you seeking?"

"Who might want to kill him...or his daughter."

Stunned, she reared back in her chair, her eyes now widened. "Kill?"

Nodding, he said, "We need to see Dr. Rhodes now. You may stay for the interview, but we need answers."

Picking up her phone, she placed a call. With a few words, she hung up, saying, "He's on his way."

Five minutes later, Kenneth stepped into the room, his eyes scanning the occupants as Jack and Patrick stood up. Introductions were made and the group settled back into chairs.

"Dr. Rhodes, I need to let you know, first of all, your daughter, Kendall, is all right but the airplane she was flying in had to land unexpectedly in Canada."

Kenneth gasped, half rising in his chair. "What? How?"

"The pilot has confirmed his aircraft was sabotaged but they landed safely. He's in charge of her security."

"But—" Kenneth's gaze jumped between the two men.

"She could not be in better hands," Patrick assured. "My teammate is the best and we're working to get her back to safety."

"Please," the older man begged, his hands fisted tightly onto the arms of his chair. "Tell me where she is and what's happening."

"They made an emergency landing and are in the Yukon area of Canada. They have food and shelter and the pilot is also a survivalist, so they'll be fine until we can arrange the pick-up."

"But who would have done this?" Kenneth asked. "Was this directed at me? I was supposed to be on that plane."

"Sir, that is what we're here to determine." Jack looked over at Estelle, noting her silence. Her impassive face gave little away, making him wonder what she was thinking.

Leaning over, rubbing his eyes, Kenneth added, "You don't understand...Kendall is delicate. She gets headaches. She's not used to being outdoors...certainly not roughing it."

"We understand, but as I said, she's in good hands.

Sir, what we need to do now, is focus on who may have had reason to want either of you harmed."

"Kendall? No one could possibly want any harm to come to her," he protested. Shrugging, he added, "But then, I can't imagine who would want me dead either." He looked over to Estelle and said, "Unless it's just someone who wants to interrupt our research."

"And what would that be, sir?" Jack asked.

Kenneth focused his attention back to Jack and Patrick as he replied, "The NCBRT is used for training as well as research, but I'm involved directly in the research of ways to combat the effects of possible mass biological terrorism. My specialty is with chemical gases, but Kendall's area of expertise is in diseases, such as ebola, cholera, MRSA, and even...plague. Lately, her team has been involved in ways to contain these bacterium and viruses in the event of mass terrorism."

"And the symposium? Did anything come out of that? Anything or anyone suspicious?"

"No, not at all...at least not that I saw and she didn't mention anything. Kendall and I presented from our organization at different sessions and then we had separate meetings with a few international representatives and, of course, the International Olympic Committee. They were interested in some new discoveries we are making with micro-organisms that can be used in terrorist attacks."

Jack took notes and said, "We need to know who here was aware of your travel plans and when people became aware of the change."

Leaning back in his seat, Kenneth's brow crinkled as he rubbed his silver goatee. "You're trying to determine if someone was after me or my daughter?"

Nodding, Jack affirmed.

Looking toward Estelle again, Kenneth replied, "As far as anyone here, I can't say. I don't know who was called when the break-in occurred. For myself, I was woken about one a.m. by an FBI agent who let me know there had been a security breach here and I would need to be brought back to Louisiana immediately. I asked about the meeting in D.C. and was told that my daughter could replace me there."

Looking up sharply, Jack questioned, "And who would have made that call? Wouldn't that have been for you to decide?"

Clearing her voice, Estelle said, "That was someone from the Department of Homeland Security. When it was determined that we needed to have Kenneth return, I was told of the decision to have Kendall flown in his place for the meeting at Homeland Security."

Silence filled the office until Estelle squirmed slightly and continued, "To be honest, it was a switch that made sense anyway." Her eyes cut over to Kenneth and she said, "Kendall is more qualified to speak to the concerns of the IOC, who is working with DHS right now on preparations for security at the next Olympics."

"Who from here knew of the exchange?" Patrick asked, watching Estelle carefully as she picked up a pen from her desk and begin to fiddle.

"I spoke with Dr. Mahdi. He's second in charge of

the research and is directly over Kendall. He agreed the switch would be appropriate, once we were told that Kenneth was being sent back here."

"Anyone else?"

Shaking her head, she said, "No. There was no reason to involve anyone else and, quite frankly, that night we were all just focusing on the break-in."

"Gentlemen, I know you have a lot of questions, but I need to know about my daughter." Kenneth's eyes filled with moisture as he admitted, "She's all I have. Her mother passed away years ago and Kendall is my life."

Softening his voice, Jack said, "I understand, sir, and you have my word that we'll keep you apprised of her situation. Right now, she is being cared for and protected. My organization is working to retrieve her."

"You asked who would want to harm either one of us, but I can't tell you of anyone. We're not political... we're researchers."

"Yes, but what you research is important to possible terrorists and that alone makes you vulnerable."

"What do you need from us?" Kenneth asked, his voice eager as he eyed the two men.

"We'd like to speak to members of her team as soon as possible," Jack replied, the steel glint in his eyes causing Estelle to halt in her refusal.

Before she had a chance to speak, Kenneth nodded his agreement. "Of course. If you gentlemen will come with me, I'll gather them together."

Standing, the three men left the office. Estelle watched as they left, hearing their footsteps as they moved down the hall. Picking up her phone, she placed a call. "Investigators are on their way to ask questions." Not waiting for a reply, she disconnected.

The gasps in the hall were the only sounds disturbing the silence as Jack and Patrick carefully observed the gathering. Kenneth had gathered a group of fellow researchers who worked in the labs closely with himself and Kendall. The news that Kendall's plane had been tampered with appeared to shock the assembly.

After introductions were made, Jack said, "We will need to interview those of you who may have any information assisting our inquiry. Dr. Rhodes will let you know if you're needed and we'll meet in the conference room." Jack and Patrick moved into the provided room, followed by Dr. Cliff Wallace, who immediately met their greeting with a scowl. His eyes darted between them as his lips thinned.

"I was stuck here, so I have no idea what information I can offer," Cliff grumbled.

"What we need to understand is what possible reasons someone could have for wanting to injure either Dr. Rhodes?" Jack asked.

"Either? I thought this was just about Kendall?"

"Well, we have no way of knowing right now if the intended victim was Kendall or her father, since he was the original person who would be traveling on the plane," Patrick explained.

"Humph. How do you even know someone was after

her…or him, for that matter? Maybe the plane just had problems?"

Cocking his head to the side, Jack asked, "Why do you think that?"

"Come on…Kendall? The bunny rabbit? Hell, she's smart, but hardly the type to be a threat to anyone."

"What about what she knows? Her research?"

"She was hardly the only one who knew the research. It wasn't a team of one!" Cliff bit out. Leaning forward, resting his forearms on the table, he shook his head. "Look, despite what her father may have told you, she's no more qualified than any of us. I could have easily gone to the symposium instead of her…or to D.C. for that matter." Shifting back in his seat, piercing Jack and Patrick with his stare, he added, "So, it would be stupid for someone to try to harm her or Kenneth… there are plenty of us here who are conducting the same research and know just what they know."

Jack's gaze sharpened on Cliff, observing the irritation flowing off the doctor. "Did you know she was being sent to D.C.?"

"No, none of us did," Cliff grumbled. "For something like that, it should have been discussed and then decided on."

After Cliff, the next person interviewed was Dr. Fahdil Mahdi. The dark haired, middle-aged man came in, appearing more eager to assist than Cliff.

"There are always those who would want to stop our work here," Fadil said. "Kendall has led a group looking for antidotes for some of the possible terrorist biologicals."

"Would harming her cause the work to cease?" Patrick asked.

Shrugging, Fadil said, "No, not at all. The work here would still go on."

"What happened the other night with the break-in?"

"I was called, since Kenneth was not here. Estelle brought in the FBI and I arrived just after they did. I suggested that we have Kenneth return here immediately."

Lifting his eyebrow, Jack asked, "Why was that?"

"Because he's the director here. If anyone should be here, it would be him."

"So you knew he was coming here early and not going on to D.C.?"

Nodding slightly, Fadil replied, "I didn't know for sure but yes, I assumed he would just send Kendall in his place."

Dr. Will Kowtaski was next and was even more forthcoming. The smiling blond sat down easily and immediately began talking before Jack or Patrick could ask questions.

"I have to tell you, I'm stunned someone would want to harm either Kenneth or Kendall. I've worked in a couple of labs before, but this is by far the best run lab and both of them are very likeable. No one here would sell them out, but we all know the security risks."

"Security risks?"

"There are those who'd love to have access to our research. We not only try to help our government in preparing for possible biological terrorists, but in how to best combat those diseases if they should happen."

"What about stopping them from getting to the Homeland Security meeting in D.C.? Would that make a difference…either in the end result or in the timing?" Jack asked.

"I don't see how," Will replied, his brow crinkled with thought. "I mean, Estelle is right here…and she's Homeland Security, so…" he looked up at Nick and shrugged before continuing, "While she's not a scientist, she's aware of everything that goes on here. Even if Kenneth, or Kendall, did not make the DHS meeting, someone else could be sent or Estelle could report."

"What about the timing? If one of the Rhodes were unable to make the meeting now, before anyone else could get there, would that make a difference?"

"That's something I'm afraid I can't say. I work in the labs but I'm not at the level to know what the DHS meeting is about."

After several more interviews, they finished with Karen. The pretty, graduate student sat in the chair, her hands clasped in front of her on the table.

"I can't believe Kendall was in a plane crash! And stuck in the wilderness! I can't imagine anyone doing this to her…you can't find a nicer person!"

Realizing Karen had no problem talking either, Patrick prompted, "Any problems here in the labs? Any professional jealousy or disagreements?"

Eyes wide, Karen leaned in and said, "Oh, yeah! Dr. Wallace has been envious of Kendall ever since he got here. I think when he was hired, he thought he would either be top dog or promoted to that spot quickly. But

Dr. Rhodes…uh, Kenneth, has no intentions of retiring soon. And he runs a tight ship. Of course, Kendall is brilliant and she could easily take over for her father, which I think drives Dr. Wallace crazy."

Jack shared a quick look with Patrick but both men remained silent as Karen continued to babble about the persons in question.

"Now, Dr. Mahdi…he's a super sweet person but I know it must be hard sometimes for him. He came from Egypt and I know he still has family over there."

"Hard how?" Patrick asked.

"Well, you know," she whispered, leaning forward. "We're here to fight terrorism and let's be honest…most of our briefings deal with the middle eastern terrorists. But he's so professional and such a nice person to work with!"

"And Dr. Kowtowski?

"Will? He's a lot of fun to work with. Never seems to worry too much about anything but extremely smart when it comes to the labwork." Leaning back, a glimpse of a smile crossed her face. "I'm really lucky to have gotten this position. I graduate this spring and hope to get employed here when I finish my degree."

"So, do you have any idea who might want either of the Dr. Rhodes killed?" Jack pursued.

The smile dropped from Karen's face immediately, to be replaced with a gasp. Shaking her head, she replied, "No, no. It couldn't be anyone from here. They're both well liked. It has to be from somewhere else."

"But who would know of their travel plans?" Patrick queried.

"The only one who would know their exact travel plans would have been Estelle."

10

"Wrap the rope over that limb," Marc instructed two hours later. They had managed to get close to the edge of the forest where it opened out to a rocky meadow. A large creek snaked through the meadow nearby, disappearing into the woods. Gray clouds billowed as snow fell, blowing in circles as the wind swept around them. As tired as Kendall was, she still offered to help set up camp. At first he declined her offer, but she set her tote down and began to work nonetheless.

Appreciating the effort, he instructed her on what needed to be done. Once more, he found two downed pine trees leaning against another tree, providing the perfect teepee shaped frame. She swept out the pine needles and branches, creating a dry floor for their structure. The tarp was roped to the trees, creating a full-sided tent. With a slight opening at the top, he knew they could have a small fire for a while.

Kendall pulled as hard as she was able but her hands

ached with the cold. The wind picked up sending stinging snow onto her cheeks. "Is this good enough?" she called.

Marc came up from behind, his long arms on either side of her, taking hold of the rope as it slipped through her fingers. "You've done great," he complimented. "I'll take it from here. Go on and get inside and out of the wind. You can help get things set up in there."

His body surrounding hers felt wonderful as the wind broke on him and did not hit her. In truth, she knew it was more than just the wind break he provided that felt so good. It had been a while since she'd had a man's arms around her for any reason, and certainly not ones belonging to a man like Marc. Chastising herself for her thoughts, she shook her head in derision, sure his mind was on their situation, not their proximity.

With a fast duck under his arm, she slipped inside the shelter. This structure was a little larger than what they had the night before. She had lost track of time, but Marc said they had a couple of hours of daylight left. *Humph— daylight?* It was already so dark with the storm she could barely see more than about ten feet in front of her.

Kneeling on the dirt floor, she spread out the blanket on one side, remembering Marc had told her they could have a little fire. Looking up at the hole in the ceiling, she thought back to elementary school when she learned how the Native Americans had fires in their structures, the smoke escaping through the top. With her tote on one side and the duffle bag on the other, she sat cross-legged, waiting for him to join her.

After a few more minutes, Marc opened the flap and crawled inside as well, dumping a pile of rocks onto the center of the floor. With his flashlight, he observed the neat interior and smiled. "You did good," he complimented. With a small spade from his emergency supplies, he dug a hole in the center of the dirt floor, lining the perimeter with stones. Reaching outside the tent, he brought some branches and twigs inside, stacking them in the center of the stone circle.

"I really want the heat," she confessed, rubbing her red nose, "but how can we keep it from catching everything on fire?"

"The stones will keep the fire contained and retain the heat, so I won't need to build it too large. It won't take much to heat this place." Smiling at her, he added, "We'll be toasty in no time."

She watched, fascinated, as he efficiently made the fire pit and lit the wood. It soon crackled to life, throwing light and heat immediately around the tent. Slipping off her gloves, she eagerly held her frozen fingers toward the flames, the heat sending tingles through her aching hands. Looking at Marc sitting across from her, his day old beard adding to his handsomeness, she rolled her eyes. *Is there anything he can't do?*

"What is it?" he asked, seeing her movement.

"I was just thinking that you probably could have done this without any tools or matches, couldn't you?"

Chuckling, he shook his head in mock humility. "Yeah, I could," he admitted. "I took a couple of survival courses and," he shrugged, "I've often spent time outdoors without a lot of conveniences."

"I'm impressed. I've never been camping or hiking."

"Hey," he said, drawing her gaze back up to his. "Everyone has different things they like to do. I'm sure you have activities you enjoy." He said it as a statement, but hoped she would share. It was going to be a long night and possibly another day before they were rescued and he figured getting to know her would help pass the time.

"I was always kind of an odd duck," she confessed, then smiled when she noted his raised eyebrows at her comment. "I never quite seemed to know which group I fit into. I liked to wear pretty clothes and makeup, but I never fit in with the sorority types. I liked to read, but no one I knew liked the same kinds of books. And professionally...well, about the only conversations I have are with other people who are interested in micro-biology, specifically staph infections. That's a real conversation killer out on dates!"

He watched her shoulder shrug as she readjusted her glasses. Her smile was genuine, if a little sad, but surprisingly it was endearing. Touched, he watched the shadows of the firelight dance on her face and noticed how beautiful she was. Certainly not the in-your-face beauty that assumed every man would be panting after her, nor the comfortable-in-the wild kind of beauty that he usually tapped while breaking up the solitary trips he enjoyed. No, Kendall's beauty was singularly her own, made more apparent by her self-deprecating smile.

"So, tell me about the books you like to read?" he

asked, wanting to keep her talking. As soon as he said the words, he fought a grimace at the odds that the professional books she probably read...and wrote... would be to his taste. Her immediate blush caught his interest. Tilting his head to the side, he waited on her answer.

"Well...I...uh...like to read for pleasure...uh...to escape."

The silence grew while he waited, a grin now spreading across his face. "Are you telling me you read romance? Like Fifty Shades?"

"No! Well, not exactly," she corrected, her eyes now focused on the fire and not his face.

"So...?" he prompted.

"Okay," she huffed, "I like to read historical romance...you know, like pirates, or Vikings, or High-landers in kilts...books like that." She spared a glance up to his face, her blush still pronounced on her cheeks, but was pleased to see he was not laughing at her. "I know it sounds stupid...but some people have the dumbest idea about romance novels."

"Hey, I have no preconceived notions," he protested, throwing his hands up while grinning. "I find it inter-esting that you like something so different from what you seem." Leaning back against the duffle bag, he stretched his long legs out, reclining with his hands behind his head. "Okay, so tell me about the pirates."

Laughing, Kendall shook her head. "They're just... um...hot guys coming to the rescue of the damsel in distress," she said. Her brow crinkled as she shrugged. "I know that sounds terribly un-feminist of me but, honestly, most of the books nowadays, the heroines are pretty kick-butt and sometimes save the hero. Though, to be truthful, often the girl does need to be rescued too."

"Kind of like us?" he joked, throwing a wink her way.

She stilled for a moment before nodding, "Yes, I guess you could say that. I was definitely a damsel in distress and, well, you've rescued me."

"You're no damsel in distress," he protested, rolling to the side with his head in his hand, observing her carefully. "You're a lot stronger than many people would be in this situation."

Sniffling from the cold, she shifted her gaze around the makeshift tent, listening to the wind howl outside. "This is so surreal, you know?" she said softly. "Almost like it is something from a book that was suddenly thrust upon us."

Nodding, he agreed. *Surreal? Yeah, it is.* Realizing he never spent much time talking to the women he shared a tent with, he was surprised how much he enjoyed hearing her talk. *And gaining the rare giggle from her was a bonus.* Blinking, he forced his thoughts to something less likely to get his cock stirring. Sitting up, he reached into the bag and said, "Let's eat and then we can make our trips outside for the necessities in plenty of time to get back before it gets too dark and we turn in for the night."

The low building sat on a lonely strip of road, mountains rising in the distance. Bart, Blaise, and Jude stepped inside Cutter's Bar in Cut Bank, Montana, having flown in an hour before. Their eyes acclimated quickly to the dim interior as the sound of country music played in the background. The bartender looked up, his face impassive at the newcomers.

"Three beers," Bart called out and, as the bartender nodded, he looked toward the back where a large man was sitting alone in a corner booth. With a head jerk indicating the beers could be delivered to that table, he and the others stalked over.

The lone man lifted his gaze, eyes crinkling as he smiled in recognition. Standing he bypassed Bart's extended hand, grabbing him in a bear hug instead. Bart was a big man, but as Jude observed, the other man met Bart in stature.

"Holy fuck, Bart," the man greeted. "How the hell did you get uglier?"

Bart laughed, knowing his womanizing reputation from years ago had earned him the jab. "Ask my wife—she thinks I'm just as handsome as ever."

"Wife? You? Well, who'dve ever thought you wouldda settled." The man stood back and peered closely at Bart and nodded. "But I can see it...she must be something special."

"That she is," Bart agreed. "Preacher, I'd like you to meet Jude Stetson. Former SEAL and now a co-worker for the Saints. He's also married to my cousin. And this is another co-worker, Blaise Hansen, former medic and veterinarian." Turning to the guys, he added, "And this is

Logan Bishop. My former Lt. Commander. We know him as Preacher."

Logan shook hands, then invited them to sit down. "I got your message and have already looked into what we need." His dark brown eyes pinned Bart as he warned, "But they just got hit with a major blizzard and it'll be at least another day before we can get a bird to them."

Bart grimaced, but nodded, sharing a glance with Jude and Blaise whose expressions matched his own. "We understand. We just want to have it planned so we can lift off at the first moment possible."

"If your co-worker is as good as you say he is, then he'll make sure the woman is taken care of until we can get in. Have your tech person keep in contact in case they move somewhere else and I'll be able to get to them. If there's no place to land, we'll send the harness down." Logan saw the tight jaw of his former Lieutenant and said, "You know the first rule of the mission: don't let it get personal."

"I know," Bart growled, "but things are different now on the outside. The men I work for are friends...their women are my friends...and my wife is my world."

Jude nodded in agreement, catching the flash of surprise rush through Logan's eyes at Bart's words. The realization that this man had most likely never been in love hit him. And living in a town of only two thousand people in the northern part of Montana probably made it easier to be a loner. *Whatever...as long as he can get us to Marc and the doctor, that's all that matters.*

"I've got a place outside of town, where I keep my

helicopter. It's a small house, but it's got three bedrooms. God knows, I only take up one and don't have many visitors out here, so you're welcome to crash with me."

"Thanks," Bart replied. "It'll make it easier to plan." He looked up as a few men strolled into the bar, greeting the bartender. "Town's kind of quiet."

"They're good people around here. They'd help someone if they needed it. But for the most part, people stay out of my business and I stay out of theirs," Logan said. "I run my air tours and pretty much keep to myself."

Jude wanted to ask if Logan found that life boring after commanding a SEALs team, but kept quiet. Too many good men came back from tours with more scars on the inside than the outside. Whatever Logan's reasons were, they were his own.

Finishing their beers, the four men tossed money on the table and left the bar. Climbing into their SUV, Bart, Blaise, and Jude followed Logan's pick-up truck as it churned up the road leading out of town.

A few miles later, they turned onto a long gravel road, a metal hangar and low-slung ranch house in the distance. The snow covered mountains rose majestically in the background, the green forest at the base.

"God's country, for sure," Jude said, surveying the vista.

"Hell, I was just thinking I'd like to bring Faith out here for a visit. She's never traveled much and I think she'd love it."

"We passed a dude ranch on our way to the bar,"

Jude said, grinning. "We could bring our wives out here and have a vacation."

Nodding, Bart was about to comment when they stopped outside Logan's home. "Not much to look at on the outside, is it?" he asked.

"Hell, it's got to be better than the hotel I saw in town," Blaise added.

Climbing out, they grabbed their bags and headed inside. The interior was old, but clean and neat. Logan showed them to their rooms and then the men met back in the kitchen where Logan pulled out some steaks and potatoes.

An hour later, after stuffing themselves with the hearty fare, Bart leaned back patting his stomach. "God, that was a good steak."

Laughing, Logan nodded. "Montana's got good meat," he said proudly. He tossed the plates into the sink, rinsing them quickly before grabbing a six-pack of beer from the refrigerator. Settling in the den, they pulled out maps and began to plan. With Luke on the phone, Bart pinpointed Marc's location, then listened as Logan worked out their mission.

"Sure as hell glad you're here," Bart said, as they finished for the night.

"No problem," Logan agreed. "It's good to be doing something besides flying tourists over the mountains."

Later that night, Logan rose from his bed, satisfied the others were fast asleep. Slipping through the house, he opened the door leading from the kitchen to the basement. At the bottom of the stairs, he bypassed the open area to the right and stood at the wall on the left.

With a few clicks to the hidden keypad, the wall slid back and he entered. Moving to his bank of computers, he double checked the weather conditions for their mission and rubbed his chin. Behind-the-scenes mission planning had always been his forte. Smiling, he got to work.

11

"What the hell is going on?" Marc growled, the wind slapping little ice crystals against his face.

"Nick's run into a roadblock with the Yukon police who aren't talking to the contacts we had with the Canadian government. We're...getting a helicopter pilot...Bart...former SEALs and Jude's with him."

"Luke, it's already snowing here! White-out conditions. I can hardly understand you." He turned to see Kendall hunkered down in the makeshift shelter he made at the edge of the trees and cursed. "Goddamnit, if it was just me, it'd be no problem, but she's not used to this."

"Marc...team ready by tomorrow morning. Nick and Monty...Alaska to see what's going on...Jack and Patrick are in Louisiana. Bart...tomorrow...get a bird up and out...get you."

Sighing, Marc agreed. "I think that was a good plan —what I heard of it. We're gonna be safe and I've got a fire going so she'll be warm. We've got some food, so we'll be good if the storm lasts a day or so."

Disconnecting, hoping Luke got most of that, he turned and hurried through the snow to the shelter they made. "Kendall?" he called out as he bent to push his way into the tent. "I've just talked to my contact and they're working on a plan to get us out, but we'll definitely be here through tomorrow." He watched her carefully, but she just nodded, her expression full of trust. "We'll be fine, I promise," and with every part of his being, he meant those words.

"I was wondering about wild animals," she said, hating to admit her fears. "Do you think we'll be bothered?"

"Well, there're mountain goats, bison, sheep, moose, deer, elk, foxes—"

"Oh, no," she protested. "I'm talking about ones that might like to eat us!"

Marc had wanted to keep her mind off the dangers, but it seemed she was determined to ferret out the truth. Leaning forward, he nodded. "Okay, you got me." Heaving a sigh, he admitted, "There are wolves and bears."

"Grizzlies?" she asked, her mouth hanging open.

"Yeah," he admitted. "Although they should be hibernating this time of year, so we shouldn't be bothered. But that's why the food we have is in a metal box that is made to keep scents from getting out, but is also hung in a tree away from us."

"Anything else I should be aware of?" she asked,

tilting her head to the side as she viewed him from across the fire.

"Lynx, cougars, coyotes, wolverines, and timber wolves, but none of them should be a problem and, remember, I have two weapons and plenty of ammunition."

"But I don't know how to shoot a gun," she confessed. "And what if you're not around—"

"I will be. I promise," he vowed, holding her gaze, willing her to lean on his strength. Needing her in a way he didn't quite understand.

"I believe you, Marc," she said, a slight smile curving her lips, her hands still out toward the small fire as she wiggled her fingers toward the flames.

He smiled in return, holding his hands out to the flames as well. Unable to help himself, he reached over and took her fingers, rubbing them briskly. The action was meant to keep the blood flowing, but the sparks he felt jolting through his body had nothing to do with the cold and everything to do with the sweet body across from him. His dick twitched at the thought of what her sweet lips could do. His gaze jumped to hers, seeing her pupils dilate in her wide eyes at their touch. Jerking his hands back, he cleared his throat, searching for something to say to cover his discomfort. *Jesus, get a grip!*

"Uh...I'm going to head out to take care of business. I'll be back in about ten minutes. I'll pick up some more fire sticks while I'm out." Gaining her nod, he shrugged into his coat and zipped it up as he opened the flap and exited the shelter in haste, leaving her inside.

Stalking away through the woods, facing the ground

to make sure where his feet were landing in the soft snow, he tried to let the cold air clear his mind and calm his erection. Disgusted with himself for his lack of professionalism, he threw his head back and yelled his frustration into the storm.

Kendall, surprised at his abrupt dismissal, clenched her fingers, already chilled now that he was no longer holding them. She unfolded her cramped legs and stretched them out toward the fire. Her toes were achy with cold and she debated taking off her boots to stick her sock-covered feet closer to the flames.

Deciding to wait until Marc came back and she had a chance to step outside one more time, she crawled on her knees, moving a few things around to make the most of their space. Tucking her things on the far side, she lay the sleeping bag on the blanket, folding the top back as though they were in a fine hotel. Rolling her eyes at her unnecessary touches, she pushed his duffle bag to the back, making sure all flammable items were away from the small fire.

Finishing that, she looked at her watch, noting that fifteen minutes had passed. Biting her lip, she wondered if he were having problems finding some dry sticks. She almost decided to go outside, but the thought of stumbling upon him as he was relieving himself immediately sent that notion right out of her head. *I'm sure Mr. Outdoors can handle himself!*

Setting a few more small sticks onto the fire, she

watched it carefully, glad for the hot stones that circled the pit. Minutes ticked by and he still didn't return. Fidgeting, she continued to stare at her watch, twenty minutes now having passed. *Okay, if he doesn't come back in five more minutes, I'll go out and look for him.* Jolting, she suddenly wondered if he had run into the people that were after them. *Surely not. If his people can't get through the storm to rescue us, then there's no way they can... can they?*

Five more minutes ticked by and Kendall could not wait any longer. She zipped her coat and pulled her gloves on. Tucking her hair up into her knit cap, she then wrapped her scarf around her neck. Opening the flap of the tent, she stared at the wind-whipped snow blowing outside and wondered if leaving the safety of the campsite was a good idea. *I won't go far,* she determined.

As soon as she got outside, she was grateful the trees helped to keep the snow from piling too high, but noted the woods still all looked the same, blanketed in snow. Stepping out, she realized at least four inches of snow had fallen, but the drifts were much higher. Her glasses immediately became useless as the snow coated them in water droplets. Grumbling, she crawled back inside the tent and dug around in her purse. Pulling off her gloves, she found her contacts case and put them in. Blinking several times as her eyes watered and burned, she was reminded why she preferred the simplicity of glasses.

Crawling back outside she stood, ready to begin her search. *Damn, everything looks the same!* Taking off her red scarf, she tied it to the tree nearest their shelter, hoping it would serve as a homing beacon if needed.

Looking at the ground, she could still see the imprints of his boot steps in the snow and began to follow. Head down, both to track Marc's steps and to keep the snow and ice from pelting her face, she continued, knowing she would be able to find her way back by following her own footsteps. The farther she walked, the more irritated she became. *He was only going to take care of business—how far did he have to wander? Geez, it's not like I was going to leave the tent to go watch him take a piss!* Snow and ice stung her face and, without her scarf, she felt the biting, frozen chips hitting her neck and dropping down inside her coat. Frustration bolted through her as she kicked at the snow on the ground.

Suddenly her right foot slipped as the ground gave away underneath her. Grabbing a low hanging limb from a nearby tree, she somehow managed to keep from falling. Pulling herself back to safety, she looked over the edge of a ditch leading about five feet down to a frozen creek, the snow covered leaves hiding the edge from her view. Heart pounding, she clung to the tree, grateful not to have tumbled down the incline. *Damnit! I should have been watching what I was doing!*

Gathering her wits, she looked down at what appeared to be a large trench dug out of the snow leading toward the creek at the bottom of the ditch. Leaning over the edge for a better view, she clung to the tree trunk for balance. Gasping as she peered through the blizzard, she saw a large, dark object at the bottom of the ditch. Jumping back, her heart pounded at the thought of a bear. *But it didn't move. Would a bear be sleeping out in the open?* Not understanding what she was seeing, she blinked several times, trying to bring the object into focus. *Oh, my God...Marc! It's Marc!*

Without a second's hesitation, she held onto the branch as long as she could as she scrambled down the embankment, slipping and sliding until she reached the bottom. Falling to her knees in the snow beside his still body, "Marc! Marc!" she screamed as she reached for him. Grabbing his head, her right glove came back red with blood. Panicked, she looked around before chastising herself, knowing there was no one to help. No one but her. Spots formed in front of her as her vision blurred, a panic-attack imminent. Gasping for air, she bent over his body, placing her forehead on his back as fear clawed at her stomach.

Forcing her body to still, she focused on the simple in and out mechanics of breathing. After a moment, as the oxygen made its way to her brain, she lifted her head slowly, relieved for her cleared vision. Looking back down at the rapidly snow-covered body of Marc, she closed her eyes as she tried to make a list of what she needed to do.

Think, think! Shit! What do I do? His chest moved up and down with breaths. *He's alive.* The wound was not large and no longer actively bleeding. Gently shaking his shoulder she tried to wake him. "Marc... Marc, you've got to get up!" Nothing. *Okay, okay. I've got to get him back.* Looking up to the top of the ditch, she wondered how she would ever get him out. *Rope!*

"Marc, if you can hear me, it's Kendall," she whispered in his ear. "I'm going back to camp but I'll be right back." His hat had fallen off with his tumble and she found it nearby, gently placing it on his head, careful of his wound.

Using the branch she had clung to, now bent partially down the side of the ditch, she pulled herself up and over the top. Stumbling as fast as she could through the snowy forest, following what was left of her footsteps, she ran back to the campsite. Diving inside, she huddled over the duffle bag, rummaging through until she found another bundle of rope. Unsure if it would be enough, she crawled back outside and untied a length from the tarp. Cursing herself for being so scatterbrained, she dashed back into the tent, wasting precious moments, grabbing the military-grade flashlight she had seen Marc use and shoving it into her pocket. Crawling back out once more, she noticed the evening shadows deepening and knew she had to hurry.

The snow created a blinding panorama, but she followed her footsteps from before. Thinking to make the path more visible when she returned, she began to drag her feet, creating a deeper trench in the snow. Coming to the ditch, she stopped at the tree, peering over the side to assess the situation. Her breath came out in frosty pants as her lungs screamed for air. *If I get out of this alive, I'm joining a gym*, she vowed, irritated at her exhaustion.

Standing in indecision for a moment, she looked around, hoping the answer to getting him to safety would just present itself. *Damnit! Think, Kendall.* Jerking her head to the side, she looked at the tree next to her and threw the end of the rope round the trunk, tying it securely. Taking the other end of the rope, she slid back down the hill, landing at Marc's motionless body.

Bending close, she brushed the snow from his face, his eyes still closed. Panic again threatened, her hand shaking as she rolled him to his back. Maneuvering the rope underneath his back and up through his armpits, she tied it tightly around his chest before climbing back up the embankment.

Looping the rope around her arms before grasping the end, she pulled as hard as she could but her feet slipped on the snowy leaves causing her to land on her ass. "Damnit!" she screamed out her frustration. Scrambling to her feet, she stepped to the back of the tree, planting her feet against its trunk, using it as leverage as she pulled again. This time, she felt Marc's full weight against the rope as he moved slightly. Pulling again, she realized he was only moving inches.

Cold, mixed with fear, clawed at her, feeling hopeless with each movement. Swallowing back the tears, she prayed as she grasped the rope and pulled again...over and over. With each heave, his body inched closer. Arms aching, she peeked over the side. *Only halfway up! Oh Jesus! And when I finally get him up, how the hell will I get him back?* Refusing to think about that, she focused on pulling on the rope one hand at a time. Just when she thought she could go no further, she saw his head and shoulders clear the top of the ditch.

With renewed effort, she continued hauling until his back was on the firm ground, only his legs still dangling below. Running over, she heaved him by his coat until he fully rested on the forest floor.

Falling by his chest, she checked his breathing. She lay her head on his shoulder as her lungs gasped for air. "Ke-nal," she heard, jerking up to see his eyes blinking.

"Marc!"

"Wha..." he moaned.

"You fell...down a ditch. It wasn't too deep but you hit your head."

"You...gah..."

"I pulled you out of the ditch with some rope, but Marc, I don't think I can drag you all the way back." She held his face in her hands, brushing the swirling snow from his cheeks as she stared into his unfocused eyes. The night was falling fast and, soon, there would be no more light. *I've got to get him back.* "Please help me," she begged, calling out both to him and to God. Untying the rope, she fumbled as she looped it over her shoulder.

His eyes blinked a few more times before staying open. "Hel...me...uh..." His head pounded but it was the pain in his ankle that shot through his leg, incapacitating him. Inwardly cursing his inability to help himself, he tried to sit up.

Squatting in the snow behind him, Kendall pushed on his shoulders as hard as she could, forcing him to a sitting position. He teetered, but she held fast, keeping him from falling back to the ground. "Come on," she pleaded as she got her shoulder under his armpit and forced him upward. His considerable weight caused her knees to buckle and she scrambled on the slick path to find her footing.

Finally getting him to his feet, she attempted to help him take a step, but he dropped back to his knees, grimacing in pain.

Oh, God. His foot's hurt too! "Marc, use me as your crutch. Hop on one foot and lean on me!" She had no idea if he was able to hear her, but he threw his heavy arm over her shoulders, nearly knocking her off balance once again.

With Marc hobbling and Kendall buried under his weight, praying every step, they slowly made their way back toward the campsite. The night had descended but with the powerful flashlight held in the hand she had wrapped around his waist and pointed toward the ground, she forced them along the path of her previous footsteps, now almost covered in fresh snow.

Staggering along the way, she blinked at the stinging ice hitting her face, her heart racing in a mixture of fear and adrenaline. "Marc? You still with me? Gotta hang with me. It's not too much further. We'll just go one step at a time, okay?" Rambling loudly with each step, she cursed as they stumbled. Without her scarf around her neck, the snow blew down the back of her jacket, making the cold even worse. Sucking in frozen air, she doubted her ability to go much further. Propping his back against a tree trunk with her hand pressing against his chest to steady him, she gasped for air for a minute before trying to continue.

The swirling snow, the dark night, the illumination from the flashlight bouncing in front of them, all created a kaleidoscope of fear, causing Kendall's tears to freeze on her face. A flash of her red scarf, still tied to the tree in the distance, finally caught her eye and she yelled, "We're there, we're there!"

At the entrance to the tent, she tried to lower him to the ground, but he tumbled forward, landing with a thud just outside the entrance. Grimacing, she peeked inside, the fire still barely burning. The warmth of the structure hit her like a furnace blast and she turned back toward Marc, whose eyes were closing.

"Marc!" she shouted, causing him to open them again focusing on her. "Crawl inside."

He tried to crawl as she kneeled in the snow, pushing and shoving against his ass, maneuvering him to the inside of the tent. He fell into a heap and she flopped down on the other side, every muscle screaming in pain as she panted.

After a few minutes, she opened her eyes to a completely blurry scene as they adjusted to the dim light and warmth. Once she had gathered her strength enough to crawl over to Marc, she peered down at his face. His eyes were once more closed as his chest heaved. "Marc?" she called.

"Yea…" he whispered.

She looked at the bruising on his temple, the dried blood crusted around the cut. "I don't know what to do to help you. You hit your head. You said when I hit mine I might have a concussion. And there's blood. And I don't know what else you injured."

"An…kle," he said, feeling what little strength he had leave him as the warmth of the tent encircled him. Closing his eyes, he fought against the desire to sleep.

Sitting back on her heels, Kendall tried to decide

what needed to be done first. *He needs to get warm. He needs to rest. He needs water. I've got to clean the wound. He can't sleep too long, gotta wake him up.* Her list halted as she came up against a blank as to where to begin.

Unzipping his coat, she was grateful to see that his shirt was dry while discovering his pockets held a bundle of sticks. Turning back to the fire, she placed several of them on the burning embers, watching as they caught fire. Digging through the duffle, she found the first aid kit and brought out the antiseptic and bandages. Carefully, she dabbed an antiseptic cotton pad onto his wound before covering it with two band aides.

His eyes fluttered open once more, but only long enough for him to say, "I sor...ry."

"No, no," she hushed. "It'll be fine. I'll take care of you," she promised, not having any idea how she was going to fulfill that oath.

Looking down at his feet, she began untying his boots. Pulling off first one and then tugging on the other, she heard him grunt loudly. "Sorry, sorry," she said, trying to remove the boot gently. Rolling down the thick sock, she gasped, seeing the bruised and swollen ankle. *Oh, God, is it broken? This needs more than a band-aide!*

Cursing her lack of first aid knowledge, she rocked back on her heels, not knowing how to help him. Rubbing her face, she heard the wind whipping as the sides of the tent flapped. Remembering she had taken the rope from the tarp, she crawled back outside.

Stinging snow pelted her body as she tried to remember how Marc had the rope before.

With frozen hands, she tied the rope back to the trees surrounding the tarp, securing their tent once more. Kicking the snow away from the ground, she gathered a few more sticks, hoping she would be able to keep the fire going through the night.

Crawling back inside, she sat, huddled in a ball, the adrenaline rush ending, leaving every muscle screaming with exhaustion and her head pounding. After a few minutes, the warmth began to penetrate and her cheeks stung with the change in temperature.

Pulling off her cap, she unzipped her coat and rolled it into a ball, placing it under Marc's injured ankle. Staring at it, she looked at his swollen foot but noted it was not bent at an odd angle. *Maybe that means it's just sprained.* Searching her memories for what to do with a sprained ankle, the only idea she could recall was to wrap it tightly. Digging through the first aid kit again, she pulled out a roll of elastic bandages. Moving to his foot, she wrapped the bandage around and around.

A grunt had her gaze jump from his foot to his eyes, seeing them open once more. She crawled over him until her face was near his. "How do you feel?"

Marc stared at the beauty, whose long hair was hanging down in a sheet, curtaining them both. He tried to remember who she was and if he had picked her up on the hike. "Whas your name?" his voice slurred as he reached out his hands and grasped her upper arms, bringing her face closer to his. Her red lips were plump and he wanted to taste them to see if they were as delectable as he hoped.

"Oh, Marc," she groaned. "I'm Kendall...please wake up and remember."

As he scrunched his face at her words, a sharp pain slashed across his forehead. *Huh?* His hands squeezed her arms for a second before he jerked his eyes open wide. *Kendall? Dr. Rhodes? Fuck! What's happened?*

"Marc, you fell and hurt yourself. Please...you need to rest."

His hands flew off her arms as though holding a hot poker. "Kendall?" he whispered. Reaching up, he touched the bandage on his pounding head, trying to make sense of what she was saying. *Oh, God, I was about to kiss her!*

"You fell and hit your head on a rock. You've been unconscious for most of the past hour," she explained.

He blinked a few more times as her words took hold. He tried to sit up but pressure from her hands on his chest kept him flat on his back. "I need to get up," he protested.

"Oh, no," she warned. "You also sprained your ankle...or at least I hope it's sprained and not broken."

"Fuck!" he cursed, dizzy from the simple exertion.

Getting one of the water bottles filled with melted snow, she lifted his head slightly so he could drink. "Marc, I don't know what to do to help you," she said. "Can you tell me?"

"I probably have a concussion," he surmised, angry at his weakened condition. "I've already gone to sleep several times, but you should wake me during the night, like I did for you, remember? Jesus, Kendall, I can't believe this happened." His mind was fuzzy but he knew he needed to try to stay as sharp as possible. "Is it still snowing?"

"Yeah," she replied, adding another stick to the fire. "Are you warm enough?"

Nodding, he had to admit, she had done an amazing job of getting him comfortable. He glanced down at his foot and wanted to check it out but raising his head sent a wave of nausea through him. Closing his eyes, he willed the tent to stop spinning. *Oh, shit...I've never failed at a mission before.* The fear of what might happen in the night with him incapacitated made him just as nauseated as trying to sit up. Feeling a warm cloth on his face, he reached up and clasped Kendall's hand as she wiped his forehead. Sleep was calling once more, but he managed to whisper, "Thank you," before slipping off.

12

Fatigue pulled at every muscle, but Kendall set her phone alarm to go off every two hours so she could check on Marc. She would like to think she would have stayed awake to watch over him without it, but did not trust herself not to fall asleep.

Hearing the wind still howling, she peeked outside, disheartened to still see the heavy snow falling by her flashlight. The darkness still blanketed the early morning, keeping her from seeing clearly how much snow had fallen.

Glancing over at Marc, she noted his steady breathing, glad he was still sleeping. Leaning over, she gently placed her hand across his forehead, breathing a sigh of relief that it was cool to the touch. Digging through the first aid kit, she came across a bottle of aspirin. *I'll get this down him when he wakes up.*

His phone vibrated and she searched to locate the sound. Her hand stilled over his crotch as she realized it was in his front pants pocket. Anxious, she jerked her gaze back to his still-sleeping face. The vibrating started up again and she carefully slid her hand in his pocket, her fingers moving along his jean-clad, thick, muscular thigh. Letting out the breath she had been holding, she latched onto the phone, sliding it out.

The vibrating had stopped, but as she checked the missed calls, she saw the name *Luke*. Not knowing the names of his co-workers, she had no idea who that person might be. *But what does it matter? I can at least let them know what is going on.*

Pressing call-back, she heard it connect on the first ring.

"Marc? I was getting worried when you didn't pick up. I've been trying and trying but haven't been able to make it through. I know it's early there, but we wanted to do a status check."

"Um…this isn't Marc. Is this—?"

"Dr. Rhodes?"

"Yes…this is Kendall Rhodes."

"Where's Marc?"

"He's…wait, who is this?"

"Dr. Rhodes, this is Luke. I'm a co-worker of Marc's and I'm here with some other co-workers. What's happening?"

"Oh, okay. Um, well, Marc fell and hit his head and has hurt his ankle. I was able to get him back to our shelter, but I don't really know how to help him."

"Dr. Rhodes, I'm putting you on speaker, so the others who are with me can hear."

"Um…okay. And you can call me Kendall."

"Kendall, this is Chad. What injuries does he have?"

Reciting what she knew and explaining what she had done, the men on the other end praised her. "It sounds like you've done an amazing job so far," Chad assured.

"I didn't know how to wrap his ankle, so I just kind of wrapped it around and around," she explained.

"Don't worry about it," Chad said. "The most important thing is...support and...swelling down. What about...head injury?"

"Wait! You're breaking up! Did you say head injury? He's got a gash on his forehead, but when I cleaned the wound, it's not as big as I was afraid."

From what she could hear, Chad once again praised her first aid attempts.

"Ma'am, this is Cam here. What is the status of your site?"

"Status?"

"What kind of shelter do you have?" he queried.

"Well, we've built a tent and Marc started a little fire inside. I've been able to keep it burning, but with the wind, I have to admit the tarp is taking a beating."

"Kendall, it's Luke again. The reason...I've now been able to get a satellite image on the location of Marc's signal...a small wooden structure about a mile south of where you are...determined this earlier, Marc could have gotten you to the site."

"You're breaking up again. There's a structure a mile south of here? Okay, but I don't know if we can make it. He can't walk on his foot. And even if I can help him, I don't know which direction to go in."

"...seen Marc use the handheld GPS system? It's about—"

"Yes," she said, digging in the duffle bag and pulling it out. "I've got it in my hands."

"Okay, I'm downloading the directions to the system and if you are holding it, it will show you the way. All you have to do is... Do you think you can do that?"

"All I have to do is what? What did you say?" Knowing this information was vital to their survival, she started to panic. *No! Not again. You can do this. You have to do this.* "Are you sure staying here isn't safer?"

A brief silence followed her question and then Chad came through. "Kendall, we don't want you to do anything you are uncomfortable with. With Marc incapacitated, you're in charge now. We just want to give you options. Following the GPS to the site is your best bet."

"Okay. I don't think I can carry everything and help him as well, but I'll do my best," she replied hesitantly, her gaze falling on Marc's sleeping form. Sucking in a deep breath, she said, "I'll see how he is when he wakes up. Can I call this number if I need?"

"Absolutely," Luke assured. "It might not go through the first time, but keep trying. We'll check in a little bit. And I promise, we have a rescue mission in the works."

Thanking him, she disconnected, closing her eyes momentarily as her mind whirled with the suggestion. A cabin sounded wonderful...*or at least a wooden structure to keep the wind at bay.* She thought about how difficult it had been to move Marc from the ditch to the tent. *How the hell can I move him again?*

Chad sat in silence for a moment as the phone line went dead. Sucking in a deep breath, the normally stoic teammate cursed loudly as he leaned back in his chair. "Fucking hell! There was more static than words from that conversation."

Charlie looked over at Luke, not knowing what to say. Being the newest member of the Saints put her at a disadvantage in feeling out the dynamics of the group as a whole. Luke glanced at her, a jerky shake of his head his only response. Sucking in her lips, she kept quiet as the men around the table erupted in a cacophony of cursing mixed with planning.

Calling them back to order, Cam said, "Okay, missions go awry all the time, but we work the problems. That's what we need to do now."

Luke called Bart, explaining the situation, knowing it could affect the rescue. Then he listened as Cam placed a call to Jack, knowing he needed to be updated on the mission as well. As Luke and Cam then circled around the maps and satellite screens, Chad called Monty.

Finally, an unsettling silence floating over the group, Charlie said, "You know, it might not be as bad as you're thinking." Gaining the, if somewhat incredulous, attention of the others, she continued.

"So what if Dr. Rhodes is a woman unused to being in the great outdoors? I mean, you all are assuming she's in over her head and can't do anything. Come on, guys.

I didn't know what I could do until I had a killer after me!"

"Yes, but—" Chad started.

"But nothing," Charlie insisted. "She's already gone out and found him, managed to get him back to their camp, and is taking charge. She's smart and it's not like she's alone. Marc might not be able to do as much, but he can guide her. I just don't think ya'll are giving her enough credit."

"We're used to being the ones who execute the missions...not having the missions take care of us," Cam said.

"I understand," she agreed. "I'm just saying that I think Kendall Rhodes is probably a lot more capable than you think." With a smile, she winked at Luke and turned back to her computers.

A howl sounded in the distance and Kendall bolted upright. *Oh, God, what was that?* She ran through the possibilities Marc had mentioned and none of them sounded good. *Bears? Should be hibernating. Should be... but not have to be. Wolves? Do they hibernate?* She listened closely, but heard nothing but the wind.

Closing her eyes, she longed to fall asleep on a soft mattress in a warm room after taking a hot shower. Just as she was about to drift off again, she heard Marc moan as he attempted to stretch. His eyes fluttered open, finally focusing on her face.

"Hey," she said softly, touching his face again to

check for a fever, relieved when only cool skin greeted her fingertips.

"Hey," he repeated, looking up at her once more leaning over him, her beautiful eyes peering deeply into his. She slid to his side, pushing his shoulders up slightly so he could accept the water she offered. "Thanks," he said, wishing his head would stop pounding. "Did I hear you talking to someone earlier or was I dreaming?"

"No, you heard. Luke called and I talked to your team. Well, sort of. The connection wasn't great."

Marc fought the urge to roll his eyes in disgust, knowing the motion would make his headache worse. He hated that his team knew he was out of commission for falling down a ditch. *Jesus, I'm a fuckin' idiot! How could I have made such a rookie mistake?* Sucking in a deep breath, he said, "What did they say?"

"Mostly, they were concerned about you."

He noticed her hesitation and prompted, "And?"

"They said they have our location on satellite and can see some type of wooden structure about a mile away from here."

Marc's mind immediately jumped into planning mode. "A mile? Which direction? Is it still snowing outside?"

"Whoa, hold on," she chastised. "There's no way I can get you there in the middle of a blizzard!"

"If I had a heavy stick that I could use as a crutch, I'd be able to make it." Grimacing, he added, "I'd need your help, but I really want to get you out of this tent and into something sturdier." He hated having to rely on her when she should be relying on him, but wanted desperately to get her out of the storm.

"Marc," she said, her face soft in the light of the small fire. "You don't have to do anything for me." Just then a gust caught the corner of the tent and the flap opened, blasting snow inside before she was able to scramble over to tie it back down.

Marc's phone vibrated an alert to an incoming message and he looked at the screen. "Luke's programed the information into the GPS. Kendall, I think we should try."

Swallowing deeply, she said, "What if we can't make it?"

"Hey," he reached out, taking her hand. "You dragged me out of a ditch and, by the way, I can't believe little you were able to do that. I'm not exactly small!"

A snort erupted as she agreed. Pondering the idea, she thought longingly about the possibility of a dry, wooden shelter. Nodding before she chickened out, she said, "Okay, but we need to plan what we're doing, because once we get outside, it will take all our strength just to move."

Grinning, Marc said, "Spoken like a true Saint!"

An hour later, they were ready to set off. They had repacked the duffle with the food box, first aid kit, dry clothes, the blanket, and whatever else Marc deemed necessary. She managed to cram most of her belongings into her large tote.

Kendall had gone back into the woods, finding a strong stick with some difficulty, causing her to rethink their attempt. But now, standing on the outside of their shelter, she could see the havoc the blizzard was wrecking on the small tarp-tent. *We'll be lucky if it lasts another day.* She untied the tarp, dismantling the structure right over Marc's head, upon his instructions. Wrestling an octopus would have been easier than untying the tarp with the wind whipping it back and forth. Finally, she managed to wad it up enough to shove it into the duffle.

Assisting him to a standing position, she groaned under his weight combined with the duffle on his back. Determined to keep her negative thoughts to herself, she swung her tote over her arm as she moved in to support his body as he hopped a few feet.

He saw the disbelief in her eyes, but steeled his resolve. *I need her assistance, but I'll be damned if I'm the reason we die out here if I can help get us to a shelter!*

13

Wind, snow, and biting cold made everything more difficult. Looking up into Marc's face, observing the grimace of pain, she wondered how they would ever make it a mile, considering she was panting and they had not taken a step.

Marc caught the doubt in her eyes, but was determined to pull his weight...or at least the duffle. With her help, he slid the straps on his shoulders to carry it like a backpack. As she handed the crutch to him, he tested its strength. He acknowledged that she had chosen well when it did not buckle under him. Testing his foot, he stuck his boot into the snow and leaned slightly, wincing when sharp pain shot up his leg. *Fuck!* Experimenting with the stick, he managed to move forward with a combination step, hobble, step, hobble.

Seeing her dubious expression, he nodded. "I'm ready." With his right hand on the makeshift crutch and his left arm across her shoulders, they set off. Step, hobble, step, hobble.

The snow was now at least six inches deep, and more, where it had drifted. Kendall tried to support as much of Marc's weight as she could, terrified of him falling and making his injury worse. Holding the GPS in her hand, she squinted so she could see their location. Looking up, she said, "We need to stay straight and we should run right into it."

Glad to have the trees catching the brunt of the wind, she tried to avoid the rocky meadow to the east and veered them into the forest. After fifteen minutes, she could hear Marc's harsh breathing as he came to a stop at a large tree. Propping him against the trunk, away from the wind, she turned her face up toward his.

"God, I'm sorry," he groaned, furious at his weakened condition. Being forced to rely on someone else when he was supposed to be protecting them went against his nature...*especially relying on a mission...and a small female at that!* Gritting his teeth, he sucked in the cold air, attempting to clear his mind.

"Don't apologize," she said, looking at his red cheeks, knowing he was winded. "We'll make it, I promise." She was not entirely sure she could keep her promise but felt that if she said it, then perhaps it would be true.

Grunting, he peered into her eyes, observing steely determination now replaced the earlier doubt. "Isn't that supposed to be my line?"

She grinned, but it was hidden behind her scarf. Pulling it down slightly, she added, "Well, looks like Paul Bunyan is just going to have to trust little 'ol me."

"Oh, I trust you, all right. I'm the one who said you were stronger than you realize."

Smiling once more, she shoved the scarf back around her mouth. "Ready?"

With his nod, they started out, shuffling through the snow once more. After another fifteen minutes, she studied the GPS noting it looked like they were half way to the structure. She figured it would take an hour to reach the shack but, at the rate they were going, it would take longer. She felt his weight on her growing heavier with each step.

Stopping once more, she watched his chest heave as frustration crossed his face. "Look, Marc, we can go faster if we leave the duffle bag here and just concentrate on getting you to safety."

He shook his head and argued, "Kendall, we need what's in this pack. It's got our supplies, first aid, food—"

"I'll come back and get it after we get you in."

"Hell, no! I'm not having you come back out in the blizzard to wander around looking for what we leave behind."

"Marc, I can—"

"No! And I mean *NO!*" he shouted. "Damnit! This is fuckin' killing me!" He looked down at her as she jerked back from his tone, immediately contrite over his vehemence and let out a deep breath.

With her lips pinched tightly, she blinked rapidly, warring between wanting to cry and wanting to kick his shins. Refusing to do the former and denying herself the pleasure of the latter, she turned and walked away for a moment. The snow stung her cheeks, as there was no place to hide from the storm. Heaving a sigh, she turned back, just in time to see the anguish on his face.

Stepping up to him, she nodded as she moved underneath his arm and they silently began the step-hobble dance once more.

Twenty minutes passed and, as she studied the GPS, she said, "We must be getting close. We should be able to see it soon!"

After another ten minutes, she looked through the woods, where the snow was less fierce as it had to battle the tree limbs to get to them, and she saw a brown structure in the distance. "Marc! Look!" she shouted.

He searched through the trees in the direction she was pointing and felt hope for the first time in the past two hours. His foot was screaming, but his head concerned him more with the pounding headache that threatened nausea with each step. Stopping to catch his breath, he lowered his eyes to the woman bravely working to get him to safety. "That's good, Kendall. You're amazing."

Her scarf had slipped down and he was able to view the brilliance of her smile as it turned toward him. *Beautiful. She's fuckin' beautiful!* For a second all he could think about was capturing her smile in a kiss, but before he could manage to do anything about that thought, her face scrunched.

"Oh, no!" she exclaimed. "There's a creek to cross!"

As he followed her pointing finger toward the shack, he could see that indeed there was a small creek, only about three feet across, which normally he could jump over. "Don't worry," he assured. "We've made it this far and will make it the rest!"

She turned and said, "Take off the duffle now and let's cross the creek. Then I can come back and get what was left."

He wanted to argue, but knew she was right. While it rankled him to have her carry the load for even part of the way, it was probably the only way he was going to get through the creek. Dropping the bag behind him, he had to admit it made the step-hobble easier.

Moving to the edge of the creek, there was no way to determine its depth, even though it appeared to be very small. Snow and ice covered the top, but there were a few exposed rocks jutting out of the surface.

"If I go first and then hold your hand, do you think you can make it?" she asked, doubt now creeping back into her voice.

Staring at the frozen surface, he nodded, unable to come up with a better plan. Looking across the way at the wooden shack, that right now looked like a slice of heaven, he vowed to get them into its safety as soon as possible.

Stepping carefully onto the first large stone, Kendall turned and faced him, holding out her hand. Aiming the limb-crutch at the ice-covered water, Marc jabbed it downward, crunching it through the frozen surface until it rested at the bottom, about ten inches deep.

"Well, if we fall in, we won't drown," he joked, but immediately felt contrite as her face registered fear. "No, no...we'll be fine."

Placing his good foot on the stone closest to her, he hobbled over until he was delicately balanced on the rock, with the crutch wobbling under his weight and her hand holding on tightly. Their eyes met, standing in the middle of the creek, a blinding snowstorm swirling around, and he felt the jolt from their gloved touch rush through his body. *How the hell can this be? We're not even skin to skin!*

Jerking her eyes away, she stepped to the next stone before turning back. Repeating the motion, he moved the crutch first and then stepped after her with his good foot. Only this time, as he wobbled, the crutch gave way leaving only Kendall's hand grasping tightly to his as he leaned precariously to the side.

Kendall felt the pull of six feet, four inches, and two hundred pounds of muscles against her arm and knew she could not keep him from falling. "Noooooo!" she screamed, refusing to let go as they toppled over together into the icy water.

Instinctively, Marc tried to twist so he would hit first and she would land on top but their bulky clothing made that impossible as they fell side by side, her tote landing in the water as well. Their clothes kept them from feeling the cold at first as she became a whirl of arms and legs trying to sit up.

"I'm so sorry," she cried, bending over to see if he was hurt. Plunging her hands in the frozen creek, she pulled as hard as she could to lift him to a sitting position. Scrambling behind him, her feet felt leaden as the water filled her boots.

Reaching to the side to grab his fallen crutch, he managed to stand with her help, pain slicing up his leg and through his head. He did not speak, unable to trust that he would not devolve into a fury of cursing. Water dripped off his arms as he jerked away from her, teetering once more.

"Don't be stupid, Marc!" she chastised, as the cold water threatened to turn her feet into blocks of ice. "You need my help!"

"You're soaking wet and freezing, Kendall, and you wouldn't be if I didn't need your help!" Marc bellowed.

His chest rising and falling in rapid succession, she held his fierce stare. After a tense moment he relented, albeit unhappily, and threw his arm over her once more. Together, they slogged the two feet to the ground and step-hobbled the last fifty yards to the shelter. "I'm going in first," Marc announced, in a desperate attempt to salvage some semblance of control.

Rolling her eyes, Kendall did not argue, too tired and cold to care. He opened the door slowly, shining the bright light inside, pleased to find it empty of critters and that, while there was only a dirt floor, it was dry. The shack was little more than four wooden walls with a sloped roof, but in the corner—*holy shit...a wood burning stove! Thank fuck for hunters!*

Pushing his way in, he hopped toward the old, crude stove, quickly assessing its usability. Turning around, he discovered Kendall was not behind him. Hobbling back to the door, he saw her heading back toward the creek to get the duffle. Taking a minute to keep his eye on her, he fought to bring his irritation under control. Irritation with himself, not her. He could not remember a time when he had not been in control on a mission and the foreign, impotent feeling left him inwardly cursing. A shiver ran over him as the icy wetness of his clothes began to penetrate. *And she's still out there...for us.*

Sucking in a deep breath, he watched as she made it to the other side of the creek and wrestled with the duffle to get it on her back. *Damn...it's almost bigger than she is!*

As Kendall finally hefted the bag on her shoulders, she turned to re-cross the creek. Chanting *Don't fall* over and over, she managed to make it without tumbling. Unable to feel her hands or feet, she trudged under the weight of the duffle back toward the shack, staring down at her boots, internally grumbling at the stubbornness of men. Finally lifting her chin, she saw Marc standing in the doorway, face contrite, his hand stretched out. After a second of hesitation, she reached out to him, their hands grasping as he pulled her inside and slammed the door behind her.

Dumping the duffle to the ground, she staggered into his embrace, her cheek planted against his wet coat. Her breaths came in great pants as her chest heaved before her mind slowly cleared and rational thoughts returned. As much as she wanted to stay in his arms, she knew they had to get dry and warm. As her eyes adjusted to the dark interior, she scanned the empty space.

"I know it's not much," he said quickly, anticipating

her disgust with their surroundings. "But it's dry and I can get a fire going."

Hearing the concern in his voice, she lifted her eyes to his face, offering a small smile. "Marc, it's fine. Honestly, it's so much better than the tent, it's like heaven."

Her teeth chattered loudly and he turned suddenly, hopping toward the stove as he pulled off his gloves. "The last inhabitants left us a present," he proclaimed, pointing to a few pieces of cut wood stacked near the stove. Grunting in pain as he knelt, he opened the duffle to pull out the fire starter, placing it in the stove first, before adding some wood. Within a few minutes, flames were crackling and warmth snaked through the small structure.

Pulling off his hat, he unzipped his coat and dropped it to the floor, thankful his flannel shirt was only slightly damp. With a lift of his hands, the long-sleeved, thermal shirt came over his head and was tossed to the floor as well. Turning around to check on Kendall's progress, he found her standing statue-still, her eyes on his chest.

Kendall gaped at the massive man in front of her, his naked chest, abs, arms—all ripped muscles—on glorious display, causing her frozen brain to short-circuit. Staring at his masculine perfection, she was not even aware he had stopped moving and was staring back until he cleared his throat. Jerking her eyes up to his, she blushed furiously, embarrassed to have been caught ogling.

"You okay?" he asked, a smile curving his lips.

"Uh…yes. I was just…" she stammered, unable to come up with a plausible lie. Sighing, she threw her hands to the side and admitted, "I was just staring at you. I've never seen a man quite so muscular as you… at least not in person." Still blushing, she added, "But I'm sure you've heard that before."

For a second, the memory of other women coyly calling him "hot" or "sexy" flew through his mind, but now they sounded contrived. The simple words of admiration from Kendall humbled him. Shrugging, he said, "My dad is a big man. His father was too. They built their muscles working on their farm. I did too, until I left home. Now, I try to stay in shape other ways."

Grateful for his humility, she smiled back. "Well, it works." Her gaze dropped to the medallion on a silver chain about his neck. She was curious, but said nothing as the cold seeped into her skin.

"Kendall," he said, softly. "You need to change and get out of those clothes. Do you have others to put on?"

Nodding, she bent to open her wet tote and pulled out her jumbled belongings. "Everything's damp," she bemoaned, wondering how she would ever get warm.

"Here," he said, bending over the duffle again, this time pulling out another thermal shirt and a pair of thermal long underwear.

Staring at the huge clothes, she raised her eyebrows, looking at the offerings suspiciously.

"Come on," he said. "They won't bite."

"No, but they'll swallow me all the same!"

"Honey, they're dry and warm…right now, that's all that matters."

Nodding, she then peeked back in the bag. "Do you have anything dry to put on?"

"Yeah," he grinned, pulling out another shirt.

She stood self-consciously for a moment, their eyes locked on each other until he blinked and moved away from the stove, turning his back to her.

"You need to get close to the fire, so I'll let you change."

She watched as he kept his back turned as she quickly stripped out of her outer garments, then her shirts and pants. Grateful for the warmth of the fire, she felt the prickly tingles as her frozen skin began to thaw. Her only bra was damp, so she dropped it to the pile of clothes and slid his thermal shirt on over her breasts. Her nipples poked through, but she thought that he might not notice. Pulling on the thermal pants, she bent to roll the legs up so that she would not trip.

Looking up, she realized he had slipped out of his pants. His tight ass, covered in thermal long underwear as well, caused her breath to catch in her throat. Whirling around before she was caught ogling again, she said, "I'm decent."

She felt him hobble closer but was afraid to look. He moved beside her, his hands extended toward the stove. Sparing a glance sideways, she was glad to see he was dressed as she was—dry thermals.

Marc did his own staring, grinning at first as he noticed his shirt hanging to her thighs. Then, as his gaze zeroed in on her nipples poking against the material, his mouth suddenly went dry. Swallowing deeply, he shook his head, trying to clear the image from his eyes but, with her sharing the small space, he knew that was a wasted effort. His cock jumped and he forced himself to think of the icy cold dip in the creek to keep from scaring her with a visible hard-on. *This is going to be a long night!*

14

"Marc?"

Jerking, he realized Kendall had asked a question. "Sorry. What did you ask?"

"I was wondering who built this. Hunters?"

"Probably." Looking around, he chuckled, "But it looks like it hasn't been used in a long time." Bringing his gaze back to her, he added, "I wish I could offer you more, but—"

"Oh, Marc," she reached out and placed her hand on his arm. "This is fabulous! We've got walls that won't blow over in a gust of wind...a way to keep out wild animals, and a stove! What more could we ask for?"

Cocking his eyebrow, he stared, causing her to laugh.

"Okay, okay! I suppose we could have a hot shower or a big bathtub to soak in, room service from a five-star restaurant, and maybe a big, soft bed!"

At the mention of a shower, tub, and bed Marc's brain short-circuited, images of a naked Kendall flashing through his mind. Willing his cock to behave, he stared at her smiling face, acknowledging how well she was handling their situation.

He felt each of her fingers burning into his arm, causing an electric jolt throughout him. He stared into her eyes, bright with the firelight flickering in their reflection, and her smile rivaling the flames. Unable to stop himself, he lifted his hand to cup her cheek, his thumb rubbing her smooth skin. "Amazing...you're amazing, Kendall."

She leaned her head slightly into his palm, loving the feel of his touch. Drawn to him like a moth to the flame, she closed her eyes for a moment, slipping into the fantasy of a man like him being interested in a woman like her. When she opened her eyes, his face was a whisper away. His gaze held hers, as though seeking permission... she hoped seeking permission. Throwing caution to the wind, she stood on her tiptoes and closed the distance.

Surprised as her lips moved over his, even though he had started it, Marc welcomed their silky warmth as her arms reached up to his shoulders. The light touch became deeper, more possessive. She moaned into his mouth and, taking advantage, he slipped his tongue inside, the unique taste of her intoxicating. As soon as his tongue stroked the inside of her mouth, hers thrust forward tangling with his. Twisting heads as their noses bumped, he breathed her in, the storm outside forgotten as she became his lifeline.

It had been a while since Kendall had been kissed— thoroughly, completely kissed. In fact, as her body reacted to the taste, texture, and touch of his mouth on hers, she no longer had any memory of any kiss before, this one rocking her to her core. Squeezing her legs together, she felt the damp at the apex as her nipples pressed against his chest. Not knowing where the kiss was leading she realized she did not care—as long as it led to the two of them together.

Instinctively he slid his arms around her, desiring to lift her in them, but the twinge in his ankle shot a dose of reality through him. "Fuck," he moaned against her lips as he shifted his weight back to his good foot.

The slight jolting of their bodies seemed to bring Kendall out of her lust-filled haze. Rocking back on her heels, her chest heaved as she gulped in air, the kiss having stolen her oxygen. Her eyes pinned his, unable to read what was in their depths, but she knew hers must have shown her acceptance of whatever the kiss was leading to.

Marc, decidedly not caring about his foot or his previous headache, recognized the desire in her eyes before his gaze dropped to her kiss-swollen lips. Licking his own, the taste of her still there, he forced his body to behave. *Jesus, I can't take advantage of her!* Even as the thought crashed through his lust, he wondered if he would be able to control himself. Sucking in a deep breath before letting it out slowly, he battled the desire to tell her they needed to get naked and horizontal as fast as possible. Instead, he said, "We should…uh…eat something and then…uh…" The survivalist part of his brain, numb with the kiss, was unable to think of what else they needed to do.

Staring at her, he hoped she retained more sense than he did.

"Yeah…" she said, her breathing slowly coming under control. "Eat…that'd be good. And then, uh…" She reluctantly pulled her eyes away from him and looked around. "We need to get things in place here… for comfort." She kept her eyes down, worried that a man like Marc would never be interested in her out in the real world. *Maybe he only kissed me back because of the crazy, intense situation we're in.* Not staring at his handsome face gave her common sense the kick it needed to spring back into place.

Stepping back, she offered him an apologetic smile, knowing she had instigated the kiss. "I'll get a place for us to sit so you can take the pressure off your foot." Glad for a purpose, she turned and walked over to the duffle, unzipping it and rummaging through the contents to see what she needed.

Marc watched her for a second before lifting his face to the roof, his hands on his hips, sighing in frustration. He wanted to howl, but figured sounding like a wild and wounded animal probably was not the best idea. *Although I feel wild and wounded!* Chastising himself for taking advantage of her and for not being able to fully take care of her, he hobbled over to the stove, determined to make sure the fire kept going. She was not like the easy girls he picked up on his hikes or camping trips and the sooner he accepted she was an important research doctor and his mission, the sooner he would get his straining cock under control.

Jack checked his phone in the Baton Rouge, Louisiana hotel room he was staying in.

"Mr. Bryant? Kenneth Rhodes here."

Glad to hear from the doctor, Jack replied, "I haven't heard anything new about your daughter yet."

"I understand but, actually, I wanted to let you know of a new development. In light of what has happened, Homeland Security is asking for a contingency from my organization to meet in D.C. since Kendall won't be there."

"I've already gotten a call from my FBI contact," Jack confided, "telling me that he thought this would happen in a few days."

"I have to make those plans and decide who will go. Please keep me up on the latest about Kendall."

Jack hesitated for a second, having been told of Marc's accident, but chose to keep that information to himself. Kendall's father would do nothing but worry and there was no new information to pass on.

"We're still in contact with our man and everything's under control. As soon as the snow stops we'll be able to extract them."

After Jack disconnected a knock on the connecting door sounded before Patrick walked in. "Got anything new?" Discussing the upcoming meeting, they turned their conversation to the possible suspects at the NCBRT.

"Cliff doesn't hide his dissention in the group, does he?"

Jack shook his head and replied, "It makes me wonder what he'd do to rise up in the organization. Or if he'd sell them out because he's disgruntled."

"Estelle Barnaby?"

"I hated like hell on our last case to think that someone from the FBI could be selling the Bureau out but, now, I have to admit, I'm more willing to take everyone at face value, as a possible suspect. So even though she's from Homeland Security, I can't rule out that she might have a hidden agenda."

"I assumed the attempt on either the elder or the younger Dr. Rhodes' lives was due to their knowledge but then, from what we've learned, they have no special knowledge that the other researchers wouldn't have."

"That brings me back to the meeting in D.C. and what DHS wanted from them," Jack stated, shaking his head. I hate like hell not knowing the motive. But let's go back and look at opportunity and means."

Patrick leaned back in his chair, scrubbing his hand over his face. "Marc said the hangar was supposed to be secured and yet the sabotage occurred there."

"I'm waiting to hear what Nick and Monty come up with from Alaska."

"Since everyone from the NCBRT was here and not there, none of them could have sabotaged the plane."

"From what Marc said, it was more than just stealing his supplies. It had to be someone with specific airplane knowledge. To drain his gas tank but tinker with the fuel gauge so that it appeared full...that takes special skill."

"So, no one from here?" Patrick asked.

"No one here...but maybe someone here directing what was happening in Alaska. Someone with serious connections," Jack surmised.

"I don't give a shit if you're pissed or not! You've had a serious security breach here, under your nose, and I want answers," Monty growled.

Kevin stood toe to toe with the Saint, both men's stances unyielding. Nick stepped forward, his granite expression just as hard.

"Look, I'm telling you I've looked at the security tapes from the hangar and there's nothing. Whoever got in knew what they were doing and blanked out the cameras. I've got my tech people on it and a contingency of agents combing over the hangar."

"Who knew about the flight?" Nick asked.

Kevin turned his gaze back to the other agent, heaving a sigh. "This did not come from the inside. I'm telling you, I know my people here and this was not an inside job."

"Someone knew my teammate was here with his plane—knew ahead of time. Someone knew what the mission was and someone had enough time to get an accomplice who was adept at sabotaging a plane. That had to have come from inside," Monty argued.

"The only people who knew about this was myself,

Hank...Henry Tomlin. One other agent, Sharon Chikuk, knew as well. She works in our Fairbanks office. Those are the only three agents who knew. I can't tell you who knew back at the Bureau's headquarters or who knew from Homeland Security. So you see, we were hardly the only ones involved. The leak wasn't from my team!"

"What about the hangar? Who takes care of the planes, refueling...all of that?"

"Airport personnel, but they're vetted by us. We know who's in here and they're not allowed here without someone with them." Kevin looked to the side, his mouth twisted in a grimace and added, "And before you ask, Hank was with them when they refueled Marc's plane."

Nick stated, "I need to talk to him."

Shaking his head, Kevin stood with his hands on his hips. "Fine. He's at the hangar right now. I'll take you over." He pierced Nick and Monty with his glare, saying, "I know this is what you have to do, but as far as I'm concerned, I know my people."

"You may know your people, but what about the threat of terrorism?" Monty asked. "We have to look at everything since one of the groups the Rhodes are working with is the International Olympic Committee."

Shoulders sagging, Kevin admitted, "Until just the last year or so, Alaska, for whatever reason, was the only state in the U.S. that did not have an active terrorist cell. Then, in 2015, we lost that designation. It's active...we keep an eye on it, but don't have the resources that other states do to monitor what's going on."

Nick glanced at Monty and gave a silent signal. As Nick followed Kevin to his vehicle, Monty detoured quickly. Placing a call to Luke, he said, "Start checking into the recent terrorist cells in Alaska. I'll give more info later but, for now, see what you and Charlie can dig up."

"On it," Luke assured before disconnecting.

Monty jogged over, climbing into the back seat of Kevin's vehicle.

"We weren't in here that long," Hank said, his eyes wide, Adam's Apple bobbing as he swallowed audibly.

Monty wasn't sure if Hank was concerned because he was being questioned or excited because something out of the ordinary was happening.

"Just walk us through what you did," Nick ordered, trying unsuccessfully to hide his irritation at the over-eager rookie agent.

Tilting his head to the side, Hank scrunched his forehead in thought. "Well, I got here about nine at night and met the two-person crew. They had badges from the airport with names matching the ones on the list I was given. I opened the door over there," he pointed to the side door near the office. "The three of us came in and they immediately got to work."

"Got to work?" Monty prodded.

"Um, yeah. You know, they started doing whatever

they do." Hank's smile dropped slightly as he continued to stare back at them.

"Can you be more specific?"

"Well, one of them walked around to the fuel tank and I remember seeing them drag the nozzle around— they were at the back of the plane."

"Did you actually watch them the whole time?" Nick pressured.

"Uh, well, not every minute. But they weren't here long," Hank protested.

Kevin interrupted, "We've got them on camera. They were here for twenty-two minutes. The missing time is after they left."

Hank smiled as he breathed a sigh of relief.

"So, when you left, you locked up and saw them leave?" Monty asked.

"Yeah, yeah," Hank replied, his head bobbing. "I was warming my car up so I sat outside the hangar for a few minutes and watched them leave right after they got in their truck."

Nodding, Monty turned back around to take a look at the hangar. He wandered around the perimeter, noting the lack of windows. The only entrances, besides the main doors, were the door by the office and a door near the back. The large, metal framed building held no secret entrances or rooms. A typical private hangar with basic security. His gaze shot up toward the cameras in the corners and he wondered about the different ways to get around the security.

Pulling his phone out once more, Luke picked up on the first ring. "Patch into the FBI's security on Hangar

23C at Fairbanks International Airport. It was breached, so see what you and Charlie can dig up."

"Damn, man, you got a lot of requests," Luke joked.

"Yeah, well, I'll buy the two of you a beer when I get back from this frozen city," Monty quipped before disconnecting. Walking back over to Nick, he gave a curt nod of his head. Nick responded and it did not pass Monty's notice that after only one case together, Agent Nick Stone seemed to already be in tune with the Saints. With a slight smile, he walked back toward the hangar's office.

15

The wind still howled against the side of the wooden hut, whistling as it seeped into the cracks between the boards, but the accommodations were far superior to the makeshift tent of the previous nights. Marc had planned on building a fire pit once there, but the presence of an old stove made him glad they did not have to rough-it more than they already were.

He watched the firelight flicker about the dark room, illuminating Kendall's pale skin and dancing off the highlights of the hair that refused to stay in her braid. The blanket had been spread on pine branches she brought in. At first, she had used a branch like a broom to sweep out the cobwebs and floor, but claimed she liked the fresh scent so well, she wanted to create a fragrant mattress.

Against his wishes, she had bundled back in her clothes and coats before disappearing into the woods nearby to gather as many armfuls of branches as she could carry. Piling them in the center of the floor, she then lay the blanket on top before standing back to survey her work.

Scrunching her nose, she complained, "Well, it's a little lumpy, but I think it'll be better than just sleeping on the hard floor."

She stripped again, down to his long thermals, and plopped down in the middle of the makeshift bed. He grinned, observing how strangely at home she appeared.

Sitting next to her, he had to admit it was not uncomfortable as they shared a meal. He watched her eat the MRE without complaining. She ate delicately, as though at a fine restaurant. *I'd love to take her out for a nice dinner when we get back.* Jolting at the thought, he shoved the idea back down. *She lives in Louisiana for fuck's sake.* Still, once the idea had taken root, it was hard to sit near her and not want to have that opportunity for a lot longer than just the time they had in the storm.

"What's your favorite food?" he asked.

Her gaze jumped to his, surprised at his question. Swallowing, she licked the sauce off her lips before answering. "Um, I guess it would be Italian. I love pasta, pizza, and anything with tons of cheese."

Marc heard words coming out of her mouth, but his gaze was still plastered to her lips where the tip of her tongue had snuck out to lick her lip. Mesmerized, he forced his eyes back to hers. "Italian, huh? Well, maybe when this craziness is over with, we can hit an Italian restaurant sometime."

Her lips curved into a smile as she nodded, bolstered by the fact that he thought about seeing her once this was all over. "I'd like that…really. But do you like it? I'd hate for you to take me somewhere and you hated the food."

Her smile warmed him as much as the fire and he could not remember the last time he enjoyed just sitting and talking with a woman. He almost proclaimed that as long as she was with him, he would not care what they were eating. Instead, he replied, "I don't think I've found any food I didn't like!"

"Well, judging by the size of you, I can imagine that's right!"

"Hey! Are you size-shaming me?" he joked, his dimples showing with his huge grin.

Rolling her eyes, she said, "Hardly! I just mean that you have the big, outdoorsy, mountain-man thing going on."

Eyes wide, he said, "That's quite a description."

"Can you deny it?"

"No," he chuckled. Then sobering, he added, "And I guess you should know, since you had to bear some of my weight yesterday."

Kendall watched the irritation cross his face and shook her head. "You have to stop feeling bad, Marc. You know, I might not be the all-American, athletic type of woman, but I'm hardly the little Miss you have to take care of all the time!"

"I know, I know," he admitted, throwing his hands in front of him in defense. "You are definitely tougher than you look." The two settled into a moment of quiet as they finished their meals before he spoke again. "I guess it's just hard for me." Seeing her tilted head as she waited for him to explain, he continued, "In my daily life, I'm used to being in control. I go where I want, take care of my needs. Food, shelter…when I'm out, I can take care of myself and pretty much anyone else who is with me. But this," he swept his hand around indicating the shack, "you've done all of this—and it was my job, my mission. You talked to my crew, got us packed, got us here, everything."

"And is there a problem with that?" she asked, her voice soft and melodic. "When we're here, dry, and somewhat warm? Safer than we were? Does it really matter who helped who?"

"When it's my job to be protecting you? " He looked at her imploringly, willing her to understand. "That matters to me. In any other situation…if we were just out camping and hiking together…" Imagining that scenario, he chuckled, finally releasing the pent-up tension. "No, not at all. You've done a great job. I'll be glad to get rescued, out of here, and to rest assured that you're safe and sound. For now, I admit that you've stepped up. You not only saved my life but now yours as well."

Settling into a comfortable silence for a moment, she leaned back on her arms and said, "You mentioned your dad and grandfather were farmers. Tell me about working on the farm."

Relaxing, he replied, "My papaw worked the farm that had been in our family for generations. My dad did a stint in the Army and then went back, married his high school sweetheart and built a house on the land as well."

"Oh, you must have had a lot of acres."

Marc nodded and said, "It was over two hundred acres. And papaw did his own crop-dusting and taught me how to fly."

Leaning back up, circling her arms around her tucked knees, she said, "So you've been flying for a long time!"

"Yep, I had my pilot's license by the time I was sixteen and hired myself out to do crop dusting as well. I studied aviation in college, flew planes for the Army, then got on with the CIA."

Eyes wide, Kendall exclaimed, "I had no idea you'd done so much. That's impressive!"

"I always wanted to travel…see the world. Flying has allowed me to do that."

"And the Saints?"

"My boss, Jack Bryant, used to be with Special Forces and on his last tour he led a multi-unit taskforce. It worked so well that, when he got out, he replicated it and created the Saints Protection & Investigations. We take on jobs from the government and private companies."

"And who sent you after me…or well, my father?"

"FBI asked us to assist, wanting the flight to be covert." Shrugging, he said, "But looks like someone knew what they were planning."

Sighing, she nodded silently. Her gaze lifted back to

his. "Can you tell me about the medallion around your neck? It looks like a saint."

Marc slipped his fingers down the neck of his shirt, pulling out the chain with the pendant dangling. "It's a St. Mark. My grandmother gave it to me."

Leaning forward, she saw the image of a lion with wings. With a smile, she said, "It fits you exactly! You're just as strong as a lion and you love to fly!"

Chuckling, he nodded. "That's exactly what my grandmother said."

The two slid into a peaceful silence until she tried to stifle a yawn. "Do you think we should turn in?" she asked.

Nodding, Marc said, "Yeah. I've sent a message letting my crew know we're alive and safe. Hopefully, the storm will pass tonight or early tomorrow so they can get to us."

Standing, Kendall bent to smooth the blanket before laying the sleeping bag to the side. Marc reached into the first aid kit, retrieving another aspirin. Taking it with a swig of water, he turned back to her as she pulled out a stick of sugarless gum from her purse. Biting off half of it, she handed the other half to him.

"Here, chew this."

He followed her instructions and then watched as she pulled out her toothbrush. She wrapped the small wad of gum into the wrapper and began to scrub her teeth. Grinning, he observed her ritual then chuckled as she looked over and blushed.

"I hate the idea of not being able to brush, so I figure the gum will help."

Nodding, he followed her lead, grabbing his tooth-brush from his bag as well. Finishing, he watched as she smoothed the blanket on the floor again.

"You lay down first," she instructed.

"You just want to get me in bed so you can have your wicked way with me," he laughed, but complied.

She covered him in the sleeping bag after putting a few more sticks into the wood stove. Laying down beside him, she quipped, "Well, with your leg out of commission, I hardly think you're in a position to do much about it!"

It was on the tip of his tongue to tell her exactly what position he would like to use to make it work between them, specifically him on his back with her riding his cock but, calling upon all of his discretion, he just smiled and remained silent. Grunting as she snuggled closely, he now wondered how he could tell his cock to behave all night long.

Pulling the sleeping bag over their two bodies, Kendall cuddled up to his large, warm body. The exhaustion of the day overpowered her nerves about sleeping so closely to the man that had taken over her fantasies.

Marc lay with Kendall curled up close to his side, their shared warmth under the sleeping bag keeping them toasty. He knew the moment she fell asleep, listening to her breathing slow. He had never talked to anyone so much...especially not a woman. Smiling, his heart warmed at the interest she showed in his life. He shifted, his ankle achy, his head achy, and his cock twitching with the feel of her thigh pressing against his hip. Fatigue finally won the battle and he drifted off to sleep.

Waking a few hours later, Marc found a weight lying across his groin and his eyes popped open. Glancing down, he saw Kendall's leg was thrown across his dick, which was now at full-mast, ready to play. Her body was curved into his with her arm across his chest and her head tucked in to his neck.

Laying there for a moment, he waited for the flight reaction to occur—the desire to get away or have the woman leave. But it did not happen. Instead, he curved his arm around her still-sleeping form and pulled her closer. She was sweet warmth and her soft breath danced across his chest as he held her tight.

He stared at her face, long dark lashes forming a crescent as they lay on her rosy cheeks. Unable to stop, he gently touched her petal soft skin, trying to convince himself he just wanted to make sure she was warm. She was—but he was still unable to control the desire to rub his thumb over her cheek.

Her eyes blinked several times and her gaze showed confusion until she focused on his face. And then she smiled. The most glorious smile he had ever seen. It soothed him, warmed him, wrapped itself around him. And he smiled back.

Sliding his hand from her cheek to underneath her silky hair to cup the back of her neck, he pulled her closer until he captured her lips. Slow…soft…a simple kiss. Using his hand, he slightly moved her head so that the angle allowed him to take the kiss deeper...wetter.

She sighed into his mouth and he took advantage, slipping his tongue deep inside, exploring every crevice. There was a moan, but he was not sure which one of them created the sound. She tasted minty from the gum she chewed mixed with the intoxicating taste that was purely Kendall.

She reached out, clinging to his shoulders, her fingers digging into the flesh as the electricity sent shock waves from her tingling lips to her core. The pressure between her legs built, but with her left leg over his, it was easy to press the ache against his thigh, seeking relief. *Right now...right here...this man.* If this was her only opportunity to have him, she was willing to take the possible heartache later just to drown in his kisses tonight.

Marc, lost in the kiss, slowly became aware of her warm core rubbing on his leg and a white-hot jolt shot straight to his already engorged cock. *Down boy...we need to take this nice and slow. If at all.* He hated the thought that they might need to stop when the desire to sink deep inside her sex was overwhelming. But this was not only physical. This was not something he wanted to walk away from.

Pulling back from her lips, he felt her fingers cling even tighter on his shoulder and watched as her brow crinkled in silent question.

"I need to let you know, Kendall, *this* is not something I really want...*you* are something I really want."

"You don't want this?" she asked, confusion marring

her face.

"No, no, that didn't come out right. I mean I do want this. Sex. But no, not just sex. I want sex with you." Huffing, he tried again. Cupping her face in his large hand, he said, "What I'm trying to say is that I do want to have sex with you, but as crazy as it sounds since we've only known each other a couple of days, I really like you. I don't just want to have sex because we're stuck in a cabin alone."

Grinning, knowing that one night would never have been enough, she said, "Shut up and kiss me again, Marc. And for the record, I really like you too!"

With that resounding declaration, Marc had no trouble doing her bidding. One hand snaked to the bottom of her shirt and slipped underneath the hem. Her warm, silky skin called to him as he skimmed his fingers up her stomach, until she screeched and jerked back.

"I'm ticklish," she giggled, before moving back in, latching onto his lips.

Not wanting to stop their progress, he moved his hand slowly upward, avoiding the sensitive spots. Halting his path with his fingers resting on the undersides of her breasts, he waited to make sure she wanted to continue. A moan slipping from deep inside of her against his tongue was all the permission he needed.

His hand cupped her breast, feeling the weight as his thumb flicked over her budded nipple. Her reaction was to grind her core against his thigh harder as her fingers gripped him, bunching his thermal shirt in their clutch.

The thin material she wore did little to keep the heat

from flaming through her as his swollen cock dug into her stomach. She slid one hand down from his shoulder, across his massive chest and ripped abs, until her fingers reached his erection. He groaned into her mouth as her hot hand clasped his girth.

Fighting the desire to come immediately like some teenager, Marc reached down to hold her hand still. "You've got to wait. I'm hanging on by a thread."

Grinning, Kendall moved swiftly and straddled his narrow hips, her hot core pressing tightly. "Is this better for your ankle?"

"Don't worry about my ankle," he said, his eyes raking over her body. "But I'm afraid you'll be too cold on top."

"Well, if I get too cold, we'll flip," she winked. With a swift movement, she grabbed the bottom of her shirt and whipped it over her head. The fire kept the cabin from freezing, but it was still cold. Her nipples beaded to hard points but he immediately claimed her breasts in his large palms, warming them.

"Sweet girl, I've got no condom…I'm clean and we have to get checked for my job, but there's always the chance of—"

"I'm clean too…and I'm on the pill. Uh…well, I didn't take it the last two days, but it should be a good time of the month, but, oh—"

"What if I pull out? I know that's not a perfect method and it's up to you. If you want to wait, honey, we'll wait."

Kendall bent low over his body, her breasts pressing

against his chest as she licked her lips. "I want you...now."

16

Growling low, Marc cinched Kendall's waist with his hands. "Hold that thought. Just let me add a little more to the fire—don't want it going out and freezing you." Gently, he lifted her off, his eyes pinned to her pink-tipped breasts as they bounced slightly. Setting her to the side, he stood up and hobbled over to the stove. Adding a few more sticks, he stoked the fire, battling back the chill in the room. As she rose and stood next to him, he snagged the waistband of her thermal under-wear and pulled it down over her hips.

"I want to take my time," he moaned, "and worship every inch of you, but I don't want you to get chilled."

"I think we'll stay warm enough," she panted, jerking her pants the rest of the way down and dropping them to the blanket.

They lay back down and his gaze roamed over her nude body, perfection in his eyes. She smiled, warmed underneath his appraisal. She knelt on her knees as he sat up, his shirt quickly shucked and next to hers on the blanket.

She drank him in, his chest more marvelous than she had remembered. Her eyes dropped to his hands as he began pulling his thermal pants off. "Let me," she whispered, her hands replacing his as she pulled them down, freeing his impressive erection.

Capturing his swollen cock in her hands she encircled him, moving her hands up and down his shaft as he groaned. Throwing her leg over his hips again, he stopped her, "Wait."

Slipping one hand between her legs the other cupped her breast. Moving between each breast, he tweaked her nipples, teasing them into aching buds. Sliding his fingers through her wet, silky folds before inserting one into her warmth, he pressed his thumb on her swollen clit. Throwing her head back, she reveled in the feelings of electricity spreading throughout her body. Panting, her release eminent, he inserted another finger, scissoring them inside. Finding the spot that would have her breath catching in her throat, he pinched her nipple at the same time he pressed harder on her swollen nub.

Crying out his name as her orgasm slammed into her, she felt her inner muscles grab his fingers as warmth spread from her core outward. He swore he had never heard a sweeter sound than his name on her lips.

She dropped her chin forward, gifting him with her smile. Chest still heaving, she seated her slick entrance over his cock and plunged him in to the hilt, causing them both to gasp. Placing her hands on his shoulders, she held on as she rode him, her breasts bouncing in rhythm.

Having always worn a condom, the feeling of being ungloved had him almost coming immediately. *Jesus, what is this woman doing to me?* Sucking in great gulps of cold air, he forced his thrusts to slow. Marc held fast to her waist, assisting in moving her up and down on his shaft. *I'm close...so fuckin' close!* "Kendall...are you—"

"Yes," she cried out.

He could tell she was tiring so, holding her tightly, he rolled them to one side, keeping her back on the padded sleeping bag. With his body over hers, he attempted to keep the chill from hitting her. *Hell, as hot as I am, the cool feels good on top!*

Taking over the thrusts, he tried to go slow but soon was overwhelmed with the desire to touch her very soul with his body. "Can you take it harder?"

Crying out once more, she dug her fingers into his shoulders before sliding them to clutch his muscular ass. Pressing him forward, she begged him to take her as hard as he could.

Barely hanging on to his control, he rocked her body until he was no longer able to tell where he ended and she began. Knowing he was close, he reached between them, pressing on her clit once more as he shifted his hips, changing the angle for deeper penetration. "Come on, baby, let go," he groaned.

She cried his name again as her tight, warm core grabbed his cock. Just as his orgasm started to hit, he remembered to pull out, shooting cum on her stomach.

Falling to the side, he panted as he held her tight, feeling her chest heaving as well.

Finally, able to maintain a somewhat coherent thought, he leaned up and grimaced as he saw the mess on her stomach. "Oh, Jesus, Kendall, I'm so sorry."

She lifted her weary head, viewed her abdomen, and closed her eyes as she fell back to the blanket with a smile on her face. "Don't worry about it," she said, waving her hand. "I'll clean up."

"No, you wait here," he protested, starting to rise.

"Marc, you've got a bum ankle. Let me get up."

Leaning over, his face directly in front of hers, he said, "Kendall, you took over when I got hurt. But I'll be damned if I let you go get cold water to clean up my cum on you. So do as you're told, sweet girl—lie here and let me take care of you."

Taking in the intensity of his gaze as it held her captive, she smiled. "Okay," she breathed out on a whisper.

Closing the distance, he placed a quick kiss on her still-swollen lips before grinning. Standing, he bent over his duffle bag and grabbed a small towel. First dipping it in the melted-snow water, he then laid it on top of the stove for a moment to warm. Moving back to the blanket, he knelt beside Kendall's body, marveling at her beauty as the firelight flickered over her skin. With his dried cum on her, he wanted to roar and pound his chest. *God, that's such a caveman notion, but damn if I don't want to claim this woman!*

He carefully wiped her stomach, making sure to clean her thoroughly while trying to avoid her tickle spots. Glancing down at the neatly trimmed hair at her apex, he stared as he saw the sticky residue between her legs. Stilling, he wracked his brain to remember if he had pulled out completely before his orgasm hit. *Jesus, being in her bareback, it's hard to remember anything other than her tight sex clenching my cock!* Wiping her gently, he tried to ascertain if it was his cum or her slick juices. Unable to tell, he looked at her sweet face smiling up at him and decided to say nothing.

His gaze dropped back to her delectable body, full breasts, narrow waist, and slender hips that curved into a delicious ass. Noting a small scar on her lower abdomen, he drew his finger over it, asking, "Appendix scar?"

Glancing down at his large tan hands moving across her pale skin, she nodded. Mesmerized by his fingers trailing along the small scar, she said, "My appendix ruptured when I was a senior in high school. I was taking an exam and felt sick. I knew I needed to finish the test so I didn't say anything until it was over. Then I passed out right in class and they took me to the hospital in an ambulance."

"Shit, Kendall," he exclaimed, his brows pulled down as he frowned at her. "What'd your parents say?"

Giggling, both from his question and the tickling of his fingers, she said, "Mom was frustrated with me and Dad wondered how it might have affected my test score!" Seeing Marc's surprise, she quickly amended, "Oh, Dad was concerned about me, but after I had surgery and was fine, he wondered about the affect."

"Is your mom a biologist as well?" His hand stilled

on her stomach as he watched her smile slide from her face.

"She was a physician...ran a free clinic in Louisiana. She was killed when I was in college." She looked up at Marc's ruggedly handsome face in the flickering firelight and lifted her hand to cup his jaw. "It's okay...I can talk about her."

"I'd like to know," he replied, leaning his face into her hand, loving the feel of her small fingers stroking his beard.

"She and my dad met in college and, even though they were both brilliant, they complemented each other so much. I was an only child but they never put pressure on me. In fact, when I was little, I took piano and dance lessons. They always said they wanted me to be happy in whatever I did."

"And science made you happy?"

"Yeah...I know, I'm a geek." Shrugging, she said, "Mom had long hours sometimes, so I would go to Dad's labs after school. I loved what he did and found that I had an aptitude for science."

Kendall dropped her hand from his face and trailed her fingers along his chest, down to his hard, six-pack abs. Finding a puckering along the way, her hand stilled. "Looks like you have a few scars as well." She held his gaze as she surmised, "Why do I get the feeling these weren't from an appendix surgery?"

Chuckling, he admitted, "No, 'fraid not."

"Gunshot?"

He searched her face, but found nothing but concern...not curious fascination as other women had expressed. Others had wanted him to talk about what he had done to get shot, *and were disappointed to find out I wasn't like a CIA operative in a movie!*

Nodding, he said, "Yeah." Offering a shrug, he added, "It was a job hazard."

"Looks like it still is," she observed, her fingers gently sliding from the scar back up to his chest. "I hate the thought of you being hurt."

Her confession shocked him...and pleased him, unused to someone caring. Before he could respond, she shivered and Marc was jolted back to the matter at hand. "Okay, you need to get dressed now," he ordered gently as he took the cloth and wiped his cock as well.

They dressed quickly in their thermal underwear and he stoked the fire once more. Standing, she blushed nervously, wondering what the protocol was for just having had cabin sex with a man she had only met a few days ago.

He watched her avoid looking at him and he shook his head as he hobbled right up to her, pulling her into his embrace. "Oh, no, sweet girl, no shyness now. And I sure as hell hope you don't regret this."

Lifting her chin, she stared into his face, seeing the concern in his eyes. "No. No regrets from me," she admitted.

"Me either," he confessed, cupping her smooth cheek. Dropping another kiss on her cooling lips, he added, "I need to get you covered up and warm."

They lay down and he pulled the sleeping bag over the top of them, encasing them in a cocoon of warmth.

Pulling her close, he wrapped his arms around her and tucked her head underneath his chin.

"Kendall?"

Warm and snuggly, she said, "Yeah?"

"This meant something, sweet girl. I don't know what all we'll need to do to keep finding out what we could have together, but you need to know...I consider this to be the start of you and me."

Smiling, with her soft breath against his chest, she fell asleep.

———

Marc's arms held Kendall close, his heartbeat against her cheek. He desired to hold her naked body tucked into his, skin to skin as they fell asleep, but did not want to take a chance with the cold. As it was, they had dressed quickly and he had built the fire back up to finish drying their wet clothes.

Now, she slept peacefully and he watched her face in slumber. *What am I feeling? Hell, I've never felt anything for a woman before other than friendship or pleasure.* But he knew this was different. *I really, really like her. More than any other woman I've ever been with. But how can we move forward after our rescue? Would she want to try? Or is this all just me?*

Finding no answer in the stark cabin in the middle of the wilderness, he drifted off to sleep.

———

Marc's eyes jerked open from a deep sleep, feeling the cool where Kendall's warm body had been. Seeing the faint light of early dawn peeking through the wooden wall slats, he wondered where Kendall was. Sitting up, noticing her bent near the stove, her pants in her hands, he called out, "What's up?"

"Sorry," she whispered. "I need to step outside to… um…well, I've got to pee."

Pushing the sleeping bag off to the side, he began to stand. "No, no," she said, pushing down on his shoulders. "I'll just be a minute."

"I don't want you out there by yourself," he said, taking her hands in his.

"Marc, I just can't do what I need to do if you're there too. Please. I'll just walk around to the side of the cabin. You can stay by the door with it open if you want, although it'll make it cold in here."

Coming to a full stand, he balanced on his good leg while grabbing his jeans and nodding. "Okay, get wrapped up and I'll wait at the front door for you. But don't wander anywhere," he warned. "Just take care of your business right by the side."

Kendall slid her now dry jeans on over the thermals and jerked her sweater over her head. Zipping up her coat, she joked, "It'll take me longer to get dressed than it will to do what I need to do!"

Smiling down at her, he placed her knit cap on her head, pulling it down to cover her ears. "I'll make the best use of this time and take care of my business too."

Pursing her lips, she agreed, but warned, "Okay, but stay on your side of the cabin!"

Laughing, he agreed as he grabbed one of his guns for protection. Opening the cabin door, they were greeted with wind-swept snow piled against the walls. The dawn's faint light glistening against the white world was blinding. Blinking, Kendall held her hand up to shade her eyes. It was still snowing, the wind tossing the flakes sideways, pummeling the couple. Stepping carefully into the first snow drift, she turned to the left and tried to hurry around the side but made slow progress, as the snow came to her knees. Marc watched her turn the corner and, now out of his sight, he headed to the right.

Taking care of his business, he was just zipping his pants when his ears perked up. Wondering what he had heard, he stilled his breathing, his ears alert for another sound. A low growl came from the distance...just before a scream pierced the storm.

Charging around the corner with his weapon out, ignoring the searing pain in his leg, he saw Kendall as she made it around the other front corner, her face a mask of terror with a huge bear in the distance charging straight for her. Unable to get a good shot, he yelled, "Drop!"

Acting on instinct, she threw herself face first into the snow at his feet just as he discharged his weapon. Firing several rounds into the head, knowing it was the only way to stop the bear, the large animal slowed before dropping to the ground. Marc fired several more rounds to be sure the bear was dead and not suffering. Moving closer, cautiously, his heart pounded as he recognized it as a grizzly. Its mouth was open, exposing long teeth, but it was the razor-sharp claws that caught his eye. *Fuck, I thought the bears would still be in hibernation for another few weeks.* The bear's thick fur was already becoming covered in the falling snow, quickly hiding the blood splatters.

Hearing a gasp, Marc twisted around and saw Kendall standing close by, eyes wide in horror staring at the bear, before she dropped to her knees and began to retch. Hustling over, he knelt next to her, supporting her shoulders. Shaking violently, she heaved into the snow before sitting back, gasping for air.

Marc swooped her up in his arms, his ankle nearly buckling under him, but he powered through the pain until he got her inside and lay her on the sleeping bag. Turning back, he shut the door, throwing the wooden bolt in place. His heart pounded out of control, the adrenaline kicking in. *Never have I felt so scared on a mission...so out of control!*

"I can't...I can't...this...I can't," she babbled as he rushed back to her side.

'You can't what, Kendall? What?" Seeing her begin to hyperventilate, he pressed against her chest. "Breathe with me, sweetheart. Breathe with me."

Lowering his face so that he was directly in her line of vision, he captured her gaze. Breathing deeply, he nodded as she began to mirror his breaths. "Good girl, keep it slow and steady."

As the adrenaline left her body, Kendall felt weak, her arms and legs shaky. Closing her eyes for a moment, she felt the cold of shock creeping through her system.

Marc laid down next to her, drawing her into his

embrace after pulling the sleeping bag over them. Whispering words of comfort, he held her close to his still rapidly beating heart. "You're safe now, sweet girl. I've got you. You're safe. You did so good…exactly what you needed to do. I've got you now."

Cocooned in warmth, she slowly felt her body return to normal, although her mind whirled. A tear slid down her cheek as she whispered, "I can't do this. I want to go home." Finally, exhausted, she drifted off.

Marc knew sleep would not come back for him. When he closed his eyes, all he could see was Kendall as she rounded the corner with the growl of the charging bear behind her. And while the bear was not very close, if he had not been able to kill it, their fates might have been very different. Kissing the top of her head softly, he pulled her tighter into his warmth. Unable to imagine life without Kendall in it now, he also wondered about her final whisper…*when she goes home, will I ever see her again?*

17

Blinking open her eyes, Kendall knew three things. One, the daylight was peeking through the slats in the cabin and if it would stop snowing today, then they might get rescued. Two, outside that door was a bear that she did not want to think about. And three, the man whose chest provided the pillow for her head was someone she did not want to leave...but she had no idea how to stay with him. *Our jobs are in different states.*

As she lay, curled into Marc's warmth listening to the steady rhythm of his breathing, she fretted. When she first met him, their differences were obvious, but after a couple of days working together to stay alive, she discovered her strength and began to feel her attraction to him might not be so impossible. But now? After last night's brush with death, Kendall knew she would never be able to be strong enough for him. *I'm an indoor girl, best suited for the laboratory...not for a survivalist who enjoys living out in nature!*

Slipping from the warm cocoon, she tiptoed to the

stove and added a few pieces of wood, stoking the dying flames back to life. Holding her hands stretched out in front of her, she reveled in the chill leaving her fingers. With a glance over her shoulder to assure Marc was still sleeping, she slid his thermal pants off and pulled her jeans and socks on. Jerking his thermal shirt over her head, she bent to grab her bra and shirt laying near the stove.

"Now that's a scene I could wake up to every morning," a low voice, still full of sleep, growled behind her.

Clutching the clothing against her chest, she twisted around, catching him rolled on his side, his head supported by his hand. "Oh! I...I thought you were still sleeping!"

With deft movement that belied his size and his injuries, he stood, making his way to her next to the fire. Eyes still twinkling in the early morning light, he lifted his eyebrow as he stared down at her. "Any reason you're sneaking around, trying to hide from me?"

Still clutching her shirt in front of her, she opened her mouth, but nothing came out. She warred between wanting to tell him to back off until she was dressed and wanting to toss her shirt to the ground and fall into his arms.

He lifted his finger to her chin and pressed upward. "You gonna say something or just stand there trying to think of an excuse?"

Snapping her mouth shut, she mumbled, "I'm just getting dressed...it's cold."

"I've got the perfect way to warm you up," he

grinned. "In fact, I was planning on it before you slipped away."

Unable to think of what to say, she dropped her gaze to his chest, battling the tears that choked her throat.

"Hey, sweet girl, what's wrong?" he asked, his eyes full of concern, reaching up to cup her cheek.

Blinking furiously, she tried to ignore the way she felt when he called her *sweet girl*. Clearing her throat, she replied with forced lightness, "Nothing!" Turning her back to him, she stepped away and slid one arm into the strap of her bra while still holding her shirt in front of her. Trying to maneuver the other arm, she heard him approach her back.

"Here, let me help," he said softly, assisting her from behind while preserving her modesty. He knew something was bothering her but hoped it was nothing more than the stress and fatigue building.

Turning back around, her shirt firmly in place, she smiled shyly. "Thanks. I'll get us something to eat."

Her eyes darted to the door and he saw fear implanted in their depths. "I'll go outside and see what's going on with the storm. And when you need to relieve yourself, I'll have you go to the right of the cabin and I'll be close by."

Her eyes widened as she exclaimed, "I don't think I can go now that I know bears can come after us!"

"Honestly, he should have still been hibernating, so I don't think we'll be bothered by another one. I don't know why he was out and about anyway, but I think he must have been a fluke. But we won't take any chances."

Nodding gratefully, she watched as he swung open

the door, the night's snow having drifted up outside even more. Sighing, she continued to keep him in her sights as he stomped through the drifts and moved toward what was now a large lump in the snow. The blizzard had completely covered the grizzly and, while she was glad not to see it's carcass, just knowing it was there had her adrenaline kicking up again.

Grabbing her coat, she pulled on her boots and moved back to the doorway. He nodded and she tromped through the drifts around to the right side of the cabin and, finding the spot he had dug out, she quickly jerked her pants down and squatted. Annoyed with the difficulty of it all, she groused about how much easier it would be to be a man and just whiz in the snow while standing instead of having her ass get frozen. Taking care of business, she pulled her pants back up before washing her hands in the snow. It was a freezing process and one that she did not think was very effective at getting rid of germs, but she at least felt cleaner performing the task.

With a quick scan of the area, glad to see nothing more than the snow covered forest, she hurried back around the front corner, slamming into a rock hard body. Bouncing back, she stumbled, grateful his arms snagged her to keep her from landing in the snow.

Chuckling, he pulled her close and said, "I forgot how fast you can move! You go on in. I'm going to try to make a call."

Nodding she hurried back inside, eager to hold her hands over the stove. After they warmed a bit, she moved to the duffle bag, pulling out two more protein bars and the bottle of snow-melted water. A few minutes later, Marc came back in, talking on his phone.

"Yeah, we're fine. She was amazing...I couldn't have had better with me," he said, winking at her. "But we were lucky and the sooner you can get us out of here, the better." Marc had called Jack, wanting to get an update on the rescue. "Does Luke have any thoughts as to who might have been circling the downed plane? There are no tracks from there to where we are now, so Bart'll have the advantage, but we're going on day three of this snow. I know it's supposed to clear in a few hours so I want to make sure Bart gets to us first."

He continued to talk for several more minutes as Kendall sat on the sleeping bag, munching her breakfast bar. She listened as he spoke to his boss and allowed herself to finally think that they could be rescued today. Her eyes were riveted to his large frame as he walked around the small hut, able to put more pressure on his ankle than the day before. He still hobbled, but he appeared to be exercising as he moved.

His body mesmerized her, from the panther-like way he moved so stealthily, to the way his arm muscles flexed just from holding the phone to his ear. His five-o'clock shadow was now a full, dark beard, untrimmed and scruffy, but it only added to the dangerous masculinity he exuded. She could not help but smile... *he's every woman's dream and I got to spend this time with him*. Swallowing her chuckle, she realized as crazy as it seemed to be glad to have been sabotaged, almost killed, stuck in a blizzard, doused in a frozen creek, chased by a grizzly, she could now only think of how lucky she had been to have the chance to get to know him.

Brushing off the crumbs from her lap, she stood just as he finished his call. Looking up, she handed him the other protein bar as she waited to see what he would tell her.

Marc reached out and took it, gratefully ripping off the wrapping and taking a bite. Chewing, he appreciated her not pestering him with questions as he worked over what he and Bart would need to coordinate. Looking down, he really thought, maybe for the first time, of how perfectly the two of them worked together. To have such different backgrounds, after such a short time they appeared seamless in their movements.

Unfortunately, that thought had him thinking of their movements the night before and his cock twitched. His eyes dropped to her ass as she bent over to shake out the blanket and the sleeping bag before replacing them back on the floor. As she turned back to him, his hungry eyes roved over her body, his cock now swelling and eager.

Stepping forward, his arms encircled her and, without a word, he bent to claim her lips. Any resistance she may have considered melted away as she leaned into him, his lips strong and pliant. He lifted her up, ignoring the twinge of pain in his ankle, and she instinctively wrapped her legs around his waist as their tongues tangled together, each losing themselves in the kiss.

Her hot core was pressed against his cock, now painfully pressed against his zipper, all other thoughts flying from his head as he slid one hand to her ass, pressing her even closer. Hefting her slightly to signal his intentions, her legs dropped back to the floor as he allowed her body to slide slowly down his front, groaning in her mouth as his hard cock ached for release. As he peeled her shirt off her body, he knew she was not just any willing woman—he only wanted her.

Kendall lifted her arms as she allowed him to strip her, knowing it would be their last time. Once rescued, he would go back to his life of missions and his cabin and his outdoor pursuits. And she would return back to the lab and her lonely existence.

Stripping from her pants and panties, she stood naked before him, her porcelain body glowing in the morning light that slipped through the cracks and the firelight as it continued to flicker. Undressing quicker than he ever had, he stood over her as she lay back on the sleeping bag. Her eyes moved over his body, every muscle ripped and defined. She saw the drop of pre-cum on his engorged cock and decided if this was going to be their last time, then she was going to make it memorable for both of them.

Shifting to her knees, she took him in her hands as she licked the pearl before swirling her tongue around the head.

"Oh, God, Kendall," he moaned, his hands clutching her head.

Grinning, she licked her lips then slid his girth into her mouth as far as she could, fisting around the base. Slowly gaining speed, she bobbed her head as she sucked and tongued in time with her hand. Reaching up with her free hand, she cupped his heavy balls.

Marc arched, his hips grinding against her face as he felt the tightness in his back. *Jesus, she's killing me.* Dropping his chin, he was undone at the look of adoration and pleasure on her face as she peered up at him. Her hands reached around to grasp his ass and she brought him closer.

Feeling his balls squeeze, he pulled back suddenly, hearing her moan in protest. "No, babe. I want inside you," he panted as he towered over her, getting to his knees as she lay back. "I'll come in your mouth sometime, but right now, I want inside your sweet body."

Her legs falling open as he moved his hips between her thighs, he plunged in with one swift movement. She gasped at the sense of fullness and stretching, but there was no ache. Only pleasure. He immediately began to piston in and out, his thrusts providing the friction her body craved. Grabbing his shoulders, she then moved her hands up and down his back from his ass to his neck, encouraging him to move faster.

"I wanted to go slow," he bit out, looking down at her flushed face.

"I want everything you've got to give," she protested, her hips arching up to meet him stroke for stroke.

Unable to deny her, he powered through, rocking her body as he worshiped her with his. Bearing his weight on one arm, he moved his hand to her breast, palming the fullness before tweaking her distended nipple. Kissing her, he swallowed her groan as he slid his hand between them, down to her sensitive clit.

Thumbing the swollen nub, he choked out, "You close?"

Another groan was her only answer, but he took that as a positive. Knowing he was about to blow, he pressed harder and felt her body buck underneath his as her orgasm rocked though her. His own orgasm blasted from his body just after he pulled out.

Continuing to thrust until there was nothing left, he dropped onto her, rolling to the side and bringing her with him. Their pounding heartbeats reverberated throughout the cabin, second only to their ragged breaths. Their sweaty bodies were quickly cooling but neither appeared ready to move.

Standing to grab a cloth, he wiped her off gently, hating that he could not come inside her. *Soon, maybe soon.*

Finally, grabbing one edge of the sleeping bag, Marc rolled her over the top of him to the other side, taking the material with him. At least partially covered now, they still lay clinging to each other in the afterglow of their lovemaking.

Kendall's soft voice whispered against his chest, "Thank you."

"Oh, sweet girl, you don't have to thank me. I'm the one who should be worshipping at your feet for even allowing me to be with you. I've never...never felt so close to someone. Never felt anything like this."

A silent tear slid down her cheek, mixed into the cooling sweat on his chest. *I thought this would be our goodbye time...but how can I think of leaving someone when I'm falling in love?*

Luke leaned over Charlie's shoulder, kissing her neck, nibbling around her jaw until he landed on her delectable lips.

"Mmmm, what are you doing?" she murmured, twisting her head for better access.

"If you don't know, then I must be doing something wrong," he whispered, his warm breath against her ear.

After a moment of pleasure, he pulled back, his groan meeting her moan. "Okay, sweetheart, playtime is over. Whatcha got for me?"

Yawning, she whirled in her swivel chair and said, "Okay, I've some things for our guys to check out." With a few clicks she added, "I've gone over the finances of the NCBRT employees and none of them are rich. Let's face it, they're either working for Homeland Security or the private lab, but I'm not finding any unusual spending or financial savings for anyone. Cliff Wallace is the one Jack said had a lot of jealousy issues, so I've been concentrating on him. Background checks out. Divorced and looks like the ex took him to the cleaners, so a chunk of his pay goes to her each month, but he still appears to live well. I'll focus on him for a bit. Estelle Barnaby has been the DHS liaison there for only a year. She came from the Dallas branch and it looks like she might plan on staying since she just bought a house in Louisiana. I'm widening the net to include off-shore accounts and I'll let you know what I find."

Looking over at Luke, she said, "What about you?"

"Nick's got concerns about the newest terrorist cell that has cropped up in Alaska and wants me to see if I can make a connection between them and the one in Louisiana. Still digging. He's also not happy with the FBI there, particularly Kevin Pierce and Hank Tomlin. Says they are *overly friendly*—"

Barking out a laugh, Charlie's eyes widened at the description. "Overly friendly? Only stodgy old Nick would call someone *overly friendly!*"

"Right?" Luke grinned back. "But it seems as though he feels they are hiding something, so I'm digging into them as well."

"Wow, I get the feeling that after the last case, Nick doesn't trust anyone, even though it turned out his fellow FBI agent was not guilty."

"Yeah, but she was caught doing a lot of investigating on her own which put others at risk...including you, I might add," he said, his grin replaced by a grimace at the memory of how he almost lost her.

Leaning over to pat his leg, she said, "Now, now... none of that." Her expression turned pensive as she lifted her gaze to his. "Honey, do you think Marc will be okay? That Bart and Jude can get to him in time?"

Luke smiled at the beautiful woman who held his heart and nodded. "If this had to happen to one of us, Marc is the best one it could have happened to. He's a true outdoorsman. Hunts, fishes, backpacks, camps, has survivalist training...I'm sure he's fine and taking care of Dr. Rhodes as well."

"Well," she said, with a sly grin, rolling her chair closer. "If I were stuck in the wilds, I'd only want to be with you. So I wonder if the good doctor and Marc are getting...close?"

Throwing his head back, Luke laughed. "Oh no, not Marc. He's only attracted to women who are just as hardy as he is...and even then, it's only physical. I have no idea what kind of woman it would take to capture his heart."

"Hmmm," Charlie said with a slight shrug of her shoulders. "I wonder..."

"You wanted to see me?"

Estelle looked up from her computer at the scowling man standing in the doorway. Pinching her lips, she said, "Come in, Dr. Wallace. And shut the door, please."

Cliff walked in and settled into the chair in front of her desk, his eyes shifting around the office. "Do you think they'll find anything?"

"You don't beat around the bush, do you?"

"Never saw any reason too," Cliff replied, his irritation showing. "We've got work to do and having the security firm Kenneth hired skulking around is not making me happy."

"My home office is still wanting the reports," Estelle bit back, "so while Kendall isn't here, you need to pull it all together."

"So, you think Kenneth will stay here and assign someone else to go?"

"Getting anxious to step into his shoes already?" she quipped. "Just don't put the cart before the horse."

He scowled once more, glaring her way. "I'll get it all ready, but I'd better be the one who goes, whether Kendall makes it out of the wilderness or not!"

Estelle pinned him with her steady gaze, cocking her head to the side. "Vicious, aren't you?"

"When I need to be…I'll do what needs to be done." Standing, he said, "Will there be anything else?"

Her lips curved slightly at the corners as she watched him walk to the door. "Not now," she conceded. "But tonight?"

Stopping, his hand on the doorknob, he nodded curtly before leaving her office.

"Looks like the Alaskan terrorist cell is growing," Luke said, looking over his shoulder at Cam and Chad. Flashing the information onto the big screen, he said, "They infiltrate the universities and rely heavily on social media to get their messages out."

"Alaska," Cam repeated, shaking his head. "What's the draw?"

"The FBI is considering various scenarios, but one of them is the oil pipelines. Perfect place for terrorists to disrupt the process, throwing the economy and environment into havoc."

Sighing heavily, Chad added, "What about the close proximity to Russia?"

Nodding, Luke agreed. "Alaska is a perfect training ground to practice activities that can affect Russia, the orient, the United States, and Canada. Quite frankly, I'm surprised they haven't discovered the benefits of working from there before recently."

"So, if someone wanted to get rid of the Rhodes, especially interrupting their reports for the Olympic committees, knowing they were in Alaska, it wouldn't be too hard to get someone to do their dirty work for them?"

"Nope, I'd say it was pretty easy," Luke nodded.

"Guys, Monty's calling in," Charlie called out, patching him through to the group.

"Here's what we've got so far," Monty said, immediately getting down to business. "The FBI supposedly vets the airport crew that services anything they need, but the cameras were disabled for a time and the rookie agent here is lying when he says he was right with them. My guess is he's either on their payroll to turn a blind eye or he royally fucked up and did so on his own. I want everything you can give me on Henry Tomlin."

"I've been checking him out since we got his name

but so far, I'm not turning up much. Charlie's working on possible offshore accounts for any of our players."

"What about the terrorist cell up here?" Monty pressed.

"Looks like they recruit heavily from college students and have their hands in the Muslim community, targeting youth. Same MO they use everywhere. But it's growing and we were just discussing their proximity to Canada, US oilfields, Russia, and all points Asian."

Nodding, Monty agreed. "That's what Nick and I figured also. So they could have had any number of people here who would disable a plane."

"But that's what's odd," Charlie piped up. "Marc's plane wasn't disabled, but specifically tampered with in a way that a seasoned pilot did not notice. That only comes from someone who either flies, knows planes, or is highly trained."

"Good point," Monty acknowledged. "Can you work that angle? And get us something on Agent Tomlin… Nick wants to nail that puppy's ass just for shirking his duties, if nothing else!"

"You'd better be telling the truth," Kevin warned, his good humor long gone. "I've got the Bureau breathing down my neck because their hot-shot agent is up here questioning how I run things!"

"I'm telling you, they just came in and worked on the plane. I didn't watch them every second," Hank confessed. "But, then, I don't know anything about planes." He slumped dejectedly in his chair, his hound-dog appearance revealing his self-pity.

Rubbing his hand over his face, feeling the scruff of too long without shaving, Kevin leaned back. "I am not going to lose my pension because of this," he fumed.

Moments later, Hank walked back down the hall to the office he shared with fellow agent Sharon Chikuk and, sitting down at his desk, leaned his head back, staring at the ceiling. A pretty native Alaskan, she looked over and asked, "How'd it go?"

After a moment he lowered his chin, allowing his gaze to roam around the small space. "This was all I ever wanted...to be an FBI agent. And, I swear, it feels like it's all coming down around me."

She swiveled in her chair to face him. "That bad?"

Nodding, he said, "They're looking at all of us. Think it was an inside job and since I was the one who was at the airport hangar with the mechanics, then I'm the one they want to pin this on."

Piercing him with her stare, she said, "So, how do you explain the missing security tapes or the tampering with the plane?"

"I don't know," he protested loudly, slamming his hand down on the desk. "But this has got to be a set up!"

Sharon's phone rang and she turned back to her desk, leaving Hank to stew in silence. Pulling out his cell phone, he typed a quick message to a friend. **Things are getting messy.**

Logan, Bart, Jude, and Blaise sat at Logan's table, maps and computers spread across the area. Looking at the others, Logan said, "I've got the coordinates of the cabin Luke said they were at. We should be able to lift off in about two hours from what I can tell. As soon as we can, my bird'll take all of us." Half-grinning at the others, he said, "It's big."

"I take it you've got something more than a little sight-seeing helicopter at the ready?" Patrick asked, his eyes trained out the window toward the large hangar on the back of the property.

"I've got a H10, light single-engine that I use for taking just a couple people around, but I've secured a Lakota for...when needed. It'll be all we need."

"Former military-grade bird? Damn," Bart whistled appreciatively. He eyed his former Lt. Commander, silently wondering what secrets Preacher was now involved in. Whatever they were, he realized with Faith at home, he no longer wished for the dangerous missions. Meeting Preacher's eyes, he nodded in silent acknowledgment before looking back at the computer monitor.

"Any chance we'll run into the ones that were after them to begin with?" Blaise asked.

Preacher rubbed his chin, watching the chatter on his own monitor, before lifting his gaze. "We'll be prepared for anything," he pronounced. "In fact, let's head out to the hangar now. I've got equipment and weapons to get ready. When we get to your friends, we'll want to get in and get them out as quickly as possible."

19

Kendall stood at the doorway of the shelter watching the snow fall lighter and the sky grow brighter. Hearing activity behind her, she turned and regarded Marc as he repacked necessities back into the duffle bag. Her gaze moved around the inside of the small shack, the wooden plank walls, stark in their appearance with slits of light peeking through the places where the boards warped away from each other. The old stove in the corner stood with its door hanging crooked off the hinges, allowing the heat to fill the cabin.

Marc finished packing and turned to observe Kendall's quiet perusal of their surroundings. Shaking his head, he said, "Bet you'll be glad to get away from here, won't you? It's about as sparse as you can get."

Her gaze lifted to his as she confessed, "Actually, I was thinking how I'll kind of miss this place in a weird sort of way."

Cocking his head to the side, he said nothing, waiting for her to explain.

Closing the door and bolting it behind her, she grinned, "Granted, I would hate to live exactly here for much longer." Her smile slid from her face as she heaved a sigh, "But, it's been…well, kind of nice to find out I can do things I never thought possible."

Walking over, placing his hands on her shoulders, Marc held her gaze, his lips curving in a smile. "Kendall, you've proven yourself far more capable than either of us ever dreamed. I confess, I was perfectly ready and, okay, determined, to provide all the protection you needed…and here I am, in your debt for saving my life."

She lifted her hand, her finger tracing his dimple before saying, "Well, considering you saved me from a grizzly bear, I'd say we're more than even."

Throwing his head back in laughter, he pulled her close, one hand cupping the back of her head as it rested on his chest and the other circling her back.

She leaned back and looked up, seeing his warm gaze beaming down on her. "When do we need to leave?"

Fighting the urge to strip her slowly and watch her as he brought her to orgasm again, he knew they needed to focus on their business. "We'll stay here until we get the signal from my crew that they are close. Then we'll leave here and it should take us about fifteen minutes to get to the clearing by the lake, where it is open but rocky. "

"Can they land a helicopter there?"

"I don't know. The pilot is experienced and will have to make that determination from his vantage point from the air."

"But—"

"Don't worry," he assured. "If they can't land, then they'll have a basket or a harness they can drop down for us."

Her eyes grew wide as her mouth dropped open. "Basket? Harness?" she squeaked. "Marc...there's no way I can sit in a basket and be raised—"

Marc interrupted again, this time with his fingers on her lips. "Sweet girl, I don't think there's anything you can't do. And I promise you, I'll keep you safe."

Blowing out a deep breath against his finger, she planted her forehead against his chest, mumbling.

"What's that?" he asked, unable to hear her response.

Leaning back a slight inch, she said, "I said, this cabin is looking better and better!"

Laughing again, he nodded. "I gotta say, being here with you has been the highlight of this mission. And Kendall?" He gave her a little squeeze and waited until she looked up at him before continuing, "I meant what I said last night...you mean something to me. I have no idea, when we're out of here, if there's any chance for us but—"

Just then, Marc's phone alerted and he hated the interruption, but he had to answer. Connecting, he said, "Speak to me."

Kendall stepped back, giving Marc a chance to focus on the call, but wondered what he had been about to tell her. Needing something to occupy her mind, she turned to her meager belongings and began to see if there was anything she could leave behind to make the walk easier.

Before she knew it, Marc was off the phone. Glancing over her shoulder up at him, she waited for him to speak.

"They're on their way. Go ahead and layer your clothes again because it's cold and we've got to trek through the high snow drifts to get to the pick-up point."

Silently, she slid out of her jeans so she could don her tights first when she felt his fingertips clutching her waist. He lifted her ponytail out of the way as he planted his lips on her neck. Leaning back against his front, she turned her head so his lips could claim hers once more. Soft and smooth, with his beard prickling her skin, she loved the feel of him close to her.

"I wish…" she breathed against his lips.

"You wish what?" he murmured, not breaking the kiss. She did not answer him, so he pulled back slightly, holding her gaze.

Swallowing back the sting of tears, she answered, "I wish we could be together. I know that sounds clingy and men don't like cling—"

"Sweet girl," he confessed, "I've never wanted clingy before…until you. But I want you."

Twisting in his embrace, she threw her arms around his neck as their lips fused together once more, breathing each other in as the kiss ignited.

After a moment, Marc reluctantly raised up, separating from her. "I hate like hell to stop this but—"

"I know," she admitted, her lips still tingling. "We have to get going."

She stepped back, pulling on her tights and then

layering her jeans over top of them. Along with two pairs of socks, she tugged her boots back on. Two shirts and then her coat with a scarf and her hat, she once more felt like a stuffed sausage. Her bag was much lighter and she easily swung it over her shoulder. Looking at Marc, her eyes grew wide.

"Good God, Marc—you're a big guy, but with all those extra clothes and that coat, you do look like Paul Bunyan!"

Chuckling, he hauled the duffle onto his back and then leaned down to kiss her nose. "Let's go get rescued." Opening the door, he led the way out.

Stopping at the entrance, Kendall took one last look back at the cabin that she was sure saved their lives. Sucking in a deep breath, she turned and began trudging in the deep snow, following his lead.

Hank sat at his desk staring at his computer, anger warring with fear. Afraid of losing his job, he was determined not to go down without a fight. Search after search only brought up what anyone could find. Glancing around, grateful the office was almost empty, he moved to the special programs he had recently been given access to for investigative purposes.

Grinning, he began sifting through more in-depth information. Engrossed in his search, he did not hear Kevin approach until he spoke.

"You working on something new?" Kevin asked, moving toward Hank's desk.

Jumping, Hank gulped as he clicked to minimize the screen. "Uh…just rechecking some info on the last case I was working on."

He held Kevin's hard stare, trying to appear nonchalant. "Hmmm," was Kevin's only response. Swallowing deeply, Hank asked, "You got something for me to work on, boss?"

Kevin continued to stare for a moment before saying, "I'd like you to work on the hangar security tapes and see what you can find."

"Me?"

"Any reason why you shouldn't work on it?"

"No, no, I'd be glad to work on it. I'm just surprised you want me on this…" his voice trailed off.

"I figure since you're the one who was there, you'll be the one who wants to find out what happened."

Nodding eagerly, Hank enthused, "Oh, absolutely. You can count on me." He smiled at Sharon, the other agent in the Fairbanks office, as she stood from her desk and left the room.

Kevin stood and walked out of the room at the same time, leaving Hank grinning as he went back to his search, pleased he no longer needed to hide what he was looking for.

Jack and Patrick walked out of the large conference room with Kenneth. Making their way down the hall to Kenneth's office, the three men entered, closing the door behind them.

Patrick ran his hand over his face before looking at Kenneth saying, "Okay, I confess that most of what was said in there was way over my head. It's been a long time since I had biology and I never studied the medical aspect of microbiology!" Jack chuckled, having to agree as they looked toward Kenneth for a layman's crash course.

"Essentially, gentlemen," Kenneth said, "The IOC is concerned that terrorists, with very little trouble, could potentially shut down the Olympics and commerce with biological warfare. Deadly, infectious bacteria could be integrated into the water, food, or even the air. And with the next three Olympics in Asian countries, it could make terrorists attacks easier. Especially in China, where a large segment of the population is poor and therefore susceptible to terrorist recruitment."

He rubbed his beard for a moment before adding, "Now, I'm not well versed in the terrorist activities, nor in the Olympics' security, but the IOC has been working with Homeland Security, who sponsors our labs here, and they are interested in what we know about the various infectious bacteria and the antidotes."

"I noticed Cliff wants to step in for Kendall at the meeting in D.C. Wouldn't that go to Dr. Mahdi as the head of that section?" Jack asked.

"Normally yes, but Fahdil's wife had surgery yesterday. Nothing life-threatening, but he had planned on taking the week off. In fact, that was the reason he did not travel to Alaska with me. It would have made sense for him to go, but he wanted to be here, of course."

"So, out of all of this, do you see any reason why someone would have wanted you or Kendall dead?"

Sighing heavily, Kenneth pulled off his glasses, rubbing his eyes before staring back at Jack. "It's no secret that Dr. Wallace...Cliff...wants my job and feels that he should be next in line. To be truthful, he's a good researcher, but as you saw today, not always the best at working with a team. He presents facts but not the way that someone else can understand them. That's why I hate to send him to D.C. alone. Kendall is very good at that type of presentation, which is why she, and not Cliff, accompanied me to Alaska when Fahdil was unable to go."

Jack and Patrick shared a look, both having noted Cliff's self-important pontificating during the meeting and the expressions of the others around the table as his words made no sense to them.

Kenneth replaced his glasses on his face and continued, "Now, please understand, I trust Cliff completely, but of anyone here, he is the only one who would benefit from either my or Kendall's demise. You see gentlemen, DHS has already confirmed the succession to Kendall when I decide to step down."

Standing, Jack shook Kenneth's hand and confirmed, "Our team is ready to extract our member and Kendall today. They will be checked out medically and she'll be able to contact you."

The older man held Jack's hand in both of his, moisture pooling in his eyes. "Mr. Bryant, you have my eternal gratitude for taking care of my daughter. She's a fragile type and would never be able to handle herself out in the wild."

"I appreciate it, but your thanks goes to my team-member who has guarded and cared for her since the beginning. Although, from what I hear, she's held her own quite well."

Kenneth appeared doubtful, but nodded just the same. As Jack and Patrick headed out of the building, Patrick was already on the phone with Luke. "Get everything you can on Dr. Cliff Wallace. Focus on him for now and see what connections we can make."

Luke glanced up as Charlie came bounding down the stairs at the Saints' compound. Sniffing the air, he grinned as his eyes landed on the large, paper sack in her hand. "Oh, sweetheart, is that what I think it is?"

"Beef and broccoli, sesame chicken, Kung Pao chicken, egg rolls, crab rangoons, and wonton soup."

"Holy moly, woman, you've just made my day!" Chad exclaimed as Cam jumped up to take the bags from her.

"Back off, gentlemen," Luke warned, placing a kiss on her lips before grinning at his co-workers all settling in around the conference table.

"How's it going?" Charlie asked as she grabbed paper plates from a cabinet.

Luke replied, "Just got a call from Patrick and he said to focus on Cliff Wallace. Says he's got motive for wanting both Dr. Rhodes out of the way."

"Means? Opportunity?" Cam asked, his mouth already surrounding an eggroll.

"Don't know," Luke confessed, "but I'm checking to see what contacts he might have had in Alaska."

"He has professional motive, but it doesn't tie into a terrorist act," Chad commented.

"Maybe we've been looking at this wrong," Luke said. "Maybe it is personal and not terrorist."

"I don't buy that," Charlie added. Seeing Luke's eyes on her, she continued, "Personal, he does something near home. Not spend the time or money to hire someone to do everything that happened in Alaska."

"What if it's both?" Chad suggested. "Terrorists want to interrupt the business of the IOC, DHS, and can do it by killing one of the Rhodes. So, they find someone at the NCBRT who could benefit from their death."

The group stopped chewing in unison as they pondered Chad's possibility, their eyes darting back and forth.

Nodding, Luke finished swallowing before turning back to his computers and said, "Looks like I need to focus on Cliff, just like Jack wants!"

20

Fifteen minutes trudging through knee high snow drifts felt like a lifetime. Kendall's legs ached from the exertion and, while the snow had stopped falling, the wind was still blowing the stinging ice crystals against her face. Add to that the snow blindness and she began to long for the tiny cabin.

She alternated between looking down where her feet were stepping to watching the back of Marc as he painfully made his way through the thick snow with his stick-crutch, knowing his ankle must be causing him agony.

Tilting her head down again, she soon bounced off his back. Looking up as she toppled backward, she discovered Marc had stopped in front of her. "Umph," she groaned as his hands steadied her.

"How're you holding up?" he asked.

"As well as you," she retorted, a grimace on her face.

Grinning at her testiness, he said, "We're almost there."

Following his hand to where he was pointing, she could see the woods beginning to clear and, though she could no longer see the rocky terrain of the meadow now that it was covered in over a foot of snow, she knew they were close. Studying the open space, she said, "They can't land, can they? Not with all the snow and ice."

Marc observed the tense muscles in her jaw as her gaze remained on the vista in front of them. Hating to make things worse, he nodded. "I'm pretty sure they'll have to send something down for us." He hated the look of despair that crossed her face so he quickly assured, "We'll be fine, Kendall. My crew is the best and I'll be right with you."

Nodding, she forced her frozen lips into a smile and said, "Alrighty then...let's go get rescued!"

Laughing, Marc turned and began to slowly make his way to the edge of the meadow. Stopping at the tree-line, they set their packs down as he scanned the area. "They'll get a lock on our location and should be here soon."

Within fifteen more minutes, they heard the sound of helicopter blades whirring as it approached.

"We're close," Logan called out to the Saints strapped into the back of his Lakota helicopter. Bart looked down, seeing nothing but the tops of the trees in the thick forests below, placing his faith in his former commander.

Jude, sitting in the co-pilot seat, kept his eye on the signal coming from Marc. "Just a few clicks away," he said, excited for the mission to be accomplished successfully.

Logan looked at the terrain as they passed over the mountains and came upon a frozen lake. Just beyond the lake lay a snow-covered area that appeared flat, but he knew underneath the snow it would be rocky and unstable. "Looks like we'll be lowering the hoist."

"If Marc's too injured, I'll go down to secure him," Bart volunteered.

"Looks like they might be okay," Blaise called out. Using binoculars, his eyes were trained on the edge of the woods, where he ascertained that two figures were coming from the forest, the smaller one supporting the much taller person. "The snow is deep and cumbersome, but Marc's managing with help from Dr. Rhodes."

"Look likes she's holding her own just fine," Bart added, his gaze now on the figures slowly trudging out from the cover of the woods.

Jude radioed to Marc's phone, "We're sending down the hoist. Can you secure Dr. Rhodes?"

As Jude received the affirmative from Marc, Bart readied the hoist, standing by the controls to send it down.

Kendall longed for the step-hobble of the other day, when the snow had not yet drifted so high. She could tell Marc was having to put more pressure on his injured ankle, so she moved up and slid underneath his arm to offer her body as a crutch. He began to scowl, but acknowledged that the high drifts of snow, now that they were out of the woods, made movement almost impossible.

Looking up, he carefully watched as the helicopter came closer, its roar sounding out over the open space. He observed the side door open and his heart felt lighter as he recognized Bart leaning out with the hoist.

"Is he crazy?" Kendall exclaimed, as she shielded her eyes and noted someone from the helicopter hanging out the open door. The blades whirled above, swirling the surface snow all about them, making visibility difficult.

"Don't worry, he's strapped in," Marc explained.

"Oh," she replied, feeling slightly foolish, until she realized the helicopter was not coming lower. "We have to make it all the way up there? With just that rope?" Twisting her neck to look up at Marc's calm face, she tried to draw strength from his lack of concern. Failing at that, she then tried to just force down the hysteria bubbling in her chest.

He felt the fear rolling off her in waves and squeezed her shoulder. "Kendall girl, you can do this. It's a steel cable and won't break. I promise I've got you and I can vouch that those men up there will care for you just as they would their own women."

Nodding, she sucked in her lips, the sting of ice against her face forcing her to accept that they needed to get out of the elements, even if that meant hanging by a steel cable harness from a helicopter. "I got this," she announced, as firmly as possible, trying to ignore her quaking legs.

Grinning, he kissed her forehead as he tucked her into his arms again. "Good girl." With a wave, he indicated to Bart that they were ready. The hoist began lowering with the harnesses and clamps.

"Fuck! We've got company!" Logan shouted, his eyes on the horizon.

"What have you got?" Bart asked, twisting his head around to see what Logan was talking about.

"Another bird coming in low, circling close to where we're going."

"We've jammed Marc's signal," Jude protested. "No fucking way anyone can tell where he is!"

"Fuckin' hell," Logan cursed. "Then someone's just waited until the storm passed and they're out scouting. And we're going to beacon them right in. Get armed."

Blaise and Bart, already armed, readied themselves, both cursing. The helicopter banked hard to the right as Logan began evasive maneuvers.

"Hang on boys, might be a shootout at the OK corral!" Logan called out, his face grim.

Seeing the helicopter swerve away, Marc's gaze scanned the sky searching for the reason, landing on the other helicopter moving in. "Get down!" he yelled, pulling Kendall down with him, face first into the snow.

"Umph!" she groaned as she lay buried in the snow, Marc's heavy body covering hers.

He raised his head just in time to hear rapid gunfire in the distance and watched as the two birds flew around each other, both aggressive and evasive, the sound of discharging weapons reverberating. Aware of Kendall's body underneath his, he warred between wanting to move off her and keeping her protected. Shifting slightly to the side, he said in her ear, "Hang on, sweet girl, I promise we'll get up out of the snow."

Twisting her head, she grunted, "What's happening?"

"Looks like someone else was waiting for the storm to end so they could find us."

Eyes widening, she gasped. "Who is it? Who's after me? I'm no one!"

Sparing a glance toward the sky again, seeing Bart firing out of his side, he looked back down at her frightened face. "I don't know…but we're gonna find out!"

The sounds in the air changed and Marc watched as the other helicopter flew away and Bart's bird moved back over them. Leaping to his feet, ignoring the pain, he bent over and pulled Kendall to a standing position. "Come on, Kendall girl, let's go. They've chased the others away for now, so we've got to get moving."

Seeing their rescue hovering over them again with the hoist lowering, Marc looked down at her and explained, "We'll go up together to save time."

Heart pounding, she fought to breathe. "Will it hold both of us?"

"No worries," he replied, keeping his eyes on the hoist waving in the wind. "You don't weigh anything. It's strong enough to easily get us up."

Reaching out to grasp the harnesses, he turned to her and began to fasten her in. She tried to help, but their hands were numb with cold and both fumbled with the clasps. Finally getting her in, he stepped into his harness, but staggered as his ankle gave out under his weight.

Kendall instinctively grabbed him, throwing her body under his arm to keep him from falling. Steadying him, she worked the clasps on his harness. He double-checked them before looking up, now seeing Blaise's face alongside Bart's. Giving them a thumbs-up, he threw his arms around Kendall, holding her close as their feet left the ground.

With a squeak, Kendall grabbed onto Marc's shoulders as they began to twirl around as they were lifted slowly. Glancing up, she saw the blades whirling on the helicopter, petrified they would somehow come in contact with them. Darting her gaze down, nausea swept over her as she watched the ground spin around.

"Keep your eyes on me. Just me. I'll be your safe place," Marc ordered, seeing the terror on her face. "Good girl," he said, at her quick acquiescence.

He looked up again and smiled, seeing the Saints' faces coming closer.

Suddenly, the helicopter swerved to the right again, taking the dangling couple on a ride over the forest, their feet barely missing the treetops.

"Shit!" he cursed and Kendall's eyelids jumped open as she screamed, their bodies flying through the air.

21

"Hold the fuck on!" Logan yelled as he banked right. Keeping the returning helicopter in his sights, he pulled up, making sure to fly high enough to keep their mission above the trees. "Get 'em up!" he ordered unnecessarily, as Bart worked the hoist at its fastest speed.

"Goddamnit," Blaise cursed, looking out the door as Marc and Kendall twirled in a fast circle, the hoist line at an angle as the couple trailed behind over the treetops.

Kendall whimpered as she clung to Marc, her life-line, as motion-sickness hit. What had begun as a slow twirling, but vertical climb, was now a spinning-dragged-through-the-air-behind-the-helicopter ascent, the cold wind slicing through her as a painful death appeared imminent.

Marc, hating the turn of events, knew they were strapped into the harnesses, but held on to her body as though he were the only thing keeping her alive at the moment. Their legs tangled together as he tried to wrap her tightly, offering his body as whatever protection he could provide.

Jude jumped to the back of the bird, hooked himself in and threw open the other sliding door, his weapon ready. Blaise took over the winch as Bart settled in with his weapon covering the other side. For most people the the ability to fire a long-range weapon out of a helicopter toward another helicopter would be an impossibility, but for the two former SEALs, their marksmanship skills took over.

"Can you get a bead on them?" Logan asked. "I can't outrun them with the hoist down—too dangerous."

As the other helicopter made a move to fly under them, in a maneuver that would kill Marc and Kendall, Bart took aim at the pilot. "Come on, come on," he breathed, waiting for just the right second. Firing, he hit his target, shooting into the front window and hitting the pilot, who immediately slumped over.

The smaller helicopter began spinning out of control in a downward path and within a few seconds, the crew of the Lakota watched as it crashed into the forest, bursting into flames. At the roar below them, Kendall jerked her eyes open in fright, sure that the noise was coming from their helicopter.

"We're good!" Marc yelled to her, but knew from her blank expression she was in shock. Looking up, he saw they were close to their rescuers.

Bart jerked around, coming up beside Blaise and Jude, peering over their shoulders. Seeing the couple getting closer, he yelled toward Logan, "Steady on... we've almost got 'em!"

As soon as Marc was within range, Bart reached out, grabbing him by the jacket arm and began to pull him toward the open door. With Jude and Blaise's assistance, they managed to maneuver Marc and Kendall into the Lakota, their bodies landing in a tangled heap on the hard floor. Once the doors were slammed shut, Logan quickly changed direction, heading to where he could refuel for the trip back to his place.

Marc felt Kendall shaking uncontrollably and refused to let her go. They lay on the helicopter floor, her arms tightly locked onto his neck, his still around her middle.

"Marc," Blaise said softly. "I've got to check you out."

"Can you get us unfastened first?" Marc replied just as quietly.

The Saints understood Kendall's shock and hands gently reached around and between the two. Jude managed to get the harness from Marc's shoulders and upper body before sliding the sling from his legs. Bart unfastened the harness clips from Kendall's chest but she burrowed tighter to Marc and he looked at his friend to see what to do.

Marc murmured words of comfort, over and over, to Kendall in an attempt to get her to relax, but to no avail. With help, he managed to sit up, pulling her onto his lap. Stroking her hair, he nodded toward his injured ankle and Blaise moved down to his foot.

Pulling off Marc's boot and unwinding the wrap, Blaise examined the swelling. "Don't think it's broken, but it's sure as hell sprained. We'll need x-rays when we get back just to be sure."

Bart slid Marc's cap off and took a look at the cut on the side of his head. "You could probably use stitches on this, but no infection has set it."

The three Saints kneeled around the couple, none of them sure how to assist Kendall. Blaise put his hand on her back while she remained tucked in Marc's embrace. "Dr. Rhodes...Kendall? I'm Blaise and I'm a medic. Can I take a look at you, please?" With a nod from Marc, Blaise unlinked her tightly clasped fingers from around Marc's neck, drawing her frozen arms down. Jude wrapped a blanket around Marc's shoulders as Bart did the same with Kendall.

Leaving her still sitting on Marc's lap, Blaise turned her toward him to shine a flashlight into her eyes. Blinking several times as if coming out of a trance, she gasped, sucking in a deep breath. Looking up at Blaise, her chest heaved as though just coming back to life.

Marc shifted slightly, murmuring continuously to her until she jerked her head around, her gaze locking onto his. "We...we're...we..." she stammered.

"We're safe, we're safe, sweet girl," he assured, his hand rubbing up and down her back. "We need to get warm and checked out...can you do that for me?"

Licking her lips, she bobbed her head as her gaze finally cleared and she looked around. As each Saint introduced themselves to her, she attempted to smile but her face still felt frozen. Assisting her to her feet, Blaise kept his hands protectively on her as her legs wobbled unsteadily.

"Y'all good?" Logan called out from the pilot's seat.

Bart affirmed their condition and introduced Marc, who had moved just enough to nod his acknowledgement to their pilot.

"Sorry about the ride I had to take you on," Logan said.

"Didn't look like you had much choice," Marc replied, "and I'm grateful you got to us instead of them!"

Logan grinned and, tossing a wave, went back to concentrating on flying. Having shucked his coat, Marc managed to get his outer layer of pants off, still hobbling on one leg. Jude indicated for Marc to sit in one of the back seats of the bird so that he could re-wrap Marc's ankle.

Marc's gaze stayed on Kendall's as she fumbled with the button on her jeans, having used Bart's assistance to slide her coat off as well. He noted her hands shaking and knew both the cold and adrenaline were at work. Before moving to the seat near Jude, he hobbled over to her and gently brushed her hands to the side, unbuttoning and then unzipping her wet pants. Hooking his thumbs into the waistband, he slid them down her legs and she stepped out of them as she held on to his arms.

Blushing slightly at the intimate touch of his hands on her with their audience, she threw him an embarrassed smile before patting his arm, indicating she was all right. With a wink, Marc sat in the seat and allowed Jude to wrap his ankle for support.

Blaise whipped out a stethoscope and began to examine Kendall. Other than her heart racing, her lungs were clear. "Were you injured during the crash or since then?"

Shaking her head, she answered, "No…just a few bruises, and I bumped my head, but that was all." Shivering, she added, "I'm just cold."

Blaise pulled the thermal blanket around her tighter and said, "You were in the snow and then dragged through the freezing temperatures traveling at a high speed. Add to that the adrenaline and shock and I'm not surprised you're cold. But we want to warm you up and get some food and water in you, okay? And we'll need to check out your head when we get back—no point taking any chances."

She nodded but her gaze jumped from Blaise's kind face over to Marc's. He smiled at her and she finally managed to get her facial muscles relaxed enough to smile in return.

Slowly looking around the inside of the helicopter, she noticed it was much bigger than the airplane she and Marc had flown in. Besides the pilot and empty co-pilot seat, which the large, curly-haired Saint climbed into, there was the cold, flat floor between the two sliding doors. Behind that were five seats, one of which Marc was in as Blaise checked him out. The other Saint had moved to a seat behind her. *We're safe? We're really safe?* After the last several days, culminating in the terrifying last half-hour, Kendall could not truly believe it was all over.

Marc watched the play of emotions move across her face and reached over to take her hand. She jumped, then blushed as she squeezed his hand in return. Behind them, Bart and Blaise grinned.

The Lakota landed easily at an outpost and as Kendall glanced out the window, she noticed an old, log cabin store with snow-covered mountains in the background. Her head swung around to Marc, but it was Logan who explained what they were doing.

"This outpost has fuel for planes and helicopters. Plus, they'll have some food and bathrooms inside."

"Are we still in Canada?" she asked, her voice full of concern.

"Yeah, but don't worry. The old coot who runs this place has been around for years. He doesn't ask questions and won't answer them either," Logan said as he pulled his headphones off and grinned back at his passengers.

"You'll be fine," Marc assured, linking his fingers with hers.

Nodding, she added, "I really could use a ladies' room right now."

Marc stepped out first then turned to assist her out of the aircraft. Linking fingers once again, he escorted her inside the old building. Once her eyes adjusted to the dim interior, she saw shelves stocked with an assortment of snacks, as well as canned goods. The scent of coffee from a pot behind the counter assaulted her nostrils and she was unable to contain her moan.

Nudging her forward, Marc said, "Looks like the restroom is back there. You go on and I'll follow."

"Is there only one?" she asked, her nose slightly wrinkled.

"Doubt he gets a lot of tour busses full of people needing to use the bathrooms," Marc joked, giving her a small push toward the door with a sign on the outside proclaiming, **Knock first – no lock inside.**

"It doesn't lock?" she squeaked, her eyes growing wide.

"I'll stand right here," Marc promised, then teased, "Of course, you've been going outside in the snow."

Throwing a glare his way, she said, "Yes, but no one else was there except you and I trusted you."

Bending to plant a quick kiss on her lips, he promised, "You can still trust me, sweet girl. I'll stand guard so no one will get in."

Desperate, Kendall opened the door and rushed inside, thrilled to be able to use an actual toilet. Pleased that the small room was clean, she reveled in being able to wash her hands with hot water and soap after finishing. Peering into the mirror over the sink, she stared at her reflection, horrified at what was looking back. Her hair, mostly out of the braid, stood up from her head in a frizzy halo. Her cheeks were ruddy and her lips were dry and cracked. Dark circles underneath her eyes and branch scratches ran along her cheek. Her clothes were wrinkled and worn, having been slept in, hiked in, and now flown through the air in. *Ugh!*

Outside the door, Bart walked over to Marc

standing guard, and smirked. "Something going on between you and the pretty doctor?"

Marc scowled, knowing his friend wasn't the only one wondering the same thing.

Bart threw up his hands and said, "Hey, don't sweat it. The rest of us have found someone when on a case. And not just any someone, but *the* someone."

"She's special," Marc admitted, "and damn if I'm not crazy about her."

"But?"

"But, it probably hasn't escaped your notice that we live in different states. Hardly a situation that makes for a strong relationship."

"So, what? You giving up…or are you going to fight for it?" Bart pushed.

Kendall heard voices just outside the door and she hesitated, curiosity taking over. She recognized Marc's voice but was unable to tell whom he was speaking with. Pinching her lips together, she realized he had been concerned over the same thing that ate at her. Whatever pull they felt toward each other was mired in the difficulty of connecting their separate lives.

Refusing to think about it now, she turned on the hot water, grabbing a few more paper towels, and washed her face. It did not help with her appearance, but she felt slightly cleaner.

Exiting the bathroom, she cast a rueful look up to Marc, seeing Bart standing to the side. "Well, it felt good to use a toilet and have hot water, but I could have done without the mirror!"

Chuckling, Marc bent to place a kiss on her lips.

"We'll both feel better after a hot shower and clean clothes," he agreed.

As Marc headed into the toilet, Bart smiled and said, "Go on and grab some food and hot coffee. Also get whatever else you might need."

She cast her eyes out toward the small store and whispered, "I don't have any money with me. My bill-fold is in my tote and I don't know where it is."

"It's in the helicopter," he replied. "Your tote was hooked on you when you came up." He leaned down, getting in her line of vision and said, "But you don't need it. Everything is charged to our account. This is business."

Wrinkling her brow as she pondered his words, he explained, "This mission is the Saints', so we cover all costs. Now get some food for you and anything else you need."

Kendall wandered over and grabbed a tube of lip balm and lotion, planning on paying them back for the personal items, before moving to the aisle with food. She was soon joined by Marc and the others as they grabbed a few items before each getting hot coffee.

Marc slipped his arm around her waist, reveling in the smile she beamed his way. Leaning down, he whispered, "How are you doing?"

"I should be asking you that question," she replied. "You're the one who was injured—"

"I'm fine," he interrupted. "But I'm worried about you."

"I have to admit, I'm dying for a hot shower or maybe a long soak in a tub and to wash my hair, but honestly?" her eyes glanced to the back of the store as she blushed, "Just using a flushing toilet and washing my hands was fabulous!"

He chuckled as he kissed the top of her head before agreeing, "Yeah, here's to indoor plumbing!"

22

A couple of hours later, Logan landed once again, only this time as the passengers looked out, they could see an old cabin with a large hangar in the back. Marc glanced at Bart, who just grinned. "Don't let Preacher's place fool you. He's got a sweet setup here."

Once inside, Logan stepped over to Kendall and Marc and said, "Make yourselves at home. I'll let the others show you where the bathrooms and bedrooms are."

Marc heard the intake of breath from her as Bart opened the door to the guest bathroom. While not large or ornate, it was clean, warm, and had a soaker tub with a shower. Looking down at her face, Marc smiled seeing her appreciative gaze. "You first, sweet girl."

Bart grinned as he left the room and she turned to Marc, "Oh, the idea of as much hot water as I want is overwhelming! What if I use it all before you get a chance?"

His cock twitched at the idea of her, naked in the

shower, and he groaned. "Well, I could join you to save the hot water, but then we'd never come out." Seeing her blush, he chuckled. "You'd better get in or I just might decide that we need that shower together after all."

Eyes alight, she asked, "Do you think Logan would mind if I soak in the bathtub later?"

The idea of her in the tub sent more shock waves to his dick and he hung his head. "No, babe. You take care of you right now." Leaning down to kiss the top of her head, he left the room quickly before he gave in to his base urges and skipped the bath to throw her on the bed immediately.

Jack had been notified as soon as the pick-up was made successfully, but as Kendall showered, Marc called his boss himself.

"Good to hear from you, man," Jack said, his voice shaking with unusual emotion. "This mission went to hell and I hated not being able to give you the support you needed."

"I kept thinking of Cam and Miriam, stuck in the Mexican jungle," Marc remembered. "It was a hell of a mission, but we did fine."

"You can tell Dr. Rhodes that her father has been informed of her rescue. I understand she handled herself well, given the circumstances."

"Absolutely," Marc enthused. "She did just what she needed to do each step of the way. I suppose you know she saved my life."

"I can't wait to meet her," Jack said, before turning back to business. "I know you just got back but we need to consider the next step. The original plan was for her to go straight to D.C. for the meeting with Homeland Security. However, they sent representatives to Louisiana and there was a meeting yesterday. I've informed the representatives of her return and they'd like to speak to her ASAP, so you can fly to Louisiana tomorrow morning and she'll meet with them tomorrow afternoon. We'll need to stay vigilant because I've got suspicions concerning some of her co-workers here and Luke's checking into them."

"What about my plane?"

"Got Nick and Monty still in Alaska checking into the FBI office there."

"I've been wanting to get back to Virginia, so I can work with Luke and Charlie there to do some digging myself, but it sounds like you need Kendall back in Louisiana."

"Yeah, after you've had a day to recuperate Bart'll charter a flight for you to come here. Bart, Jude, and Blaise will head back to Virginia."

"You want me in Louisiana too?"

Chuckling, Jack replied, "Figured you'd like to keep the security mission until we know where the threat to her is coming from. And if Bart is to be believed, you and Dr. Rhodes have gotten close."

"Bart and his fuckin', gossipin' mouth!" Marc growled, shaking his head. "He's worse than the women!"

Jack laughed and said, "Well, just remember her father is here. See you when you arrive."

Disconnecting, Marc sat on the bed for a moment

until interrupted by Kendall walking out of the bathroom, steam billowing out of the room all around her. All thoughts of her in danger flew out of his mind as he watched her glow with pink-tinged skin and her wet hair hanging down her back. Standing, he moved swiftly to her, his arms encircling her as he pulled her into his chest.

"God, you smell good," he exclaimed, inhaling the scent of her shampoo. "I hate to let you go, but with you this clean, I've got to take a shower as well." Pushing her back slightly so he could see her face, he teased, "Did you leave any hot water for me?"

Playfully slapping him on the arm, she moved away and stepped over to the bed. "Yes! I skipped the bath so there'd be sure to be some left and you could get in sooner. What's the plan?" she asked, as she ran a comb through her hair.

"Well, we'll stay here tonight, get a good night's sleep, and then tomorrow you and I'll take a charter flight back to Louisiana."

At those words, she whirled around, eyes wide. "Another plane?" she moaned, her expression falling. "Can't we drive?"

"That's over thirty hours of driving, Kendall," he said shaking his head. His heart ached at her fear. "Sweet girl, if I had a magic wand to get you there without having to fly, I would use it…but we need to get you back."

Rubbing his chin, he looked up sharply when she asked, "What?"

Before he could speak, she added, "When you are trying to think of what to say to me, you rub your chin."

Barking out a laugh, he said, "Okay, Miss Observant, you're right." He told her about the meeting and watched closely as her eyes morphed from fear to shrewd.

"I'm sure Dr. Wallace was more than happy to share our information," she said, her eyes narrowed in irritation.

Cocking his head, Marc queried, "When I asked you about your work and why someone would want you out of the picture, you said that you all worked on the projects and you weren't the only one responsible."

"That's true, but he's never hidden the fact that he'd like to take over the lab. I'm sure he thought my dad would retire earlier." Shrugging, she said, "He always got pissy when I was the one who presented at conferences, but that's just professional envy...not a threat."

Marc said nothing, but tucked that information away to investigate later. *I'll be able to talk to the good Dr. Wallace myself when I get to Louisiana.*

"Speaking of tonight," she said drawing his thoughts back to the present. "Um...where will we all sleep?"

Grinning, he replied, "Logan's got his own room, obviously, plus two spare rooms. Bart's already said he'll take the pullout in the den and Blaise and Jude'll share the bunks in the other room."

"Bunks? All of your friends are huge! They'll never fit in bunks!" As she pursed her lips and looked at the double bed next to her, she turned her gaze back to his. "Are we sharing this room?" she gasped, blushing.

"You got a problem sharing a bed with me?" he teased.

"No…but, what about them?" she lowered her voice to a whisper.

"They know we've been sleeping on the ground and they'd all like us to get a good night's sleep on a good mattress. There's no hotel around that's safe, so it's the best solution." Smirking, he added, "I've got no problem sleeping with you."

Rolling her eyes, she said, "Do they know that we've, um…"

Placing his hands on her shoulders, he said, "There's no locker room talk happening between me and my co-workers, so rest easy. What's happening between you and me is private. My friends respect that and they'll respect you."

Biting her lip, she looked uncertain as she asked, "I wasn't sure…about…us. Um…you know…when we got back." Throwing her hands to her sides, she said, "God, I sound so stupid when I'm nervous."

Sliding his hands from her shoulders, down her arms, so that he could link his fingers with hers, he bent forward resting his forehead against hers. "I know the past days have been crazy. But for me, I think you know you mean something…not just a fun time on a fucked-up mission."

Nodding, she smiled, letting out a long breath. "I know. And me too. I'm just worried about the logistics of this whole thing." Squeezing his fingers, she added, "Okay, go take your shower and I'll wander out and see if I can help in the kitchen. I'm still starving."

Thirty minutes later, Marc emerged from the back rooms and found Kendall happily ensconced in the kitchen with Logan, delectable smells emanating from the stove. Blaise was in the den, talking on his phone. Bart and Jude were sitting at the kitchen bar, chatting with Logan.

"Oh, my God," Marc moaned, "what am I smelling?"

"Tacos," Kendall answered, her eyes glowing as she twisted her head around to look at him. They smiled at each other, both knowing how much the scent of the spicy food was teasing their appetites.

Logan grabbed some paper plates from a cabinet and tossed them on the counter. "Come and get it," he called out. The other Saints stepped back, allowing Kendall and Marc to fill their plates first. Sitting at a long table, with benches instead of chairs, the group dug in, moans of appreciation coming from all, but loudest from Kendall and Marc.

"Don't you get lonely out here?" Kendall asked between bites.

Marc knew Logan had been Bart's SEAL commander and, while he was grateful for the rescue, knew not to ask about his work. As he glanced around the simple, but comfortable, log cabin, he wondered what secrets it held. *Not many people have a former Army Lakota helicopter in their hangar along with a smaller, tourist bird.*

"I like it secluded," Logan answered, a smile dancing at the corners of his mouth.

"Do you do a lot of rescuing?" she continued.

Marc started to interrupt, but Logan replied, "Yeah, I

MARYANN JORDAN

do some ski and hiker rescues in the mountains around here."

Licking her lips, drawing Marc's undivided attention to her mouth, she nodded, "I wondered why you had such a big helicopter."

The other Saints smiled indulgently, knowing Kendall's curiosity would soon pass and Logan was perfectly able to handle her inquisition with enough facts to be believable and enough fiction to keep his business secret.

The topic of conversation soon moved over to the reason they were there. "I just have such a hard time believing that anyone would want me or my dad harmed," she exclaimed.

Bart had briefed Marc on the Saints' findings but left it up to him to choose what to disclose to Kendall. Marc wanted to keep her up on all information, knowing her insight would be needed.

Turning toward her, trying to ignore the moans she made while her lips closed around a taco, he said, "We've got co-workers in Alaska working on the angle of who up there would have tampered with the plane. And we've got co-workers in Louisiana who are investigating the facility where you and your dad work."

Her eyebrows dipped into a "V" as she shook her head slightly. "But no one there would profit from our being killed."

"Kendall," Jude interjected, gaining her attention. "You never know what's going on in someone's personal life that can impact their professional life." Seeing her still-confused expression, he added, "Something that would make them sell out...their co-workers or their country."

Eyes wide at the implication, she almost responded negatively, but instead mulled his words over in her mind. "As a scientist, I have to be open to all types of possibilities when determining the outcome of an experiment." Slowly letting out a long breath, she twisted back toward Marc. "I'll be open to whatever I need to consider, to make sure we get who we're after."

The other men chuckled at her determination, respect in their eyes. Marc held her gaze and for the first time on a mission, his heart beat erratically at the thought of her in danger.

Later that night, Marc sat up with the others discussing the case as Kendall went to bed. She had hugged each man in thanks and then gratefully headed to the bed in the guest room, excited for a mattress. She wondered when Marc would join her, but sleep claimed her long before he made it in.

After she left the room, Marc said, "Okay, you've given me the overview, now I want everything you've got. I'm torn between wanting to head back to Alaska to kick the ass of whoever fucked with my plane and heading to Louisiana to see who set her up."

"That all?" Bart asked, a smirk on his lips.

Holding his gaze, Marc grinned. "Nope, I'd also like to head back to Virginia...with her at my side." His friends grinned while Logan simply shook his head.

Slipping underneath the covers with her a few hours later, Marc reveled in the feel of the soft sheets and the warm body that snuggled up to him, pillowed with the comfortable mattress. Wrapping his arms around her, he closed his eyes as the scent of her shampoo teased his nostrils. He had thought about this moment for the past several days and had to admit it was better than he had imagined...and he had imagined it as perfect.

I may never be able to sleep with her in my arms again. That was the last thought he had before slipping into slumber.

Waking up the next morning, he knew he had to do something because it was different...she was different. All he wanted to do was to lie there, wrapped up in her.

23

Kendall clung to the Saints and Logan as she said good-bye, offering tearful thanks for her rescue once more. Then she clung to Marc's hand during most of their chartered flight, although it was peacefully uneventful as they landed in Baton Rouge by early afternoon. Planting a kiss on her lips as they taxied into the hangar, Marc whispered, "You good?"

Smiling against his lips, she murmured, "With you beside me? Always."

Hoping her words were true, he grinned as the plane came to a stop.

Marc alighted first, seeing Jack standing near Kenneth Rhodes. A flash of doubt flew through his mind at the thought of her life in Louisiana and his in Virginia. Moving slightly to allow Kendall a chance to see her father also, he watched as she screamed, "Dad!"

Running to her father, he captured her in his embrace, tears filling his eyes.

Marc headed over to Jack and Patrick, shaking their

hands as he shot a glance to the side, ascertaining Kendall was all right. She was tearful, but smiling. As he turned back, Jack and Patrick both smirked at him. "Yeah, yeah," he said, rubbing his chin as he grinned at them.

Kendall dragged her father over to Marc, making the introductions. Kenneth shook Marc's hand vigorously, thanking him for saving his daughter. As the group made their way to the SUV, Kendall slipped her hand into Marc's. He dropped his gaze down to their hands before lifting his head, cocking his eyebrow at her. She replied with a smile of her own as she linked her fingers tightly with his. As he assisted her into the back seat of the vehicle, he noted her father's gaze was latched on their hands as well.

It did not take long to drive into town, Kendall insisting they go to the NCBRT first, against Kenneth's protests.

"Dad, I had a chance to shower and rest last night. I've got work to do today." Turning to Marc she asked, "Do you think there's any reason not to go in?"

His jaw tight, he replied, "I hate like hell to put you in danger, but it's probably no secret that you're still alive."

"Will you stay with me?" she asked, her voice less sure.

"You got it," he replied.

"Kendall," her dad interrupted. "Plans have changed. We have a meeting scheduled with the representatives from Homeland Security for this afternoon, but they still want us to come to D.C. as well. We've decided to send a contingency. Cliff wants to go, but he's not a good presenter, so Will and Fahdil are going as well."

"Then I'm going too!" Kendall stated emphatically. As soon as her father opened his mouth, she argued, "No, Dad. I'm not having him step all over my research. Will and Fahdil are good, but I know the research implications better than anyone!"

Unable to disagree with her assessment, Kenneth looked over at his daughter, taking her hand in his. "I just want you safe," he said, his voice breaking with emotion.

Leaning her head onto her father's shoulder, she said, "Dad, with Marc I'll be as safe as I could ever hope to be."

Jack and Patrick shared a smile as the Saints' boss said, "Looks like we'll be heading back to Virginia sooner rather than later!"

Stepping into the conference room full of co-workers, Kendall smiled at the group, noting the expressions of both shock and happiness. She wished Marc had not insinuated that someone from the NCBRT might be behind the sabotage, but now the thought stuck with her. Determined to take charge, she said, "Well, I'm back from the wilds of Canada and ready to get to work. I understand Kenneth is getting a contingency of us together to attend the meeting in D.C.— "

"There's no need for you to go," Cliff interrupted, his

glower firmly in place. Estelle shot him a glare, but he continued to insist. "I can handle the meeting."

"I'm sure you can handle the technical aspect just fine, but we will be going as a group, nonetheless."

Will grinned before attempting to cover his amusement behind his hand. Cliff was too angry to notice, but Kendall observed Estelle looking around the room, her mouth in a tight line of disapproval.

Turning to Fahdil, Kendall asked, "How's your wife?"

Smiling his appreciation, Fahdil replied, "Much better thank you. It was minor surgery and my daughter has come to check on her. I'm also expecting my son to come and visit as well, so I'll be able to make the trip with you."

"Perfect," she replied before turning back to the group. "Okay, you have your presentations to prepare and we will leave first thing tomorrow morning. Estelle will have the flight arrangements, right?"

Estelle forced a smile on her face as she nodded. "My assistant will email you with the details."

At that, the group dispersed with many coming to hug Kendall and to offer their thanks for her safe return.

Finally, turning to Marc, who was standing by the door, she walked over to his embrace. Leaning her head back to look into his face, she reached up to touch his dimple. "What are you smiling about?"

"Seeing you come in here and take charge was sexy as fuck!"

Laughing, she said, "Would you believe that before

the trip to Alaska and everything that happened over the past days, I wouldn't have done this?"

"So what's changed?"

Taking a deep breath, she shook her head slowly. "I don't know exactly, but managing to survive in the wilderness...let's just say, I found my backbone!"

"I'd say it shook some sass into you," Marc pronounced as he lowered his head to capture her lips. After a moment, he pulled back reluctantly and asked, "So what do you need to do today?"

"Mmm, I'll get Karen to pull together my notes and then let's head to my place. I've got plants to water, packing to do, and I'm dying for some Chinese food!"

"Anything else?" he murmured against her lips.

"And I think I can just fit in making love to my mountain man," she replied, her giggle cut off as his lips descended once more.

Jack and Patrick landed in Virginia and smiled as Cam picked them up at the airport. Shaking hands, they piled into the Saints' SUV and headed back to the compound.

"Anything new?" Cam asked as he maneuvered the large vehicle along the country roads.

"Marc and Kendall will be coming here after all," Jack said, gaining a lifted eyebrow from Cam. Chuckling, Jack explained. "Dr. Kenneth Rhodes needs to send a group to D.C. tomorrow and Kendall will head it up. So, Marc will be accompanying the scientists to D.C."

Shaking his head, Cam said, "And I thought you

were indicating there was something between Marc and the younger Dr. Rhodes." He caught the shared look between Jack and Patrick and grinned. "Oh, so I see I might be right after all."

Jack, getting back to business, asked, "Charlie and Luke find anything?"

Nodding, Cam said, "I heard her say this morning that she was finally getting somewhere. I think they'll have a report for all of us as soon as we get back."

Stepping into Kendall's apartment, Marc did a quick walkthrough for security before allowing her to step through the door. As he watched her enter, his gaze roamed around the space, curious about her home. The apartment was not large, although it was in a nice part of town. Boring beige carpeting and white walls were broken up with a colorful sofa and comfortable chair facing a television, flanked with floor to ceiling book-shelves. A large window overlooked a nearby park, offering a view of trees and a small pond.

She watched him take in her apartment before shrugging, "It's not much, but it's home."

Grinning, he stalked over to her and, with a kiss to her forehead, said, "Anywhere with you is home, sweet girl."

"I chose this one because of the park view." Laughing, she said, "Now that I've camped in the wilds, my little park seems kind of tame." Holding his gaze, she added, "I'm really glad you're here with me."

"Nowhere else I'd rather be," he admitted, fighting the urge to lead her into the bedroom and peeling her clothes off one by one.

Blushing slightly, she said, "Um...I know I wanted to order Chinese, but I wondered if maybe you'd like to...um—"

Grinning, he pulled her tightly into his body, his erection pressing into her stomach, and watched her eyes light. "You asking if I want to take you to bed before Chinese?" Seeing her lips curve into a delicious smile as she nodded, he scooped her up into his arms, stalking down the hall before depositing her in the middle of her bed.

"It's only a double and not a king," she apologized, considering his large body fitting onto her bed.

"Then, darlin'," he mumbled as he kissed her, "we'll just have to get closer."

Peeling her clothes off slowly, he fought the urge to hurry, knowing he wanted to take his time to savor every moment. Not knowing how long they would have together, he vowed to make sure he spent his time worshiping her body. He moved his hand from her hips to grasp the material of her shirt, pulling it upward. She leaned forward just enough to allow him to slide it over her head before he tossed it to the side.

Her silky breasts spilled out of the top of her lacy bra and he trailed his lips from hers, kissing his way tortuously down her neck into her cleavage. Kendall's skin came alive as his lips moved over her breasts. Unfastening her bra, he peeled it away and it joined her shirt as it was tossed over the edge of the bed.

Sliding down her body, he tugged her pants down past her hips, snagging her panties as he went. With her body spread out before him, a feast to be savored, he leaned over while resting his weight on one hand as he admired her perfection.

Her rosy tipped nipples beckoned and he obliged. Sucking one deeply into his mouth, he nipped with his teeth before soothing the sting with his tongue. She writhed as the sensation shot straight from her breasts to her core.

She giggled in shock as he stood up and grabbed her ankles to pull her to the side of the bed. Raising her head, she watched as he laid a trail of open-mouth, wet kisses from her breasts down her stomach, ending between her legs. With her spread wide, he feasted on her wet folds, sliding his tongue deep inside.

Throwing her head back on the mattress as the sensations swept over her, her fingers clutched the comforter. Her sex throbbed as his tongue continued its thrusts. She rocked her hips upward, unable to keep still. He chuckled, placing his large hand on her stomach to hold her in place. Licking her folds, he pressed his tongue inside her sex before moving up slightly to pull her clit into his mouth. One hand slid towards her breasts, slightly pinching a nipple.

Kendall cried out as sparks flew out from her core in all directions. Her fingers left the covers to move over his head, still between her legs. He lapped up her juices as the orgasm created the flow he had been waiting for.

Unsure if she could move, her legs flopped to the sides as her heart pounded erratically. Standing, Marc jerked his t-shirt over his head before shucking his jeans and boxers, freeing his erection. Crawling back over her body, he dragged her higher on the bed. Lifting her head, she admired the physique towering over her. Seeing him naked in the light of day, his muscular body proudly on display, her chest heaved as she sucked in a deep breath. Over six feet of honed muscles, his six-pack abs led downward to his massive legs, his cock standing out ready to join his body with hers.

With the scent of her sex filling the air, he kissed her legs as he moved up her body, nipping at her stomach before moving to her breasts. Lowering his hips between her legs after rolling on a condom, his dick strained to enter her. Gazing down at the face of this beautiful woman, so unlike any woman he had ever been with, he marveled at how well they fit. "Hey, sweet girl," he whispered against her smiling lips.

Plunging his straining cock deep inside her in one thrust, he groaned at the sensation of her hot, tight core squeezing him. Her hips moved upwards to meet his as his thrusts became more forceful. With wild abandon, he pumped furiously, as though reaching for a secret place inside of her that he wanted to touch. With that intensity, it did not take long until she was moaning his name, her climax roaring through her.

He pumped until her sex stopped milking him, then he quickly pulled out, much to her dismay. Before she could question him, he flipped her over onto her stomach and grasped her hips to pull them up and back.

"Just lay down on your side," he said, his hand gently

guiding her. Cuddling her from the back, he lifted her top leg as he slid his fingers back through her drenched folds, giving her clit a light pinch. Immediately, she felt her sex clench and moisture pooled again. She gasped and he leaned over her back.

"Is that okay, sweet girl?" he asked, not wanting to make any assumptions.

Moaning in pleasure was the only answer she was able to give, and he chuckled again as he thrust his engorged dick into her waiting core.

This angle brought new sensations and she felt as though her world was tipping on its axis. His fingers gripped her hips, digging in to hold her as he moved slowly at first and then more swiftly.

He held her tightly, one hand on her breast, as his body dove into hers, over and over. Loving the friction inside, she desired to feel the sensations on her clit. Slowly moving her hand down between her legs, she fingered herself.

"Oh, babe. Seeing you touch yourself is gonna make me harder," he panted, between thrusts.

Sliding her fingers back to her clit, she rubbed and pulled on the swollen nub, feeling her inner core tighten with need.

Wanting her to come again before he did, he tugged gently on her sensitive nipple, eliciting whimpers from her.

"Are you close?" he asked roughly.

"Yes," she panted. The gripping sensations from her sex sent sparks outward as the pressure began to build, straining until she found her release.

Her inner walls convulsed around his cock as he gave over to his own climax. Head thrown back, thick neck muscles straining, he pulsated into her waiting body, experiencing a release unlike any he had ever felt in his life.

Laying with legs and arms tangled, no words came as their sweaty bodies slowly cooled in the lazy afternoon. At that moment, nothing else mattered—not the distance between their homes or jobs and not the fact that he needed to protect her from harm. He dealt with the condom, eager to not have anything between them again once they were sure her birth control was back in place.

As the lust-filled haze slowly lifted, she cupped his face and, with a grin, asked, "So...Chinese or round two?"

With a loud whoop, Marc opted for round two.

24

The next morning found Marc and Kendall once more settled into airplane seats for the flight to D.C. As she boarded, she was surprised to find that they were all sitting in business class. Watching Marc easily store their carry-on luggage in the large bin above, she locked her eyes on the way his muscles flexed against the sleeves of his shirt. Blinking out of her lust induced stupor, she said, "Estelle must have added this perk to our flight."

Marc, grinning down at her as he caught her gaze traveling over his body, replied, "This'll be a lot more comfortable for you than our first trip together."

Settling into the seat, she placed her hand on his arm, confessing, "Looking back, I'll always be grateful for flying with you in your plane."

Across the aisle sat Will and Fahdil, chatting amicably, and in front of them Estelle and Cliff talked, their heads bent together.

Karen and another intern, Bob, chosen by Kenneth,

were sitting in front of Marc and Kendall, excitedly talking about the flight.

Enjoying her coffee and pastry, Kendall licked the powdered sugar off her lips, capturing Marc's attention. Staring at her mouth as her pink tongue flicked out to slide along her upper lip, his cock stirred. Taking a deep breath before letting it out slowly, he willed his dick to behave. *It's gonna be a long flight!*

"Marc?"

Jerking as she called his name, his gaze jumped to hers. "Sorry," he mumbled.

Grinning, she said, "Hmmm, where was your mind? On last night, perhaps?"

His gaze raked across her face as he growled, "Girl, if you don't want me to introduce you to the mile-high club, then don't talk about last night, 'cause this flight will be damn uncomfortable!"

Giggling, she agreed, "You're right. If I think about it I'll be dragging you to the bathroom myself!" As she sobered, she glanced around the airplane cabin and, lowering her voice, she whispered, "Do you think any of us are in danger?"

His jaw tightened as he replied, "I'll assume the worst so that I'll be prepared for anything." Seeing the light in her eyes dim, he added, "That's what I'm here for—so you can focus on your meeting."

"It'll be hard not to continually look over my shoulder all the time."

"Good," he confirmed, gaining a surprised look from her. "That way you'll be cautious. Until we know what the threat is and where it's coming from, I need you vigilant."

The flight passed with no problems and Kendall breathed a sigh of relief as they disembarked, heading to the taxis waiting to take them to their hotel. Walking into the two story lobby of the four-star hotel, Marc scoped out the area as she moved toward the reception desk.

Calling out to the group, Kendall reminded them to meet back at one o'clock in the lobby to taxi over to the Department of Homeland Security.

Grumbling under his breath, Cliff mocked, "We know what to do."

Estelle moved to the reception desk as well, her lips continually pursed, and Kendall wondered if sitting next to the dour Cliff caused her to be even more irritable.

Standing back slightly, Marc viewed nothing untoward, but kept his eyes on the others in their group just the same. Fahdil and Will got their rooms first and Marc noted that Will and Karen were on the same floor. Bob ended up with a room on the first floor. Cliff and Estelle also received rooms near each other.

Unsure if any of their room placements were significant, Marc nonetheless noted the whereabouts of all in their party. Kendall checked in and turned as the others made their way to the elevator. Grinning, she handed Marc the room key. "Guess you're bunking with me," she gloated.

Laughing, he was pleased for the empty elevator,

since the others took the first one that came to the lobby. Once inside, he walked her backward until she pressed up against the wall, his body moving in to claim hers. With his hands on either side of her head, he dipped down until his lips captured hers. His kiss was dominant as his tongue thrust inside of her mouth, relishing the taste of coffee and the mint gum she was so fond of chewing. Breathing her in, he backed away only when the elevator dinged their arrival at their floor.

Licking her kiss-swollen lips, she breathed heavily. Reluctantly moving out of the privacy of the elevator, they hurried down the hall of the seventh floor to find their room. Opening the door, Marc stepped through first, his gaze sweeping the room, first for security and then in appreciation.

The room was elegant with heavy wooden furniture, a thick, cream-colored down comforter on the king-sized bed, and windows that gave a view of some of the grand, stone government buildings' architecture. Turning, he lifted his eyebrow, observing Kendall as she stepped up next to him peering out the window.

"You usually travel this way?"

"No," she laughed, wrapping her arms around his waist as she snuggled close. "I decided to upgrade." Looking into his face, her heart skipped a beat as she took in his rugged handsomeness, unable to believe he was here with her. "I wanted to treat you since you're doing all you can to protect me."

Pulling her close, he replied, "Sweet girl, you don't owe me anything." Seeing doubt flash through her eyes, he rushed to explain. "No, no, not just because this is my job. But because you've got to know that I'd do anything to keep you safe." Bending down to hold her gaze, he promised, "You're in my heart."

Lifting on her toes, she kissed him, soft and gentle, letting her lips say what her heart was feeling. As she settled back on her heels, she glanced at the clock. "Do we have time to play before we have to be back downstairs?"

"Oh, yeah…plenty of time to play."

With that, he scooped her up and deposited her in the middle of the bed, both willing to skip lunch for time together.

Nick and Monty met with Hank at a restaurant in town at the insistence of the young FBI agent. They had been planning on returning to Virginia, when Hank contacted them early in the morning for a meeting.

Hank was already in a booth when they arrived, his eyes darting around as they slid into the booth opposite of him. Neither spoke, waiting to see what Hank had to say.

"Look, I know you all suspect me, but I had nothing to do with Marc's plane—"

"You weren't there? You didn't walk away and not continually observe them?" Nick interrupted, his eyes glaring at the agent sitting across from him.

Hank dropped his head as he sighed. "Yes, yes…I know. I fucked up and I'll be paying for that mistake for a long time. But I've learned from it and I can't believe you never made a mistake."

The tic in Nick's jaw was the only outward expression of irritation. He opened his mouth to speak, but Monty stepped in. "You found something?"

Hank nodded several times before leaning in and saying, "I've been checking into everything. Kevin asked me to work on 'cause, like everyone else, he's pissed at me, but he was the only one in our office to know that Dr. Kenneth Rhodes was being flown back to Louisiana." Rubbing his hand over his face, he added, "I don't know who to trust other than you two."

"And…" Monty prodded.

"I've checked the IDs of the men who were supposed to show up that night and it's no surprise that they weren't the two men I let in. Obviously the names were the same and they had fake badges. I've been trying to figure out who they were and started with some of the known members of the terrorist cell we have here in Alaska."

Nick, calmer now that Hank was making sense and not excuses, nodded for him to continue.

"Okay, so far I haven't identified them, but in doing more research, I have learned that the cell recruits heavily from universities, especially the young who might be gullible or financially needy. I've been going through the database of who we know is there."

"No hits yet?" Nick asked.

"Not positive, but I've compiled a list of some names, though I don't have pictures of all of them." Sighing heavily, he added, "We're a small office and Kevin's already given me another case to work on. I just thought that maybe with your resources you would be able to help."

"Give me what you've got and I'll send it to my people," Monty said, glancing at the list that Hank immediately pushed across the table. Lifting his gaze back to Hank, he said, "We were going to leave today, but I think we should stay at least another day, to give my group a chance to look this over." Nick nodded, but stayed mute.

Hank heaved a sigh and, with a look at his watch, said, "I've got to get back to the office." Standing, he added, "Thank you," before he left the restaurant.

Nick moved to the now empty side of the booth and asked, "You believe him? Or is he blowing smoke to take suspicion away from himself?"

Rubbing his chin, Monty shook his head. "Don't know. But let me get this to Luke and see if we can start making sense of it all."

Jack and Patrick settled around the conference table with the other Saints. Looking over to his computer experts, Jack asked, "What have you got for us?"

Luke smiled at Charlie and said, "Take it away."

Rolling her eyes at his comment, she turned her focus to the others around the table. "As you know, Luke and I focused originally on the security feeds from the hangar to see what we could discern, but they had been interrupted. So, while we knew we were dealing with professionals, we had no way to counter what they had done to protect their identity. So, next, we went after the financials of any and all possible suspects. We began combing through the agents in the FBI office in Fairbanks and the people who worked in the NCBRT."

"And," Luke interjected, "as you know, there are a lot of people to consider and it takes a long time to work through all the possible money routes. But, we have made a few connections worth digging into further."

"As far as the Alaskan group, we haven't found any money concerns with Kevin, Hank, or Sharon. But we did find that Sharon Chikuk's family has been involved in protests against the government taking over native Alaskan territories for oil routes. No terrorists' activities, but something to note in case she would be susceptible to blackmail. So far, we've found nothing overtly suspicious with Kevin or Hank, but I'm still digging," Charlie reported.

Flashing more information onto the wall screen, she continued. "Now, here's where it gets interesting, and it's with the people in Louisiana. I finally found an account with a significant amount of money deposited into it, in the name of Fahdil Mahdi." At that, only the sounds of the Saints cursing could be heard.

"Hang on guys," Luke interrupted, gaining their attention once more. "The problem is that the account is not set up with his social security number—it's a fake one. So, we don't know if it's his account, and that's how he's hiding things, or if it's someone else's account and they are using his name."

"How do we find out?" Blaise asked.

"We're still working on it," Charlie admitted. "Like I said, these things take some time."

"Is he the only one right now that's suspicious?" Chad queried.

Shaking his head, Luke admitted, "Nope. Estelle Barnaby has not hidden her displeasure at being assigned to the *backwaters of Louisiana*." His fingers made air quotes around her description of her assignment.

Charlie added, "I'm also looking into Dr. Cliff Wallace. His unhappiness at being under Dr. Kenneth Rhodes is well documented and he'd be a perfect candidate for wanting to get rid of both Dr. Rhodes. Now, whether or not either his or Estelle's professional dissatisfaction comes out strong enough to want to kill...we're still trying to find out."

Jack nodded thoughtfully for a moment before continuing assignments. "Charlie, you keep working the financial angle to see who might have the money to pay to have Marc's plane sabotaged. Chad, you and Patrick work with Luke to compile the pictures of all known ISIS members, from any and all databases, and get them to Monty. He's informed me that one of the agents there is trying to identify the men who came into the hangar. Since he's not sure he trusts the other agents, he's working rogue with Monty and Nick. Cam and Bart, you two head up to D.C. and assist Marc in keeping an eye on the NCBRT delegation. We're missing a link... somewhere there's a connection and we're not seeing it yet. Keep on it."

With those orders, the group went back to work.

Marc was allowed entry into the Homeland Security meeting, but sat near the back as he watched the proceedings with great interest. The large room held a massive wooden table in the middle with comfortable leather chairs all around. Along the walls was another row of chairs, filled with those taking notes and supporting the main delegates at the table. He observed Kendall as she sat in between Cliff and Fahdil. Estelle was sitting with some of the DHS personnel and members of the IOC that filled out the table. Will, Karen, and Bob sat behind the others from the NCBRT. Karen held some of Kendall's papers and handed them to her as needed.

Cliff began speaking but as he began to babble in techno-terms the other could not understand, Fahdil interrupted, suggesting Kendall present her research findings. Cliff's eyes narrowed in anger as he shot Estelle a pointed glare, but he kept silent.

Marc knew Kendall preferred the lab to public

meetings but noted with pride as she spoke eloquently, captivating the audience.

"As Dr. Wallace was saying, we all recognize the potential for terrorism to come not from a bomb, but in a way that would be designed to overwhelm our emergency rooms, hospitals, doctors, and build terror in people who would not know if their food, water, or even air was safe. And obviously, at an event such as the Olympics, where you have a large gathering of people from all over the world, the threat of such a terrorist act is concerning."

Looking directly at the members of the IOC, she continued, "Most of these biological causes need an incubation period. This affords the terrorist time to escape or to keep terrorizing before anyone knew what had happened. It could take the medical community days to even realize what they were looking at was a biological terrorists' attack."

"So the symptoms could look like something else?"

Nodding, she looked behind her to indicate Karen should begin the PowerPoint. As it flashed on the boards on either side of the room, allowing all occupants a chance to view it easily, Kendall continued.

"As you can see, many of the symptoms could look like food poisoning or flu—"

"But not necessarily death?" another person asked.

Nodding, Kendall agreed. "The attack does not have to cause a large number of deaths to be effective since the intent is terror, which causes panic and chaos. In fact, many of the biological agents on the lists you have been provided are not fatal."

Fahdil continued with the presentation, reviewing the different agents to be aware of and the potential symptoms they could cause. Cliff jumped in as well, at times talking over Fahdil, causing Marc to grin at the pompous scientist's fight for attention. As his eyes wandered back to Kendall, he saw her gaze land on him, her lips curving ever so slightly. They shared a quick smile before the IOC began asking about prevention and treatments, areas of Kendall's expertise.

Nodding to Karen and Bob to continue to the next presentation, Kendall said, "As long as incapacitating agents aren't used, making sure to have national planning for these attacks is effective. Recognizing the signs and symptoms early is paramount. The strategic stockpile of antibiotics and antivirals, which can be expensive, would be beneficial. Although a terrorist group might be able to create a variant that is resistant to most antibiotics, this is unlikely."

The others around the table began to murmur as she mentioned, "Anthrax, Ebola, Plague, Botulism, Smallpox, and Cholera are, of course, on the lethal end of the spectrum. On the low end is Brucellosis, Tularemia, Q fever, Mycoplasma, and Mycotoin."

As the meeting droned on, Marc studied the participants carefully but was unable to ascertain any overt discord or danger. As the meeting came to a close, another session was planned for the next day.

Walking over to Marc, Kendall smiled up at him, leaning back as she asked, "Were you bored silly?"

"Not at all," he replied, honestly. "It was nice to see you at work."

Scrunching her nose, she replied, "I prefer my lab work, but the dissemination of my lab results is important."

"I thought you were sexy as fuck," he whispered, his breath tickling warm against her ear. Looking at the now empty room, he said, "Do we need to go back to the hotel with the others?"

Sighing, she nodded. "Yeah, we were all going to have dinner together to make sure we're ready for tomorrow's summit." Cutting her eyes upward, she peeked at him through her long lashes. "But after we eat, you and I can disappear to our room."

With a quick kiss, Marc leered his agreement.

A few minutes later the group left the building and stepped outside to hail taxis. Kendall's phone vibrated and she stepped away from the noisy group to answer the call.

"Hello? Hello? I can't hear you," she said, stepping further away. The sound of squealing tires brought the group's attention toward the road behind where the taxis were lined up against the curb. Several pedestrians screamed out a warning as a black sedan with dark-tinted windows jumped the curb, heading straight for Kendall.

Marc sprinted toward her, his arms outstretched as he took her down, twisting mid-air so that he landed on his back, taking the brunt of the fall. Grunting as he rolled quickly, he placed her underneath him before jumping up to pursue the vehicle, but it had already bounced back onto the road, swiping the taxi nearest them. With no identifiable license tag, he cursed as his head swiveled around toward Kendall again. He ran to her noting her disheveled hair and torn stockings.

Kneeling by her side, he noticed her skinned arms and knees. Scooping her into his arms, he placed her in one of the waiting taxis and, turning to the others standing open-mouthed, he shouted, "Get back to the hotel. I've got her and I'm taking her somewhere safe."

Karen ran over with Kendall's purse and shoved it into the back seat. Marc thanked the intern then slid into the seat next to Kendall. Giving the driver an address, he turned to assess her injuries. They appeared to be superficial but she was holding her wrist, which was beginning to swell. Bending swiftly, he slipped off his shoe and unwound the elastic bandage tape from his ankle.

"Marc, don't. You need that!" she protested through gritted teeth. She kept her eyes on him, not wanting to look down at her wrist and seeing what she was afraid she would see.

With the tape in his hand, he said, "Right now, you need this more than I do. Come on, sweetheart, let me have your hand."

Afraid to let go, she twisted around to face him. She grimaced again and his gaze jumped to her face. "Where else does it hurt?"

"Just some aches," she replied. "My wrist is the worst of it."

He gently wrapped her swollen wrist in the bandage, keeping just the right amount of tension on it. He lifted his gaze and saw pain flash through her eyes.

"I'm sorry," she murmured, her focus on her wrist and not his face.

"You're sorry?" he said, eyes wide. "Kendall, I'm the one who's sorry." Seeing her confusion, he shook his head, cursing. "I took my eyes off you. I allowed you to step away to take the call. Then, in my haste to get you safe, I didn't get my arms wrapped around you low enough for you to fall without you hurting your wrist—"

"Marc," she stopped his tirade, her eyes focused on the man who had saved her life, more than once, sacrificing his own body to do so. Gaining his attention, she continued. "This is not your fault. This is the fault of the asshole who tried to run me down."

Sucking in a deep breath as his nostrils flared, he nodded. "You're right, and I'm not giving him another chance."

After the taxi dropped them off at the hotel, he rushed her into the elevator and said, "We're going to the room and then I'm calling my co-workers. We'll get someone to pick us up and then we're getting out of here."

"But the meetings—"

"Your team can handle them. I want you out of here."

"Where are we going?" she asked, her brain having trouble keeping up with his plans.

"My place," he announced.

Several hours later, Kendall gazed out of the window of the SUV as Bart drove her and Marc along the country road toward his house. Blaise was in the front seat, having come along to check her out. He had re-wrapped her wrist as well as Marc's ankle, having had the forethought to bring along a first aid kit. She had wanted to make a quip about them always rescuing her, but the words stuck in her throat as the enormity of the situation hit her. Instead, she had melted into Marc's embrace as they sat in the back seat. She remained quiet as the men talked around her and about her. It should have been offensive but, truthfully, she was glad someone else was in control because out-of-control was all she felt right now.

Marc breathed easier as they approached his drive-way. He had insisted Kendall call Kenneth and, after assuring her father that she was fine, Marc took the phone and told Kenneth of his plans, letting him know that the rest of the delegation would finish the week of presentations, but she was going home with him while the Saints continued to work on discovering who was after her.

After gaining Kenneth's unequivocal appreciation, Marc had disconnected and handed the phone back to Kendall, noting the way she quietly cradled her injured wrist with her hand. Wrapping his arms around her shoulder, he had pulled her in, allowing her to rest her head on his chest.

Now, as Bart turned the SUV onto Marc's driveway, Kendall moved slightly so she could see more. The winter had stripped the leaves from many of the trees, allowing the evergreens to stand out in stark relief, their lush, green branches creating a backdrop for the log cabin coming into view. Smiling for the first time in hours, she leaned closer to the window, amazed at the picturesque scene. Whirling around, she grinned toward Marc. "When you said you lived in a cabin, you really meant a true, log cabin, didn't you?"

"He built it by himself," Blaise commented from the front seat.

"I had some help, as I recall," Marc replied.

"Yeah, but only with the heavy stuff. We helped with the framing, but you did everything else," Bart stated.

"I think it's wonderful," she gushed.

"You haven't seen the inside yet," Marc joked.

Giving him a pretend glare, she said, "I've lived in a true shack in the middle of the woods during a blizzard. I have a feeling this is much more than that!"

The group laughed as Bart came to a stop outside the front porch. Sobering, Bart added, "Jack wants the two of you at the compound as soon as you can make it."

Marc nodded but his eyes cut in doubt toward Kendall. Bart noticed and added, "No worries. The women'll be there too."

Doubt was replaced by mirth as he realized that, after watching each Saint fall for a woman and those women becoming family, he was about to bring Kendall into that fold. Knowing what the other women would assume with the introduction to her, he felt panic hit his chest for a second. *Is this what I want? Kendall?* Then a resounding affirmation hit him and he grinned as he alighted from the vehicle and jogged to her side. *Yes, this is exactly what, and who, I want in my life.*

As Kendall's door opened, she watched as Marc's handsome face slid into a broad smile, sending her pulse into overdrive. She squeaked as he reached in, plucked her from the seat and held her against his chest. Laughing, she protested, "It's my hand that's hurt, not my legs."

"I couldn't figure out how to assist you out of the car without hurting your wrist more," he confessed as he bent to kiss the end of her nose. "Welcome to my home," he said, taking her elbow and escorting her up the front steps to the porch. Looking over his shoulder, he called out, "Tell Jack we'll be there in about an hour. I'd like to get her settled first."

Stepping through the front door, Kendall was enchanted. Thick logs lined the walls of the open floor plan. The living room, with it's red and brown braided rug in front of a stone fireplace, was to the left. To her right was a kitchen and dining area, separated from the living room by an L-shaped counter. The furniture was rustic and masculine. "Oh, my gosh! Your home is charming!" she enthused.

Marc lifted his eyebrow in surprise. "Charming? Never thought of my house as being described as charming."

Whirling around, she looked up at him, her forehead scrunched. "No? And what do your other lady friends call it?"

Holding her gaze, he admitted, "I've never had any

MARYANN JORDAN

women here…other than the Saints' girlfriends or wives."

Her mouth opened to respond but then snapped closed just as quickly. Finally, offering a small smile, she said, "So, are you going to show me around?"

Grinning, he waved his arm in an expansive circle and said, "Well, you've seen the living room and kitchen." He watched as she stepped around the counter and viewed his kitchen.

"I'm impressed," she admitted, her gaze landing on the modern appliances, granite counter tops, and the view out his window of the surrounding woods. Moving back toward him, she followed him down a hall, past a door on the left that opened into a small office filled with books, and two doors on the right, one for a small bathroom and the other for the laundry and mud room. A door leading to the yard on the side of the garage was beyond the washer and dryer.

She noted the room was neat, but not overly so. Muddy boots lay against a wall with a mop and broom hanging from hooks. Some dirty clothes were piled on top of the washing machine and the room had a musty odor.

"Sorry," he mumbled. "I haven't been home since I left to fly to Alaska to meet you."

Giggling, she replied, "It's fine. I love your house…it feels like a real home." Sighing, she added, "I never felt very invested in my apartment in Louisiana, so it has a bit of a sterile appearance."

Moving back into the hall, he began to ascend the L-shaped staircase to the second floor. Upstairs, two doors led from a small landing. "Here's the guest room," he announced throwing open the door to a large room, simply furnished, and through another open door she could see a bathroom. The iron bedframe held a double mattress with a multi-colored, patchwork quilt as the covering. Smiling, she then followed him into the master bedroom, complete with king-sized, log bedframe and another patchwork quilt as it's cover. Through a doorway, she stepped into a huge master bathroom, with separate shower and deep bathtub. Turning back, she observed Marc leaning against the doorframe, a mixture of pride and uncertainty in his eyes. Rubbing his hand over his head, he shrugged as he said, "It's not much, but it's home."

Rushing to him, almost knocking him over in her enthusiasm as she threw her arms around his neck, she gushed, "I love it! I can't believe you built this place yourself. Oh, Marc, it's gorgeous."

As the uncertainty left his face, leaving pride in its place, he bent, sealing his lips over hers. They stood in the doorway of the master bathroom for several minutes, their kiss speaking volumes.

His lips were strong and soft. Firm and yielding. Powerful. Masterful. As she clung to his shoulders, she knew whatever she needed to do to make this relationship work, she would do it.

He groaned as his tongue swept inside her warmth, tasting her essence, and mint, all at once. He loved this house...loved the Saints...but was falling in love with this woman.

Their lips continued to plunder each other's mouths

as their bodies pressed tightly together. Sighing softly, she lowered her heels and he held her against his pounding heartbeat while she touched her swollen lips. She had felt lost in his kiss...and then found, all at the same time.

As stunned as Kendall was at the charm of Marc's log cabin, she was speechless as they drove in Marc's truck through the security gates of Jack's house and compound. As they came out of the woods along the driveway, an enormous log home stood against the backdrop of the Blue Ridge Mountains, a long front porch gracing the front. Marc pulled up and parked next to a multitude of other vehicles.

"Who all is here?" she asked, jerking her head from gawking out the window over to Marc.

Reaching across the console to take her fingers in his hand, carefully avoiding the bandage, he assured, "Just the Saints and some of their women. You'll be fine, I promise."

This time, stepping inside, Kendall was overwhelmed. The first thing she noticed was the two-story stone fireplace and the wall of windows extending from the floor to the vaulted ceiling with the mountain view.

Before she took another step, her gaze landed on a large crowd of men and women sitting around the room.

Her chest heaved as she took a deep breath, attempting to quell her nerves. Warmth invaded her back and she knew Marc had stepped directly behind her even before she felt his hands on her shoulders and his breath wash against her ear in a whisper.

"Breathe, sweet girl. Everyone here is a friend." A slight nod was her only response. Taking her by the hand, he led her over to where the gathering sat, lounging comfortably.

A pretty blonde, with girl-next-door looks, bounded toward the couple, her hands outstretched. "Welcome to our home, Kendall." Hugging Marc, she welcomed him home as well, before turning back to Kendall. "I'm Bethany, Jack's wife."

Jack slid in behind his wife, his hands placed on her shoulders and nodded toward Kendall. "I'm Jack Bryant. You're among friends here, Kendall."

She smiled, saying, "That's just what Marc said." His eyes dropped to her wrapped wrist and she noticed they narrowed as his mouth tightened before he met her gaze and gave a short smile.

"Well, it's true. Let's introduce you to the rest of the group, then we've got some information to go over with you."

Nodding, she followed the pair toward the others, Marc's hand on the small of her back. His fingers felt intimate, comforting. Taking in the large gathering of smiling face, she returned their smiles. A stunning woman with light blonde hair, streaked with pink, purple, and teal rose from her seat and approached first.

"Hi! I'm Angel. My husband, Monty, isn't here. He's in Alaska, still checking things out there. Hopefully you'll get to meet him soon."

Since she had already met Bart, Jude, and Blaise, they introduced their wives and fiancés, Faith, Sabrina, and Grace.

Overwhelmed, she then met Chad and his wife, Dani; Cam and his wife, Miriam; and Patrick and his wife, Evie. Last, she was introduced to Luke and Charlie. It only took her a moment to realize that, not only were they a couple, but they were also both the computer experts for the Saints.

Head spinning, she sat in the chair provided, Marc at her side, and wondered what was next. Bethany and Angel disappeared into the kitchen, plated some desserts for the group and returned to pass them out. Kendall watched, amazed, as the group settled into the camaraderie of old friends. As she quietly observed, she noticed the men were all muscular with a strange combination of don't-fuck-with-me and adoration for their wife or fiancé. *Just like Marc is with me.*

As she continued to watch the group, she wondered what it would be like to have these people as friends and not just a company that wanted to protect her. *I have friends back home...well, more like acquaintances. But I do have friends in the lab...well, more like friendly co-workers.* Blinking rapidly, she realized her life in Louisiana was a bit stale, whereas this gathering was lively. She felt

Marc's hand rest on her shoulder and forced herself to relax.

"Kendall," Bethany called out. "I know you need to work with the Saints but when you're finished, please come back here with us for a while. We get so little time to just hang out and we'd love for you to join us."

Before she could respond, Miriam said, "We also know that you were rushed here and hadn't planned on staying long. If there's anything you need, please let us know. We have lots to share!"

Smiling her acceptance, Kendall started to rise from her seat as the other women did, but Marc's fingers on her shoulder pushed her down slightly, indicating she should remain. The women left the room, heading toward the back hall, leaving only Kendall and Charlie with the men. Nervously she looked to the side, calming as she saw Marc's gentle smile.

"Kendall," Jack stated, "in full disclosure, we have a separate place where we work, but when we have someone we need to talk with, we do it here. My living room is less formal, but secure. No one will know you are here, talking to us. We need to let you know where we are in the investigation and gain information from you that only you might know."

Nodding her understanding, she rubbed her hands on her slacks before posing her face in what she hoped was not a nervous expression when, in fact, her heart was pounding.

Charlie smiled at Kendall and was the first to speak. "At first, we had no idea if your father or you were the intended victim of the plane sabotage. Either way, it was a carefully planned and executed endeavor. Part of it was to use someone in Louisiana to break into the NCBRT building, just enough to set off alarms but not to do any damage or theft. It was enough to disrupt the travel plans of the head of the NCBRT-- your father. And, of course, you as well. It also took someone in Alaska who had the technical know-how to damage a plane in a way that it did not appear damaged at takeoff."

Kendall listened carefully, nodding occasionally, even though what had been said was information she was already aware of. Uncertain what was expected of her, she tried to focus carefully.

Jack took over, "To be able to do that, someone had to have the ability to get badges that appeared to have the right security, and to also know how to disrupt the hangar cameras. So, while the people in Louisiana did not need any technical skill, the ones in Alaska did."

Listening intently, Kendall's hands lay in her lap, fingers twisting, showing that her heart was racing. Marc did not need to look at her face to see her distress. Her muscles, underneath his hand, radiated tension. He gently rubbed his fingers along her neck and shoulder, massaging away the stress in a desire to communicate she was not alone. She spared a small smile toward him and he grinned in return as he felt her relax back against him slightly.

"I understand what you're explaining, but if you are asking if I know anyone with that…um…expertise, I don't."

"What we need from you, Kendall," Luke began, "is your impressions of the people you work with."

Squinting, she replied, "But why? Wouldn't this be done by someone who wants..." Shrugging in frustration, "Oh, I don't know. Maybe they want the NCBRT's lab reports."

"Why?" Bart interjected, leaning forward so that his forearms were resting on his knees.

"I'm sorry? I...I don't understand?"

"Why would someone want the lab reports?" he asked again. "What do you have that someone would want?"

Sucking in her lips for a moment as she churned the possible reasons over in her mind, she finally replied, "Well, we have a lot of information about biological agents that can be used for terrorism. And we have ways of prevention as well as management. Especially for a large population."

"Okay, good," Chad nodded, "but now think of why someone might want that information, or who would be able to use that information."

Wrapping her mind around the prompt, she said, "While a lot of layman's information on the subject can be found with any Google search, we have the definitive scientific evidence of what works, what doesn't work, what to look for, and what to do." Her gaze jumped up to the group before she twisted her head to look at Marc sitting next to her. "While we aren't the only ones in the world working on this, we have one of the premier labs. If some of our information was in the wrong hands, it could advance someone's knowledge of how to release a biological terrorist act. And if they knew the specific antidotes and controlled those, they could keep the affected population from being treated."

"So, essentially, being in the wrong hands could also allow them to sell this information to others interested," Jack added.

Swallowing deeply as understanding swept over her, Kendall nodded.

An hour later, Kendall's frustration was at an all time high. "No, no, no," she repeated. "I work with these people and none of them would sell us out!"

As her gaze landed on the dubious faces of the Saints, she heaved a sigh and repeated, "Maybe it's some low level person who works there, but Drs. Wallace, Mahdi, and Kowtowski would never do this. I may not always like Estelle Barnaby, but she runs that place with an iron fist when it comes to hiring and security." Shrugging, she added, "And it's a good thing, because I know my father is buried in his research and the institution as a whole—not the security or personnel aspects."

"Anyone talk about family problems, money issues? Buying expensive items...things that you were surprised they could afford on their salary? Affairs or dating a lot? Traveling beyond what they do for work?" Luke prompted.

Rubbing her head, Kendall felt the tension headache pounding. Marc silently stood and walked into Jack's kitchen. Pulling down a glass, he filled it with water before walking back and kneeling in front of her. Getting close enough so that his face was the only thing in her line of vision, he said, "Here. I'll get your pills." Digging through her purse, he pulled out the headache tablets and dumped two into her hand.

"I'm sorry," Charlie said softly. "We had no idea you were ill."

Smiling wearily, Kendall explained. "I get headaches from tension, but as long as I take these, it won't go into a migraine."

"Do we need to stop?" Jack asked, brows lifted in concern.

"Baby, we can stop anytime," Marc assured her, his hand cupping the back of her neck.

Drinking more of the water, she shook her head. "No, no. We need to figure this out and I need to be more open to the idea that someone I know may have instigated...or even organized this." With another deep breath, she plunged ahead, "Cliff Wallace wants to head up the NCBRT and, while I know he wants my father's job, so far he's been willing to wait until Dad steps down. I know he thinks I want the job, but that's ridiculous. All I want is to do the research not run the organization." Holding up her hand, she quickly added, "And I have made this clear."

"Estelle Barnaby had to have a security clearance for her position and I doubt she has any skeletons in her closet. Will Kowtowski..." Kendall smiled, causing an unfamiliar flash of jealously to spear Marc.

"He's so laid back. And I think he and Karen, my

research intern, might have a thing going on. But they're both unmarried, so a little office romance wouldn't be harmful since they are not in the same lab and he is not her supervisor." Rubbing her head again, she said, "And Fahdil is such a good man. He's been in the country for several years. He's a family man, with a wife and two children."

Charlie looked up sharply. "Two children?" she questioned.

"Well, yeah...sort of. He has a daughter that is their biological child and his wife's nephew...or some relative, came over several years ago and Fahdil took him in. He refers to him as his son, so I just think of him that way."

The Saints all turned their eyes toward Charlie whose lips were tight with irritation. "Damn," she cursed. "Somehow I missed him!"

"Well, I don't think that he'd be who you're looking for," Kendall stammered, turning to look back toward Marc.

He viewed the worried crease on her brow and said, "We have to look at any possibility."

Leaning closer, she confessed, "But what if my words cause someone to be looked at erroneously? What if I'm creating havoc with someone's life for no reason?"

Sliding his hand from her shoulder down her arm and back again, he tried to infuse his warmth into her stiff limbs. As she let out a deep breath and nodded, he squeezed her gently.

Charlie and Luke began typing on their laptops as

the others waited. Looking back up, Charlie said, "Does he have a different last name?"

"Yeah, but I'm afraid I don't know what it is."

"No worries, it should show up. I'll keep digging." A moment later, she looked up again. "Tariq Mustafa. It says he's twenty years old."

"Yes, he came here to attend school," Kendall explained.

"In Louisiana?"

Shaking her head, Kendall said, "He started in Louisiana, before transferring somewhere else, but I have no idea where. I'm sorry," she said, her hands clasped tightly in her hands. "I just never really paid attention. It never came up in conversation…or if it did, I was probably preoccupied and it went in one ear and out the other."

Her shoulders slumped and it was Patrick, watching her body language, who spoke. "Kendall, don't beat yourself up. Most of us aren't used to being tuned into what everyone says. There's so much that goes on in our daily lives and work, that we naturally filter out what doesn't seem important." He smiled before explaining, "I was in the military before becoming an investigator. I was used to paying attention to what was going on in the field, but, believe me, I had to learn to pay more attention to what was being said, and not being said, before I could investigate with any skill."

Suddenly jerking to attention, Kendall said, "I did see his picture on Fahdil's desk!"

Luke smiled and said, "Perfect. I've just pulled up something…tell me if it's him." Flipping his laptop around, he showed a picture of a young man, dark hair and dark eyes, smiling at the camera, his arm around another man at what appeared to be a fraternity party."

Moving closer, Kendall knelt in front of the laptop he was holding, to carefully study the photograph. Nodding, she replied, "Yes, that's him. That's the boy in Fahdil's family picture."

Luke added, "He lives in Alaska."

Face planting into her palm, she added, "Oh, my God! Now I remember why Dad said something about how Fahdil would be perfect for the Alaskan symposium but he couldn't go because of his wife's surgery. It never occurred to me that he was talking about his son being there."

"You're doing fine. This is good information," Marc said, reaching for her fingers as she stood again. He knew he was echoing the others' pleasure, hoping they were now one step closer.

"So what now?" she asked. "I don't want to falsely accuse anyone of anything."

"You're not," Marc assured, holding her gaze steadily. "You're just giving us what may be another piece of the puzzle.

Charlie, still shaking her head, said, "Well, we're going to see what we can find out about him. But for him to be connected to someone at your research lab and to be in Alaska at the time that Marc's plane was sabotaged is highly suspect."

Kendall fiddled with her purse strap as she sat in the large sunroom overlooking the back patio of Bethany and Jack's house. The Saints had retired to wherever it was they actually met and she was relegated to sitting with the women. It seemed rather segregated and, working in a male dominated field, she was uncertain how she felt about it.

"It was so nice to take a day off," Evie said, stretching her legs out in front of her chair, a cup of tea in her hand.

"Where do you work?" Kendall ventured to ask.

Smiling, Evie said, "I'm a geotechnical engineer with a munitions plant near here."

Eyes wide, Kendall was unable to hide her surprise. Evie laughed and said, "Don't worry if you've never heard of that! I often get that response." Shrugging a little, she said, "But I love what I do."

"And you took today off for..." Kendall prompted.

"Hey, when Bethany calls and says that the last Saint

is showing up with a woman who might need help… well, we all answered that call!"

Blinking in shock, Kendall was unable to think of a reply.

Evie motioned toward the woman sitting next to her and said, "Dani works at the same company, but we work in different areas."

Nodding, Dani added, "I used to work for the ATF with Chad, but left the agency."

"I own my own business," Angel said, "so it was easy for me to take a break. Plus, I was at the bakery at six a.m. so I was ready for a chance to get out." Looking at Kendall, she explained, "I own Angel's Cupcake Heaven."

"Those were your confections we enjoyed earlier? Oh, my goodness, they were fabulous!" Kendall gushed. Now curious about the others, she shifted her gaze around the group.

Cam's ebony-haired wife, Miriam, smiled as she said, "I'm a nurse. I work in a nursing home now instead of a hospital. It's an easier schedule since we have a baby."

"I work two part-time jobs," Faith said softly. "I teach art at a school and work as an illustrator for the local police department.

The perfectly put-together woman amongst them was next. "I know it's hard to remember everyone's name. I'm Sabrina, Jude's wife. And I run my own interior design business."

The last woman in the gathering to speak was wearing comfortable jeans with her blonde hair pulled back from her face. "I'm Grace," she said, her smile beaming toward Kendall. "I run a companion dog company."

Sitting back in her chair, Kendall sipped her tea. Marc had mentioned that Jack's wife owned the cabin rentals, as well as a successful wedding venue, next door. "I'm stunned all of you would take time out of your busy lives to come here today." Smiling at the others, she added, "I'm humbled and don't actually know what to say."

"Honey, we've all been right where you are!" Angel pronounced. "We've all been caught in something out of our control and ended up meeting the man that was right for us. And it just so happened that that man was a Saint."

"Why the name Saints?" Kendall asked. "I did ask Marc when I saw his medallion but he only said it meant something different to each of them."

Bethany nodded and said, "Jack's mom had told him of his namesake, who was her father, Jacques. And the Saint that he was also named for became important to him. When he started his own security company, the name fit for him. He never required it to be special to anyone else, but as it turned out...each of these men—"

"And Charlie," Angel threw out.

Laughing, Bethany agreed, "Yes, and Charlie, all have Saints that are special to them."

"You're a very unique group," Kendall observed aloud.

"We owe that to Bethany," Miriam explained. "When she and Jack got together, she mother-henned the rest of the Saints and have brought us women together in a group as well."

Shrugging, Bethany smiled. "I never planned it this way…it just happened organically." Sobering, she held Kendall's gaze. "It takes a special woman to be with a Saint. Someone supportive, but completely strong on their own."

Kendall regarded the nods of agreement from all the other women. Each smart, independent, and brought together in their diversity by the love for their man… and each other. A strange emotion began blooming inside of her, one that she could not identify at first. As they began talking and laughing with each other, including her in their conversations, Kendall realized that what she felt was a sense of belonging. *I want to be a part of this group. I want to be with Marc.* The thoughts caused her to gasp softly, but as she blushed she was glad that no one seemed to notice. Joining in their conversations, she relaxed for the first time in days.

"With him right now…send what you've got." Monty held his tablet in his hands, lifting his gaze to Nick. Hank was sitting at the table with them, nervously glancing around the small diner.

After a few more seconds of silence, Monty held the tablet out so that the other two men were able to see the photograph. "This is Tariq Mustafa. Recognize him?"

Hank's eyes widened as he swallowed deeply. Nodding, he said, "That's one of the men who was in the hangar with me." His gaze jumped up to Monty's. "Who the hell is he?"

"He's a university student here." Monty added, "And he has ties to one of the researchers who works under Dr. Rhodes."

Nick, leaning his tall frame back in his seat, pierced Hank with his eyes. "We just came from Kevin, where we learned that the terrorist cell here in Fairbanks is growing in number and, even though your office is small, he's trying to keep his eye on them. He said they're organized and appear to have numerous backers with money."

Hank's hound dog eyes lasted a moment before he sighed heavily. "Okay, look. There's more I haven't told anyone. Once we got inside the hangar, my phone rang. The two men were making a lot of noise with the re-fueling equipment and one of the—not this guy, but the other one—shouted that I might be able to hear better if I was in the office." Shrugging, he added, "It made sense. I saw no reason to stand there and keep watching them. So I went into the office."

"Who called?" Nick asked, his sharp gaze assessing Hank's sincerity.

"I'm not sure. I could hear a woman speaking, but the voice was hard to understand. She kept rattling on about how the FBI office was hard to get into and she had an issue she wanted looked into. I was on the phone for probably six or seven minutes before I could finally get her to hang up and call the main office the next day. By the time I got back out, the men were almost finished. One was wrapping the fuel line back up and the other one was in the cockpit, but I had no reason to doubt what they were doing."

"Why did you keep this quiet?" Monty asked. "You made it sound as though you were only out of the hangar area for just a moment."

Finally losing control, Hank barked out, "I was a chicken-shit, okay? Kevin was pissed. I was afraid of losing my job...and still might." Running his hand over his hair, he shook his head dejectedly. "I just plain fucked up." At the silence, he finally looked up and said, "So what now? What do we do now?"

"You?" Nick asked, his lips pinched together. "Nothing. It's been determined that Tariq's not in Alaska right now. We've been told where he's gone and we'll be investigating him there."

With that, Nick and Monty left the restaurant, leaving Hank slumping in his seat, appearing more dejected than ever.

"Jack? We're checking out of the hotel and getting ready to fly back to D.C. We've been to the university—Tariq never returned this semester. His bills were paid by Fahdil, but Tariq's roommates said he packed up and left several weeks ago. At this point, Nick's got to get back...this is Kevin's jurisdiction. I'm not sure about this FBI office here, but nonetheless, it's their territory. Nick and I've reported our findings to them. From what they tell me, they're focusing more attention on the terrorist cell here."

"Understood," Jack responded. "You flying straight back to D.C.?"

"Yeah, we'll be back in the area this evening. Nick's alerted the FBI office in Baton Rouge, Louisiana to be on the lookout for Tariq in case he tries to make a visit."

"According to Kenneth, Fahdil expected Tariq to stay with Fahdil's wife as she recuperates. Again, that's the local office's jurisdiction. I've been in contact with them to pick him up."

"That was the information we were given as well, Monty," Jack acknowledged. "Charlie's tracking his money."

"Think there'll be much money to track?"

"Maybe not, but Luke's checking out the university security cameras and has found him with some students that are suspect."

"Send me what you've got and I'll pass it on to the agent here," Monty added.

"Thought you weren't too sure about him," Jack queried.

"Right now, the main agent here hasn't given us a reason not to trust him. And the younger one seems intent on trying to make amends. Quite frankly, Nick doesn't trust either of them, but dealing with the terrorist cell here is in their hands, not ours."

"You got that right," Jack acknowledged. "Okay, I'll have Luke work on Tariq's location as well and get that to you as soon as we can."

Marc appeared at the doorway of Jack's sunroom, his gaze immediately seeking out Kendall. He had wondered how she would handle the other women, knowing they would be easy with her, but also knowing that being thrown into the whole group at one time could be overwhelming. Watching Kendall laughing and talking warmed his heart. He wanted her there…with him.

Standing, she greeted him with a smile as she stepped forward, her arms naturally seeking to wrap around him as his did the same. Enveloped together, they were both lost in each other's gaze, everyone else in the room disappearing from thought.

"You okay?" he whispered.

Nodding, she replied softly, "Yeah, I'm good."

"We're finishing up some things here."

She searched his face for any clues, but all he offered was a small smile as he pulled her head closer and kissed her forehead. "Can you tell me anything?"

"We've got the FBI fully involved now, since there is an active terrorist cell in Alaska. We're also looking into both Fahdil and his son. We know the son is involved… he was one of the ones in the hangar the night my plane was tampered with."

Shocked at this information, Kendall's brows drew down in anger, knowing how personal Marc felt about the assault.

"And we're going to be sending someone up to D.C. to work with the FBI in detaining Fahdil."

At that, she sucked in a gasp, her forehead creasing further. "It's not him, Marc. There's no way the man I have worked with for several years has anything to do with terrorist acts."

"We have to be willing to check all possible leads," he said, his voice low and soft as he tucked a strand of hair behind her ear. His finger trailed over her ear and down her jaw, sending ripples of warmth down her spine. "As soon as we're finished, you and I'll head back to my place."

That thought curved her lips into a smile.

"You like that idea?" he whispered, his lips now replacing his fingers on her ear.

Shivering lightly, she looked up. "You know I do."

With a squeeze, he grinned. "Good. I'll be back in just a bit and we'll go spend the night in a cabin that will be a lot more comfortable than what we had during the blizzard!" Bending to place a quick kiss on her lips, he turned and stalked back down the hall.

Kendall stood for a moment observing his retreat. His back was as impressive as his front. The way his jeans cupped his ass. The way his long-sleeved polo stretched over his muscles. The neat trim of his hair that made her wish it was slightly longer so she could slide her fingers through it.

Someone clearing their throat had her whirling around, blushing furiously as she noted the women all smiling at her.

"Watching something interesting?" Bethany asked, tossing her long, blonde braid over one shoulder.

"I'd say, from that kiss, she's already found something interesting!" Angel laughed.

Pulling in her lips as she sought in vain for a witty

comeback, Kendall finally gave up and allowed a giggle to escape. "Okay, busted. Yes, I was definitely watching something interesting…and yes, I've found something interesting." Moving back into the sunroom, she sat down, picking up her tea once more.

Miriam reached over and patted her leg. "Don't be embarrassed. Like we said earlier, we've all been in your shoes."

"Do you know how long you'll be staying?" Faith asked, her gentle expression holding curiosity.

Kendall stared at the dark-haired beauty, feeling as though the woman had the ability to see inside her tumultuous feelings. "Um…well…I don't really know. I mean, Marc wants me here as long as there's a threat. Or until they get the person who…but, I don't…" Giving her head a slight shake, she smiled ruefully. "I'm not really making any sense, am I?"

The others rushed to express understanding, but as she looked back at Faith, she suddenly declared, "I have no idea. My job is in Louisiana, but now the idea of trying to have a long-distance relationship doesn't seem very appealing."

Faith smiled gently, as though holding on to a secret. The other women looked over at Faith as Bethany asked her, "What do you see?"

Shrugging her sender shoulders, she waved her hand delicately. "I simply see change coming." Her gaze sought Kendall's as she smiled. "But good change."

Kendall stared, uncertain what was transpiring but, her thoughts were interrupted when Evie offered, "I was also considering a long-distance relationship, with

Patrick." Kendall turned to face her. "We met in California where he was stationed and I lived. I worked for a geo-technical firm and, when he was getting out of the Army, he was moving back east."

"Patrick is my brother," Angel explained, tucking a colorful strip of hair behind her ear as she folded her bright red leggings-covered legs underneath her body, settling into her seat.

Kendall returned her gaze to Evie, curious as to how she made her decision. "What made you choose to follow him?"

"I was disillusioned with my workplace and my mom had moved to the east coast. But, all in all, it really came down to me wanting to be with him."

Biting her lip, Kendall pondered what lay ahead. She cared for Marc, but liked working in the lab. And then there was her father to consider. If she left Louisiana, he would have no family nearby. Sighing audibly, she saw Marc walking toward the sunroom, many of the other Saints following. As she stood to say her goodbyes, she watched in awe at the men, who appeared larger than life, as they each immediately focused on their partner.

Angel pretended to pout since Monty was not present, but Hollywood-handsome Patrick threw his arm around her after he kissed Evie. "Come on, sis. You're coming home with us until Monty is back."

Chad, referred to by his wife as a gentle giant, hugged Dani from behind, his hands resting on her stomach and Kendall wondered if they had a secret as Dani twisted her head back and gifted her husband with a smile.

Blaise tucked Grace underneath his arm and said, "We've got to go feed the animals," and, with a nod to everyone, they headed out.

Cam grinned down at Miriam, asking, "Who's got the baby? Your mom or mine?" Miriam laughing, replied, "We can just head home, 'cause they're both at our house playing grandma!"

Jude bounded into the room, pouncing on Sabrina, bending her back over his arm to place a kiss on her lips. "Let's go, darlin'."

Luke and Charlie were standing in the doorway saying goodbye to everyone as Bethany called out, "Ladies, don't forget we're meeting at Mountville Cabins tomorrow. Gotta figure out the arrangements for Angel and Monty's wedding!" Turning to Kendall, she added, "And you need to come too!"

Jack's stern countenance softened as he pulled Bethany into his embrace. With his lumberjack looks and her girl-next-door beauty, they looked like a commercial for Outdoor Living Magazine. With that thought, she swung her gaze swiftly back to Marc, worry settling in her stomach. *He's so different from me. Can I ever be what he needs?*

Bart walked into the room last, pulling Faith into his embrace tightly. As they turned to walk out, Faith touched Kendall's arm gently. With a faraway smile on her face, she whispered, "Don't despair. All will work out the way it should."

Leaning her hips against the counter in Marc's kitchen, Kendall could not hold the grin back as she viewed him standing at the stove, stirring the marinara sauce. Now in a short-sleeve, black t-shirt and worn jeans with his bare feet sticking out from the bottom, her eyes enjoyed their feast. But the growl of her stomach reminded her she needed to eat.

"What can I do to help?"

Grinning over his shoulder at her, he said, "Just grab some plates. The bread's in the oven and the noodles are ready." Looking at her wrist, he asked, "How's your wrist?"

"It's good as long as I don't bend it too much." Dropping her gaze to his feet, she asked, "How's your ankle?"

"Not bad," he grinned. "I'm not gonna lie and say it's perfect. Blaise says it can take weeks for a sprain to heal, but it's all good." Turning around with a platter in his hand, he kissed her nose on the way to the table. "Still can't believe you pulled my ass outta that ditch."

Chuckling, she sat down and replied, "Well, it wasn't easy. But I was desperate." Looking over at him, she said, "I definitely discovered I was stronger than I ever thought possible. And I don't mean just physically."

"Babe, you were fuckin' amazing during the whole ordeal."

Ducking her head, the pleasure of his words flowed over her as the scent of the spaghetti teased her senses. "I have to admit, even though we were only trapped for a few days, I don't think I'll ever take food for granted again!" Taking a bite, she moaned as her tongue flicked out to lick the sauce from the side of her mouth.

Casting a glance toward Marc, she noticed his fork was halted halfway to his open mouth, a pained expression on his face.

"What? What is it?" she asked, concern filling her voice.

Swallowing as he blinked, Marc shook his head. "Damn, girl. Hearing you moan like that shot straight to my dick."

Eyes wide, she burst out laughing. "I'm not sure what to say to that!"

Leaning forward, he took her mouth in an open, hard, wet kiss, stealing her breath. Pulling back, he grinned as she mewed at the loss of his lips. "There," he pronounced. "Now, let's get through this meal so we can get on to better things."

"Better things?"

"Oh, yeah, sweet girl. Better things."

His voice held promise and she squeezed her legs tightly to ease the ache.

Kendall's last bite was barely finished when Marc leaped from his chair, grabbing her plate. As he tossed it into the sink she winced, hearing the clatter. He chuckled as he stalked back to her.

"Don't worry. I've got the non-breakable shit."

"Only a man would call dinnerware 'shit'—"

Her quip was interrupted by his lips claiming hers. The kiss was possessive as he held the back of her head with his large hand, angling it so he had maximum contact. His tongue thrust inside her mouth, searching her warmth, tangling with hers. She tasted of spice, wine, and woman. He realized that he rarely kissed... not like this. With casual hookups, kissing was too intimate. For a man, action with their dick could somehow be separated from emotion. But kissing like this...pure heaven.

Hearing her moan, he captured the sound with his mouth as his arm banded tightly around her. Her breasts crushed against his broad chest as her arms wound their way around his neck. Lifting her in his arms, he whirled around so her back was against the wall as she wrapped her legs around his waist. His erection pressed against her core and he knew they needed to get to the bedroom soon.

Carrying her, he backed away from the wall only to have tighten her arms around him even more. Mewling in distress, she grabbed his head, fusing her lips to his.

He mumbled against her mouth as he banged into a chair on his way out of the kitchen. She weighed nothing to him, but he still managed to hit her back against the stair rail-post as he rounded the bottom of the steps.

Giggles erupted and he felt them travel from her lips down to his chest. Lifting his head, he noted her bright, lust-filled eyes as he confessed, "Never taken a woman in my arms upstairs before. Guess you can tell that."

Her giggles melted into a deep smile as she replied, "Does it make me sound needy if I said I was glad?"

"Glad I just ran you into the stairs?" he asked, a chuckle dying in his throat as he searched her eyes deeply.

"No...but that you're telling me in a round-about way that you've never had a woman in your bed here." She hesitated for a second, moving her lips to a whisper from his, before adding, "It makes me feel special."

As he ascended the steps with her still tightly in his embrace, he said, "Kendall, you are special." At the top of the stairs, he turned into his bedroom, his lips once more on hers. With a gentle heft he indicated for her to loosen her legs. Holding her as her feet slid to the floor, he thrust his tongue inside her mouth, continuing to plunder her essence.

Unsure her legs would hold her, Kendall gripped his shirt in her fists, not wanting to lose his mouth. Dark beer mingled with spices and something completely masculine, filling her senses. Her fingers continued to move from his hair down his thickly muscled back and up again. From the moment she had first laid eyes on him in Alaska she knew he was huge, but every time she had her hands on him, she was awed at the strength in his body. Thick muscles bunched under her fingers, but with the t-shirt in the way, she felt deprived.

Grabbing the bottom with her good hand, she began lifting his shirt upwards but was too short to make it all the way. He took pity on her as she lifted to her toes to reach and jerked the offensive material away. Her hands stilled for a moment, hovering over his chest but not touching. Raking her gaze over his chest and abs, she suddenly felt unworthy of the man in front of her.

Sensing a hesitation, Marc lifted her chin, raising her gaze to his. Cocking his head, he asked, "What's wrong?"

"Nothing," she replied honestly. "You're perfect."

Grinning in response, he leaned down, his tongue flicking out to lightly trace her lips. "Then we're well suited, 'cause you're as perfect as they come."

Having never been called perfect before, except when acing a test in school, his words moved over her slowly, filling every part of her.

His hands moved to her sweater, lifting it upward. It caught on her breasts for just a second before he slid it the rest of the way over her head and tossed it onto the floor. She loved the idea of her clothes lying on the floor next to his and was surprised when he asked if it needed to be hung up.

As his fingers unsnapped her bra, she shook her head. "No. I don't own any fussy clothes."

Freeing her breasts, he grinned as his eyes devoured her pink-tipped mounds. "I like that. Non-fussy clothes."

Laughing, she felt his eyes hot on her breasts just

before he bent to take one nipple deeply into his mouth. She no longer felt mirth as the jolt shot from her breast to her core. Gasping as he continued his assault, moving from one nipple to the other, she clutched his shoulders, her fingers digging in tightly. Her nails, normally short for the work in the lab, had grown in the past week and now left tiny marks.

Lost in the feel and taste of her skin, Marc unfastened her pants and slipped them down her legs far enough for her to kick them off, landing in the ever-growing pile of clothes. Her silky panties were now the only thing between him and the prize.

Stepping forward, he backed her toward the bed until her legs hit the mattress and with his palm planted on her chest he gave a little push, grinning as she bounced. Grabbing her ankles, he dragged her toward him until her ass hit the edge and her legs were wrapped around his neck.

Leaning over, he kissed his way from her breasts down her stomach, chuckling as she squirmed.

"Ticklish," she gasped, caught between wanting his lips to move down and wanting to prolong every sensation.

He acquiesced to her first desire and slowly dragged his tongue to the edge of her panties. Slipping his hands in the elastic, he lifted her up just enough to slide the satin over her ass before shifting to the side, allowing them to fall off the end of her legs and onto the floor. Now, with her completely exposed to his view, he raked his gaze over her beauty as the scent of her arousal filled his nostrils.

Kendall had never felt so exposed or so beautiful in her life. Every inch of skin he perused felt warm and began to tingle. This was not a man who was simply trapped with her, but a man who wanted to cherish... and devour her. His eyes were dark as they dropped to between her legs and, before she could beg, he licked her folds before latching onto her clit.

What had been tingles erupted into bolts of electricity as he licked and sucked until she was writhing underneath his ministrations. One large palm placed on her tummy held her firmly in place as his lips and tongue continued their assault. Tighter and tighter her inner muscles coiled. He added a finger to move deep inside and, with one last suck on her sensitive bud, she cried out his name as her fingers clutched the bedspread.

Waves of pleasure crashed over her as her orgasm slowly ebbed. Her breathing ragged, she managed to lift her head and found his penetrating eyes staring at her. A slow grin moved across his face as he licked his lips while standing.

Unbuttoning his jeans, he slid the zipper over his aching erection, quickly shucking the denim down his legs. His boxers followed and the pile of clothes on the wooden floor grew. Leaning over her once again, he slid his hand underneath her body as he flipped the bedspread downward. Shifting her in the bed, he crawled over the top.

The cool sheets now underneath her back helped to tamp down the heat that had built in her body. Watching the play of muscles as he rested his bulk on his forearms, she eagerly spread her legs, her feet resting against his tight ass.

"Take me now, Marc," she begged, desperate to have him inside.

With a desperation that matched hers, he plunged into her warm body after rolling on a condom, stretching her inner core as it tightly grabbed his cock. Slowly at first and then with more vigor, he thrust deeply as he held her cheeks in his hands. She had adoration mixed with ecstasy in her gaze and he closed his eyes in awe of the beauty that was all her. His fingers clutched her face, careful not to bruise, but desiring to crush her lips to him.

She reveled in the exquisite torture of tightness as her slick channel grabbed him, causing her entire body to tingle. As the friction increased her fingers clutched his shoulders, moving over the play of muscles, attempting hold her body in place. As his thrusts pushed her backwards she dug her heels into his ass, going along for whatever ride he wanted to take her on. The movements were hard, but not harsh, tying owner-ship and sensuality into one package.

His balls tightened as he was close to coming. With a final thrust, he powered through his orgasm as his thumb pressed on her clit, pulling her along with him. Emptying into her, he thrusted until every drop was gone, emotion mingling with the physical release he needed. Rolling to the side, taking her with him, he observed her tousled hair, her kiss-swollen lips, her sated gaze and, her flushed body as he moved his hand over her curves. *Hell yeah!* Acknowledging the caveman emotions filling his chest, his heart pounded knowing he had fallen for this woman who would soon be going back to her life in Louisiana.

Marc's breathing patterned had morphed from gasps to a much slower pace and as Kendall watched him closely, she noticed the change in his expression from one of intense power to concern.

"Hey," she whispered, her fingers gliding over the stubble of his jaw. "Where'd you go?"

Smiling, just inches from her face, he replied, "Nowhere. I'm still right here, sweet girl."

Her thoughts tangled as they rolled around and, without thinking, she blurted, "I love being here with you." Not one for spontaneous outbursts, she immediately blushed, wondering how to pull the words back into her mouth.

His brows drew down as he repeated, "You love being here...with me?"

Deciding it was too late to retreat and knowing she did not want to, she nodded. "I know I've only been here a day, but..." offering a delicate shrug, she continued, "I just love being with you."

"Kendall, I need you to speak plainly because I don't want to misunderstand what you're saying," he said, brushing her hair back from her sweat-slicked forehead.

Now unsure, she sucked in her lips, dropping her gaze to his chin. He lifted her still-wrapped wrist and placed a soft kiss on the bandage before cupping her cheek and lifting her face to his. "Just say it…whatever it is, just say it."

"I've been thinking we would try a long-distance relationship, but every time I think about it my heart sinks." Sitting up on the bed, she tucked the sheet over her breasts as she rested her forearms on her drawn up knees. "Working in Louisiana with Dad was all I've wanted to do, but I realize my life was boring. I had some friends, but nothing like the groups of women I was with earlier at Jack and Bethany's place. I dated, but nothing like this. Nothing that made me really feel beautiful or…or…or alive!"

She turned her gaze to his, determined to face whatever he was thinking, even if it was going to be rejection. Deeply inhaling a fortifying breath before letting it out slowly, she said, "Then I came here, to this beautiful place. What you've built here is a home, not just a place to hang out and sleep. Your friends are real and supportive. They're like family."

"So…" Marc began tentatively, his fingers tracing a path along her arm, "are you saying you want to stay in Virginia?"

Assessing his eyes, noting the warmth permeating from them, she groaned. "Yeah. I mean, maybe." Rolling her eyes, she huffed, "What if all this is just the whole *we saved each other's lives and killed a grizzly together*—"

Placing his fingers on her lips, he shushed her. "What does your heart tell you?"

Letting out a long sigh, she admitted, "That I'm interested…in you…and in staying. That is, if you're interested. I'm scared to death to leave Dad and I don't know where I'd work, but I'd really love to consider the possibility of staying."

Chuckling, he ran his thumb over her lips, the skin petal-soft against his work-worn finger. "Consider the possibility? That's sounds like you're fearful."

"Honestly? I am. We've only known each other a little over a week and I'm thinking of turning my life around completely for you. Is that crazy?" Shaking her head, she moaned, "I must be crazy! Nobody falls for someone that fast!"

Marc moved his thumb over her cheek now, feeling the warmth of her blush. "If you're crazy, then so am I. I was wondering if I could be a long-distance Saint."

Gasping, eyes wide, she exclaimed, "You were?" The pair smiled wordlessly for a moment at each other, knowing whatever was happening was larger than either had ever experienced before. Shaking her head slightly, she said, "No, Marc. Your world is here. With your friends. With your work." Her gaze roamed around the comfortable room as she added, "With your beautiful home."

Sitting up in the bed next to her, he kissed her forehead before pulling back to peer deeply into her eyes. "Sweet girl, I want you here with me, no doubt. But we can put this on hold until we sort out who's after you."

Nodding, her eyes twinkling, she agreed. "Then let's hope you catch them fast!"

Waking up in a tangle of legs and arms, Kendall was aware of Marc moving from the bed as he grabbed his vibrating phone from his jean's pocket. His voice was sleep-rough as he talked, and she leaned up on her elbow to stare at the man whose bed she just shared. Grinning, she loved the way his gruff voice caressed her, but as he stood and walked toward the bathroom, his tight ass and muscular back grabbed her attention.

Throwing back the covers, she jumped up and grabbed her clothes from the floor. Looking them over, she decided to just slide on her panties before grabbing Marc's t-shirt from the pile, pulling it over her head as he came back into the room. His gazed drifted slowly from her sex-tousled hair to her nipples, prominently displayed against the soft cotton of his shirt.

"Good morning," she grinned as she stepped closer and lifting on her toes, placed a light kiss on his lips.

"Mornin'," he growled, pulling her body close.

Tugging on her shirt, he said, "I like seeing you in my clothes."

"I remember wearing your clothes in Canada when mine were wet," she reminded. Shaking her head, she said, "Was that just a few days past? It seems like it was ages ago." Looking up suddenly, she said, "Oh, Marc, maybe I am crazy! We've only known each other for such a short time and it was all surreal."

Shushing her with his fingers on her lips, he said, "It's okay. We don't need to make any lasting promises right now. No changing lives at the moment. Let's just get through the next days and we'll take it slow. I'll go at your pace." Feeling her relax underneath his fingertips, he added, "But I know what I feel is real. It may have happened fast, but it's real."

With another kiss, he bent to grab his clothes and said, "I've got to go to D.C. this morning. Me and a couple of the guys are going to talk to Fahdil at the hotel. We want to talk to him about Tariq."

The sweet moment fled from her mind as Kendall's stomach clenched at the thought of her co-worker's relative being involved in terrorist activities. Knowing she needed something to take her mind off the situation, she headed down to the kitchen, determined to fix Marc breakfast before he left.

A few minutes later, Marc came downstairs, the scent of bacon and coffee filling the cabin. With an appreciative kiss, they sat down to eat.

Nibbling a slice of bacon as Marc dug into his eggs with gusto, she reminded, "I'll be going to Mountville today with the women."

Stopping mid-bite, he frowned thoughtfully. Leaning back, his eyes moved between the door and her. Reaching underneath the collar of his shirt, he pulled out the silver chain with the St. Mark medallion dangling in his fingertips. Pulling it over his head, he said, "Come here, babe."

Brows scrunched down, she nonetheless leaned forward, allowing him to slip it over her head. Looking down at the winged-lion pendant now resting between her breasts, she fingered it before gazing back up at him. "Why?"

"I hate leaving you but I'm the one who needs to be with Nick today as he interviews Fahdil. It's personal now. It was my mission, my airplane, and my woman."

"Marc, I wasn't your woman when all this happened," she reminded, her voice gentle.

He reached over and cupped the back of her head and said, "It doesn't matter the timing. You are now and that makes it my battle."

"That's kind of scary," she admitted, her gaze on the hard line of his jaw.

"Girl, with you I'm all sweet. But with anyone who tries to hurt you...I'm all kinds of scary."

Not sure what to do with that pronouncement, she dropped her gaze back to the medallion, but before she could ask, he said, "There's a tracer in the back of that. I know you'll be with the women today, but I'll still have Luke pick you up and drop you off."

She started to interrupt, but he placed his finger on her lips and continued, "Not until we know exactly what's going on. I want you safe. Can you do that for me?" Leaning forward again, he replaced his finger with his lips and the argument went out of her.

"It's little enough for all you're doing for me," she agreed, taking another bite of bacon as she watched a beautiful smile cross his face.

A few minutes later as Marc was ready to leave, he reviewed the security panel by the front door. He left after another kiss, this one long, hard, and definitely swoon-worthy.

Two hours later, answering the knock on the door after being alerted that Luke was coming to pick her up, Kendall swung the front door open, greeting Luke and Charlie like old friends. Stepping outside, she was not offended when Luke double checked the security.

It did not take long to get to Bethany's property and soon they drove under the wooden sign listing the Mountville Rental Cabins and Wedding Venue. Pulling into the driveway, Kendall felt the location was similar to getting to Jack's property.

"Look familiar?" asked Charlie from the front seat. "Bethany's place is right next to Jack's property."

"Oh, that's convenient," Kendall noted.

Luke laughed, adding, "That's how they met. Bethany's grandmother got lost, came crashing through Jack's woods, which were alarmed, and we all went charging out to see who the intruder was. What we found was an older lady, who seemed confused, and then Bethany, who came barreling out of the woods like a mama lion. She and Jack squared off and it was quite a sight to see, the two of them go at it!"

"They were really angry with each other?" Kendall asked, her mind unable to reconcile the sweet, in-love couple she met yesterday with Luke's description.

"Yes," Luke confirmed, "but it didn't take long for them to fall for each other."

"From what I can tell, that's happened with all the Saints," Charlie quipped, winking at Luke.

Kendall was no longer listening as she peeked out the window, viewing the glorious woods on either side of the wide gravel drive. They parked in front of an older, large, two-story, wooden building alongside several other vehicles. Charlie leaned over to kiss Luke goodbye as Kendall stepped out of the SUV.

Opening the front door, they passed by the reception desk, hearing laughter coming from the back room. Walking into what appeared to be a living room, Kendall noted the gathering. All the women were present, along with a middle-aged woman who was sitting on one of the chairs with a note-pad in her hand.

Bethany cried out, "Come join us! Margery is just taking the last notes for Angel's wedding reception."

Kendall quickly learned that Margery and her husband were the live-in managers for Bethany's business and Margery also served as a wedding planner. An afternoon tea was prepared, complete with sandwiches and small cakes. The group dove into the food and it did not take long for Kendall to feel right at home again.

"So, I hear you met Jack when you crashed onto his

property," Kendall mentioned, licking the icing from the cake off her lips.

Bethany laughed while nodding. "Oh, yeah. Jack and I had a real hate-to-love relationship." Looking around the room, she smiled as she added, "But then, everyone here has their own story to tell. Ladies, why don't you fill Kendall in?"

"My grandmother was being rooked by a scam artist and Jude caught him." Grinning, Sabrina said, "We'd dated before that, but it was during that time that we fell in love."

"Bart and I were thrown together by the FBI to find a kidnapped child," Faith explained, a gentle smile on her face.

"Chad and I worked together for the ATF, but it wasn't until I began working for a munitions plant where there were problems that he and I got together," Dani said.

"My dog brought us together," Grace smiled. Shrugging slightly, she continued, "I was in an accident and had amnesia. Blaise found me and, with the Saints' help discovering who was after me, we fell in love."

Kendall shook her head, amazed at the stories she was hearing. She looked over at Evie and said, "I know you worked in California when you met Patrick."

Nodding, Evie agreed, "Yes, and there was a theft ring going on between my company and his Army base. He got involved with me as we tried to figure out what was happening."

Charlie was sitting next to Kendall and said, "You

know that Luke and I were brought together by a love of cyber mystery-solving."

Tossing her colorful hair over her shoulder, Angel said, "Monty came to my rescue when members of my former sorority were being killed."

Miriam, sitting on the floor with her plate in her lap, replied, "I was a Red Cross nurse working in Mexico when I was kidnapped—"

The gasp from Kendall interrupted Miriam. "Seriously?"

Nodding, Miriam replied, "Yes…it was awful, but Cam came to rescue me. We spent days escaping through the jungle until Marc could pick us up." She smiled softly toward Kendall and said, "That's why I have a particular soft spot for Marc and I'm so glad he's found you."

By the time the women had all given their recounting of meeting their Saint, Kendall leaned back in her seat, not knowing what to say. *Is this where I am with Marc? Is that why I feel so at home here?* Before she had time to ponder her inner questions further, Bethany stood and called out, "Let's take a walk to the gazebo!"

As they meandered along the gravel road that wound around the small lake in the center of the property, Kendall's gaze roamed constantly over the beauty. Thick woods filled with evergreens, lush and green, peaking through the leafless oaks and maples. They passed small, A-frame, rental cabins and a pier jutting out onto the lake.

The cloudless sky allowed the sun to warm them

slightly as they walked around the lake. "Bethany, this is gorgeous!" Kendall enthused.

Bethany, walking nearby, turned and smiled, pride evident on her face. "Thanks! My grandparents bought this land and had the idea of vacation rentals. They built the cabins themselves and lived in the first one as they built the others. Then they built the main reception building."

"Did you grow up here?"

"Only during the summers, but a few years ago, after my grandfather died, my grandmother needed help. So I came back and now I run it as a rental and wedding venue."

Miriam grinned, "And so far all the Saints who are married had their ceremonies or receptions here!"

The conversations flowed but Kendall continued the walk in silence as she viewed the Blue Ridge Mountains in the background with the cool, crisp air filling her lungs. Inhaling deeply, she could smell the cedars and pines. Feeling a touch on her arm, her eyes flew open as she startled, seeing Faith standing next to her.

"Are you all right?" Faith asked, her soft voice floating through the air.

Smiling, Kendall nodded. "Yeah, I'm fine. I'm just... I'm..." laughing, she said, "I don't know what I am!" They walked in silence for a moment before Kendall spoke again. "This area is so beautiful, but what I can't understand is how at home I feel." Faith said nothing, allowing Kendall to continue her thoughts. "My parents had moved around some but, once my dad landed in

Louisiana, we stayed. But honestly, I never felt there the way I do here."

"Is it the place or the people?" Faith queried.

Kendall smiled widely, her face shining as she replied, "Honestly? Both!" Now that they were at the gazebo, the women stopped, enjoying the view once more. Kendall breathed in deeply, the view sinking into her being.

Walking back to the main cabin, the women's conversations revolved around weddings, babies, and careers. And Kendall found she did not mind the topics at all.

Estelle and Cliff stood at the hotel's reception desk as they checked out. The elevator doors opened and they were soon joined by Will and Karen.

Looking at her watch, Estelle said, "Where is Fahdil? We have a tight schedule to get to the airport and the receptionist already said there was an accident on the highway."

"I think he's still in his room," Karen replied.

"Well, he's on his own if he misses the flight," Estelle bit out, moving to grab her bag, leaving Will and Karen rolling their eyes behind her back.

"Dr. Mahdi? Agent Nick Stone." Nick stood in the doorway of Fahdil's hotel room and flashed his FBI badge. Marc noted the doctor's viewing it warily before turning his gaze up to him, recognition in his eyes.

"Mr. Jenkins, you're with the FBI too?"

Marc replied, "No, sir. When you saw me with Kendall, I was just as introduced: with a security company hired to see to her and her father's safe journey."

"Doctor, we need to talk to you about Tariq Mustafa," Nick cut in, getting right to the point.

"Tariq?" Fahdil repeated, his voice first surprised and then confused. "Is there something wrong? Is he all right?" Eyes wide, he looked between the men standing at his hotel door.

"We have no information about his condition, sir, but we do need to talk to you. Is there somewhere we can meet privately?"

Fahdil opened his mouth but closed it quickly. Glancing back into his hotel room, he nodded toward the table by the window. "We can meet in here if it's acceptable."

Nick, Marc, and Chad stepped inside and followed Fahdil to the table where the morning's coffee service sat. Marc introduced Chad as they took their seats. Offering to pour coffee, Fahdil's hands fluttered nervously when they politely refused. Finally, taking a seat himself, his eyes moved quickly amongst the three men as they settled. His expression wary, he said, "Some of my co-workers have already checked out of the hotel. I have a plane to catch in a few hours—"

"Doctor, we will try to make this as succinct as possible."

Without mincing words, Marc began. "Dr. Mahdi, you know I was originally contracted to escort Kenneth Rhodes and then, as things progressed, it became

Kendall Rhodes. With everything that happened, we were uncertain which of the two was the original intended victim and now the FBI is looking to see who sabotaged my plane."

Fahdil nervously stared at Marc, his mouth working, a protest building. "And you suspect my son, Tariq?"

"We know that he has been recently studying at the University of Alaska. Were you aware that he did not return to his classes this semester?"

"Did...did not return? I don't understand."

"He stayed in Alaska, but moved out of the dorm and withdrew from the university," Marc continued, his gaze carefully assessing the man in front of him.

Licking his lips, Fahdil shook his head slowly. "That can't be. I...I talk to him. He tells me how his classes are going."

"All which can be pretenses," Chad added.

"But why? Why would he pretend to still be at the university if he's not? Why stay up there?" Fahdil's voice grew louder, his chest heaving with each breath.

"That's what we were hoping you could tell us," Nick said, pulling a folder out of his briefcase and placing it on the table.

Fahdil's gaze dropped to the file, eyes wide as though afraid of its contents. He said nothing, but clasped his hands together on top of the table, his knuckles white.

Nick opened the folder, pulled out a photograph of several young men and pushed it over to Fahdil. "Do you recognize any of these people?"

"That's Tariq," Fahdil answered as his gaze roved

over the picture, "but I don't know the others. I never met any of his friends from Alaska." He lifted his eyes back to Nick, his brows drawn down.

"Those other men are suspected terrorists in a growing cell in Alaska," came the reply. "They recruit from universities."

Seeing Fahdil about to contest, Marc jumped in, tapping his finger on the image of Tariq. "And he was positively identified by an FBI agent as one of the two men who sabotaged my plane."

"No!" Fahdil said vehemently, pushing back in his chair, his face a mask of disbelief.

"Yes," Marc growled, "and there's more." Gaining a nod from Nick, he continued, "We have traced a bank account in your name to Tariq. The account is in your name, but not your social security number. It appears he used fake identification to set it up but the money you've been sending to him ends up in this account. And, what's more...he then transfers it to another man." Tapping his finger on one of the people in the photograph, he said, "This man right here. One that is on the FBI's top list of persons of interest as a possible terrorist."

Blinking as he looked at the copies of bank receipts, Fahdil stared wordlessly for a moment. Finally coming out of his trance, his voice broken, he said, "I...don't know what to say. He...Tariq was always a good boy... from a good home. We took him in when he came to America. Never...never would I have thought of this." Closing his eyes as a tear slid down his cheek, he shook his head in agony. "This will devastate my wife...we think of him as a son."

Nick added, "Dr. Mahdi, we have also found cyber evidence that he had hacked into your NCBRT account, the assumption being that he was looking for your research and perhaps did not find what he was ordered to find."

Marc observed as Fahdil swallowed deeply, a slow expression of understanding coming over his face.

"Last fall, during a break when he was home visiting, he had a lot of questions about my work. I was flattered," Fahdil explained begging for understanding. "I thought perhaps he wanted to go into the sciences and possibly research. Of course," he quickly qualified, "I did not tell him anything that was secure, but gave him basic information." With a grimace, he added, "Tariq had more questions and I told him that Dr. Rhodes was the one with all the data." As though understanding was falling all around, his voice became strident as he said, "We had a party and I introduced him to Kendall and Kenneth."

Covering his face in his hands, his shoulders shook as he said, "What have I done?"

Nick stood after a moment and said, "Dr. Mahdi, considering what you've told us, I'll need you to come to the FBI headquarters with me. We need to get your official statement." Seeing the older man's wide eyed face, he added, "You're not under suspicion at this time, but you have had contact with a known terrorist and are a person of interest. You may certainly obtain legal council if you wish."

"And Tariq?" Fahdil inquired.

"All of this has been turned over to the FBI in Alaska and in Louisiana. They will find him and detain him since it is their jurisdiction."

His brow furrowed, Fahdil said suddenly, "Can I call my wife? She's been unwell and I do not want her upset when they come looking for Tariq!"

"I'm sorry, doctor, but we cannot take the chance that he'll flee."

His face downcast, Fahdil followed Nick out of the room.

A few minutes later Marc and Chad climbed back into their SUV and began the trip homeward. As Chad drove, Marc leaned back in the seat, his mind on thoughts of Kendall back in his home. Grinning, he realized once more that the image did not bother him.

"Stay here."

Kendall, standing behind Luke, looked over at Charlie who just smiled as she shrugged.

"You know, Luke...you could actually say 'please'," Charlie quipped, earning a slight scowl from him.

Stepping inside Marc's house, Luke turned back to Kendall and said, "Please."

Unable to stop her snort of laughter, she stayed on the front porch as Luke continued through the house, searching as he went. Walking back to the front, where Charlie and Kendall had not entered, he reported, "All clear."

Somber, after watching the activity, Kendall said, "It seems so remote that someone wants to harm me and that they would follow me here."

"You can never be too sure," Luke replied, as Charlie nodded.

"Do you want me to stay until Marc gets home?"

"Nah, but thanks anyway," Kendall answered. "I've... I've got some thinking to do and I do it best alone."

Nodding her understanding, Charlie embraced Kendall tightly and whispered, "Only you can decide what you want in life and whether or not change is right."

Blinking back tears, Kendall nodded, unsure of her voice. With a wave, she watched as Luke alarmed the panel and tucked Charlie under his arm. Closing the door, she locked it carefully and walked into the living room, continuing to observe as Luke and Charlie drove down the driveway. Sighing heavily, she made her way into the kitchen to fix a cup of tea. Sitting down at the table, she sipped while staring out the window, wondering if the scenery would provide answers to her tumultuous thoughts.

An hour later, Kendall still sat at the table only, this time, her eyes were glued to her laptop. The University of Virginia had a doctoral program in Biodefense and as she scrolled through the information she wondered about their lab facilities.

Curious, she emailed the department chair, asking

for more information. Her legs screamed in stiffness as she realized she had sat too long with them tucked up underneath her. Standing, she stretched before walking into the kitchen to make another cup of tea.

Her phone rang and racing back to the table, hoping it was Marc, she stared at the unfamiliar number. Connecting, she said, "Hello?"

"Dr. Rhodes?"

"Yes?"

"I'm Dr. Thomas Johnston...chair of the Biodefense department at UVA. I'm so sorry to call you out of the blue, but I received your email and wanted to reach out to you."

Laughing, Kendall replied, "I just sent it a few minutes ago and didn't expect a reply so soon!"

"Well, I happened to see it on my phone and told my wife I needed to call you instantly. Of course, I'm well aware of your credentials and the work you and your father have done. We have positons that need to be filled on our faculty staff and research labs."

Stunned, Kendall said, "Dr. Johnston, I have to be honest...I'm just putting out feelers right now. I have no idea if I'm actually moving to the area."

"I totally understand, but we'd love to have you come and visit as soon as you could."

"I don't have a resume prepared—"

"No, no. We can just make it an informal visit, for you to have a chance to see if you would even be interested."

Smiling slightly, Kendall nodded, even though she was alone in the room. "Yes, I'd like that very much.

Thank you." Making arrangements for a visit two days later, she hung up the phone, her lips now curving into a full-blown smile. Biting her lip, she walked over to the sofa and dialed.

"Sweetheart!"

"Hey, Dad."

"How are you?" he asked suddenly and she heard the concern in his voice.

"I'm good, I'm good. Don't worry."

He was quiet for a few seconds and then said, "Your voice sounds like you want to talk."

Chuckling, she replied, "Oh, yeah? Think you know me so well?"

Her dad's voice gentled as he replied, "What's going on, Kendall?"

Sighing heavily, she said, "I'm trying to make a huge decision and wanted to talk to you first."

"Ahh," he said. "You're thinking about moving to Virginia, aren't you?"

Shocked, she did not know what to say so she said nothing as he continued.

"Kendall, working with you here in Louisiana has been a dream come true for me, but I've always known that, one day, your journey would take you somewhere else. And honey, my dream never had to be your forever."

Blinking rapidly in an attempt to hold the tears at bay, she failed as several ran down her cheeks. "Oh, Dad, I've never thought beyond the research at NCBRT. I guess I just figured it was a place where I was comfortable and content." Leaning her head back on the sofa, she cast her eyes around Marc's welcoming cabin, feeling more at home than she had in years.

"And now?" he asked, interrupting her musings.

"I'm not sure comfortable and content is where I want to be," she replied. Sighing heavily, she added, "I've contacted the University of Virginia and they want me to come in and look around. They have positions for faculty in their doctoral program."

"So what's holding you back? I only had to look at you and Marc to know how you two feel about each other."

"But Dad, it happened so fast."

"Did you know that your mother and I only dated three months before we got married?"

"Three months?" Kendall responded, her voice almost shrill. Somehow the thought of her careful father being impetuous had never entered her mind.

"We met in college and I'd never met a more beautiful or smarter woman. I was a goner right from the start. And the fact that she fell for me, too, made me the luckiest man in the world."

"What are you trying to tell me, Dad?" her voice now filled with emotion thinking of their love and the love that was cut short when her mother died.

"Not everything can be found in a laboratory, sweetheart. Not everything can be answered by science. Sometimes, the heart tells us what we need."

Swallowing deeply having never heard her father express himself quite so eloquently, she choked out, "I love you, Dad."

"I love you too. And who knows? After this mess

blows over with the NCBRT, I might decide to find a new position myself! Virginia might just be a place for this old researcher!"

Laughing for a few more minutes, she said, "I guess the others will be flying back today. Dad, I need to tell you that Fahdil's son might be in trouble with the law. I have no idea what has happened but I know the FBI will be visiting Fahdil's wife to talk to him."

"But he's not here," Kenneth reminded. "I was just at her house, visiting last night. Their daughter was there but when I asked about Tariq, she said he had visited but already left."

"Oh," Kendall said, as she finished her call. Staring out into the room, a strange slithering began in her stomach. *If he's not there...where is he?*

31

"You gonna ask me what's on your mind or are you gonna just keep looking over at me?" Marc growled his question as Chad grinned, his eyes now back on the road.

"I'm driving as fast as I dare, but I get the feeling you wish I'd go faster to get you back to the pretty lady waiting for you back at your place," Chad said.

Blowing out a breath, Marc leaned back in the seat, rubbing his hand over his face. Looking out the passenger window for a few silent minutes, he said, "I watched it happen...over and over with each of you. I just didn't expect it to happen to me."

Snorting, Chad glanced to the side. "What? Fall in love?"

"Yeah," Marc answered. "She's nothing like what I thought I wanted...and yet everything I need."

Chad agreed as he moved though the southbound traffic. "Do you think she'll stay?"

"I don't know," Marc admitted. "I want her to but I

don't want to limit her career. We'll just have to see what happens—"

Interrupted by his phone ringing, Marc pulled it out of his pocket and grinned as he saw the caller. "Hey, sweet girl. Did you have a good day?"

"Yeah," she said, "but that's not why I called. I just talked to my dad and he told me that he had been to Fahdil's house to visit with his wife. Their daughter was there, but not Tariq. Dad said that Mrs. Mahdi said Tariq's not there now."

"Fuck!" Marc cursed, gaining the immediate attention of Chad. Looking over, he said, "Tariq's not in Louisiana...or at least not at his home." Putting the phone back to his mouth, he said, "Babe, where are you? Are you locked in? Security on?"

"Yes, yes, I'm fine," she exclaimed. "I just thought you should know. Should I call someone?"

"No, I'll call both Nick and Jack. Listen, I'm calling Jack first and sending someone to the house to stay with you." Hearing her about to object, he interrupted, "Non-negotiable, Kendall. But don't open the door to anyone until you see them on the porch and recognize one of the Saints."

Gaining her acquiescence, he looked over to Chad. "How much longer?"

"Only about thirty minutes," he replied, his voice as hard as his stare.

Relaying that information to Kendall, he hung up after gaining her promise to call him if she heard anything.

Disconnecting, he looked over at Chad, his jaw so

tight he thought his teeth would crack. "We know that asshole fucked with my plane to get rid of Kendall and now he's missing. I've got a sick feeling he's coming here."

"He'd be crazy to try to get into your place," Chad replied, shaking his head. "But then, he's got nothing to lose."

Dialing Jack, Marc quickly barked out the information gaining Jack's assurance someone would be at his house in fifteen minutes. Then he called Nick, unsure he would be able to get hold of him. Sighing in relief he was thankful when Nick answered immediately. Relaying the information, he heard Nick curse in response.

"I've got Fahdil here and I'll see if he has any idea where Tariq is."

"We've got Charlie and Luke trying to see if he was on a plane but, with false documents, they'll have to work through security cameras."

"I'll get the agency on it as well and see if we can find him," Nick said. "Fuckin' hell. I'll also get the Louisiana office to see if he's still there just not at the Mahdi's home. I'll get someone on Kenneth Rhodes also."

"Appreciate it," Marc replied, angry that he had not thought of that himself. Looking at the time on his phone, he growled to Chad, "Twenty-five minutes. Can you shave any time off that?"

Jack immediately sent the Saints into action, sending them to Marc's house while ordering Luke and Charlie to check Marc's security system.

"If he hacked the security at NCBRT, I want to make sure what we've got on Marc's house is working."

Charlie narrowed her eyes as she turned to her computer, Luke already tapping on his keys. "Nobody better fuck with my system!" A few seconds later, she yelled, "Damnit! Someone's bypassed the first line!"

"Lay the phone down where I can see it."

Kendall's gaze jumped toward the hall, where a figure stood in the shadows. Gasping, she did not move, the phone still stuck in her hand.

"Lay the phone down and keep your hands where I can see them," the man repeated.

Heart pounding, she placed the phone on the sofa as her eyes stayed glued to the figure. She recognized an accent, but could not distinguish the features. Gaze not wavering, she said nothing, waiting for him to speak again. Her body quivered with adrenaline and she swallowed deeply, willing her nerves to steady.

"You're not going to ask how I got in?"

She replied with a jerky shake of her head.

The figure stepped forward into the light and she recognized the young man. "Tariq," she stated with no surprise.

"Were you expecting me?"

Her stomach dropped as she nodded slowly while

she tried to discern if he had a weapon. He was not holding anything in his hands but a bulge in his jacket pocket appeared ominous. A smile spread across his handsome face as his black eyes bore into hers.

"Your man's system is good...real good...but I managed to get past it." When she made no comment, his lips pinched as he continued, "Just like I got by my *father's* work security system."

"Father? Fahdil?" she breathed, her voice exposing her nerves.

Sneering, Tariq repeated, "Yes, my *father*. I'm thankful he's not my real father or I'd be ashamed."

Her mind reeling, she sat trying to reconcile his words with his obvious disgust but understanding did not come. "I don't know what you want from me."

"I listened to him talk about the work he was doing...how you all were researching ways to keep us from being able to accomplish our great jihad." His face contorted as he continued, "From his emails, I was able to hack into his work, but only to a certain degree. I found someone who would help. Someone on the inside who wanted more...wanted to be more."

His words tangled inside her mind as she tried to piece together what he was saying. "Inside?" she asked.

Spit flew from his mouth as he growled, "Yes, *inside*, you stupid woman!" Moving a step closer he grinned, saying, "I just needed to ply him with alcohol and he let me know what Fahdil had not—you were the one whose research was the most dangerous to our cause. You needed to be taken out."

The two watched each other in silence for a

moment, before he chuckled. "You still don't get it, do you?"

Shaking her head, she replied, "No. No, I don't. I'm not the only one with research knowledge against bioterrorism. That is what we're talking about, isn't it?"

"Give the good doctor a gold star," he sneered again. "My group wanted to get to you before you had a chance to talk to the Olympic Committee." Leaning forward, he asked, "If we could take out either you or your father, then we could disrupt the work you are doing."

"Disrupt?"

Shrugging, he answered, "We kill you, your father wouldn't be able to go on for a while…if ever. If he was killed, then the same would happen to you. Either way, it furthers our cause."

"Your cause?"

"I was recruited in Louisiana and sent to Alaska. I was seen as having potential. Smart. Driven. None of the simple activities for me. No, I was destined for greatness."

"I'm not the only one researching. Why focus on me?"

"The ways to cause bioterrorism are well known," he said, stepping closer. "But the ways to counteract are more specific. Your research needed to be interrupted… halted. Our insider let us know that the rest of the group did not know all of your findings, as you were still working on them. I even know that what you just presented to Homeland Security is not complete until your theories are more researched."

"Who's on the inside?" she asked, this time her words barely a whisper.

"Oh, no," he chuckled. "This isn't like some stupid American movie where someone finds out everything right before they're killed."

All other thoughts flew out of Kendall's mind as soon as he spoke the word "killed". The roar of her blood rushing through her ears almost drowned out the audible pounding of her heart. She remembered the party Fahdil and his wife gave when Tariq first came to live with them. Nostrils flaring, she said, "You were given everything...everything! And you're throwing it all back in their faces."

"When a higher call comes, you answer it," Tariq clipped, his words harsh.

"If you've got your hands on my research, then what are you doing here?"

Irritation mixed with anger settled in his eyes. "I had help, but found that I was unable to get completely into your system. So the decision was made to get rid of you. And by getting rid of you, your father would soon follow."

Jumping to her feet at the mention of her father, she stood, hands clenched in fists as she eyed the man in front of her. "You won't get away with this. The FBI is already looking for you."

A slow smile curved his lips. "You still don't understand. Maybe I will get away...maybe not. But for me, death would only bring me honor."

"There's no honor if you're in prison," she bit back, unable to keep her anger in check.

"I won't end up in prison," he said, his smile reducing to a smirk as his dark eyes continued to bore into her.

The Saints rendezvoused at the end of Marc's long driveway. Jack jumped out, racing over to where Marc and Chad had just screeched to a halt. Grabbing Marc's arm, he held fast.

"Hold on! We've got Luke patched into your place. Tariq is in there. It's just he and Kendall and it appears they're in the living room. Tariq's got no idea that when he disabled the first round of security, it tripped the next level. Luke's sending the feed straight to Nick."

Marc felt the punch to his stomach as his heart fell. "Fuck," he breathed as anger penetrated every fiber of his being. Pulling his weapon out, he only managed to take one step before being faced with a line of Saints blocking him.

"Bro," Cam said calmly. "We do this smart. You know that. Fucked up missions happen because we get ahead of ourselves."

Marc's lips tightly pressed together as he fought to tell his fellow Saints to get out of his way, but he reined himself in. Jude and Bart slipped through the woods around to the left as Monty hustled toward the right. Monty, on the phone with the local FBI agent stepping in for Nick, filled him in on the situation.

Chad, a former bomb disposal expert, grabbed the suit Jack had brought for him. Looking at Marc's anguished face, he said, "Just being prepared, man. That's all."

Sucking in a deep breath before letting it out slowly, Marc's eyes cut over to Patrick as he called out, "Listen!"

Patrick turned up the volume on the receiver from Marc's security system and the group listened, Marc's heart pounding in frustration...and fear.

3 2

With only slightly more bravado than fear, Kendall asked, "What have you got planned?" Her eyes grew wide as she watched in terror as Tariq slowly unzipped his jacket. The bulge she had thought was in his pocket was actually an object taped to his waist. She swallowed hard as her mind raced to accept what her eyes were latched onto. "Wh…"

"Oh, I'm not planning on using this unless I have to," he stated, his gaze dropping to his belt. "I only plan on you dying and…" he cast his gaze around, his sneer back in place, "burning this place to the ground. I'll be long gone and this will just seem like an unfortunate accident."

"I thought you were supposed to make a statement," she bit back, the thought of his plans twisting around in her stomach.

"This is just in case there's no way out," he said, patting the object gently. "Unlike you, I'm not afraid to die. But as I said, that's not my intent. I still have much to do for my cause."

"Your cause?" Kendall asked, forcing her gaze to stay steady on his as her mind raced to think of a way to get away. *If I can get out of here, he'll have to follow me. I'm the one he wants.*

"I'm becoming necessary for my group," he bragged. "My skills with software, plus my family connections, made me the perfect person for this. And now," he waved his arm around, grinning, "killing you and then getting rid of your father will give me the perfect opportunity to stop the research."

"Even if Dad and I are gone, Fahdil will never help you," she exclaimed, her brow furrowed. "Surely you know that."

"Hmph, who needs him? You forget, I already have an ace in the hole there. Someone who has helped me in the past and will continue to assist."

Biting her lip as she allowed her gaze to drop slightly to keep an eye on his hands, she asked, "Who? Who is helping you?"

"Nope…told you, that was my secret. Enough talk—"

Tariq's phone vibrated and his gaze faltered as he moved to pull it out. Not recognizing the number, he hesitated before answering. "Yeah?"

Just as he brought the phone to his ear, Kendall shoved his shoulders, forcing him backwards over the coffee table.

Whirling around, she raced to the front door, fumbling with the deadbolt. Hearing Tariq cursing as he scrambled to his feet, she threw open the door.

Making it to the front porch, his voice shouted right behind her.

"Stop, bitch, or I will use this!"

She halted, her face contorted in frustration at her inability to get away. Just then she heard her name called and she lifted her head to look straight ahead. Heaving a gasp, she cried, "No! Marc, go away! He's got something strapped to him!"

Tariq's eyes darted around but he stayed in the door-frame, protected by the house behind and her body in front. With a satisfied smirk, he called out, "I've got it all planned out. You fools are too late."

Marc's weapon, raised toward Kendall who was in the direct line of fire between he and Tariq, watched as her anguished face never left his. She mouthed *I love you* as a tear slid down her cheek.

Shaking in fright, she wished she were braver, or at least knew what to do, but standing and staring at Marc's hard face was all she could accomplish. Hearing Tariq right behind her caused her to lose all thoughts except of the man who wanted her dead.

"Kendall?" Marc called out, but with a glance realized shock had rendered her slow to react. Sucking in a breath in an attempt at calm, he tried a different approach. "Hey, sweet girl?"

He watched her blink in recognition, her focus back on him. "That's it, sweet girl. You wanna know what I was just thinking of?"

She barely shook her head as Tariq screamed, "Shut up!"

"I was thinking about grizzlies in Canada. Remember?" He watched as her eyes lit and her breathing increased. *Atta girl. You've got it.*

With a quick blink, she flung herself down onto the hard wood of the porch, heedless of the pain flaring in her wrist and knees as the immediate sounds of shots whizzing overhead filled her ears. Then a thud behind her. Squeezing her eyes tight to brace for the explosion, she panted as her ears roared.

In an instant, Marc was scooping her up in his arms, racing back up the driveway toward Blaise as Chad approached the front. Monty and Jack escorted the FBI toward the house.

Her arms wound tightly around his neck as she buried her face in his neck. His warm skin with the scent of sweat felt familiar...and comforting. She was barely aware of Marc sitting down as he kept her safely tucked in his embrace.

"Kendall?" Blaise said gently. "Can you let me look at you?"

Raising her head slightly, she replied, "This is getting to be a habit, isn't it?"

Chuckling, Blaise said, "You're cracking a joke? Girl, you are something special if you can joke about this now!"

Swallowing back a nervous laugh, she loosened her arms but found Marc tightened his in response. "I'm fine, honestly. It's just my wrist and knees again. He didn't touch me. He just talked."

Jack, standing over them with several of the Saints around, added, "Very smart. You kept him talking. That gave us enough time to get here."

Blaise added, "Then, I'd say you're very lucky too, but I want to check your wrist again." He frowned as he unwrapped the bandage and saw more swelling. Shaking his head, he advised, "Marc, I think you might want to get this x-rayed, just to make sure this time you did not break it."

Marc nodded, his face tight with anger. "Damn, Kendall," he growled, "I'm so sorry."

Eyes wide, she held Marc's face in her hands and confessed, "I just knew you'd come for me. I knew you'd save me."

Forgetting their audience, Marc leaned in, his breath warm against her lips as he said, "Always, sweet girl. Always."

As the group from the NCBRT stood at the luggage pick-up in the Baton Rouge airport they chatted among themselves.

"Anyone hear from Fahdil?" Will asked.

Karen stood next to him but a respectable foot apart as her eyes cut over to his and she fought to keep a flirtatious smile from her lips.

Estelle, her lips in a typical pinch, said, "I simply got a text that said he had something come up and he would be taking a later flight."

Cliff, tapping his foot impatiently, glared at the luggage belt. "How long does it take to get the luggage off the plane," he grumbled.

"What's your hurry? You got somewhere important

to be?" Will laughed. "For me, I'm going to grab something to eat, hit the shower, and then fall into bed." Cutting his eyes toward Karen, he grinned as she blushed.

"Dr. Kowtowski?"

As the group turned toward the speaker, they saw four men in dark suits. All serious. No smiles. And all four holding out FBI badges.

Will's eyes darted to the side but he realized all avenues of escape had been cut off. Facing the speaker, he said, "Yes?"

"You need to come with us."

"What is this?" Estelle cut in, her attempts at superiority coming through. "I'm with Homeland Security for the National Center for Biological Research and Training. Dr. Kowtowski works at the center under me."

"Ma'am, then you'll be interested in our findings. We have evidence of Dr. Kowtowski illegally tampering with your security system, hiring the persons who broke into your center last week, and selling information to a known terrorist group."

"Will?" Karen stood shell-shocked, her mouth open.

"What the hell?" Cliff said, turning toward Will. "You goddamn traitor!"

Estelle's shoulders slumped at the realization her career was over with a traitor under her nose, her eyes closing for a moment as she pulled herself together. With a final sigh, she straightened her shoulders, casting her glare toward Will.

"I want a fucking lawyer," Will stated, his easy demeanor gone, defiance in its place.

"You'll get your chance," the agent said. "Now, if you'll come this way."

The luggage conveyor belt had started and passengers all around grabbed their bags, but Karen, Estelle, and Cliff stood frozen in place as they watched Will being escorted away.

33

TWO WEEKS LATER

Sitting in Jack's large living room, surrounded by all the Saints and their women, Kendall looked over at Marc as he stepped around a travel bassinet and scooped her up, plopping her down in his lap. Careful of her wrist, now in a brace, he handed her a glass of iced tea. Smiling her thanks, she cast her gaze around the large gathering, falling in love with the camaraderie all around.

"Any word on what's going on in Alaska?" she asked. Nudging Marc, she added, "This guy won't tell me much."

Jack nodded toward Marc and said, "There's not much we know to tell. I will say that the terrorist cell went underground and by the time the FBI closed in, they were only able to round up a few of them."

Moans came from the group as he continued, "It seems that once they realized Tariq had come to Virginia, acting on his own, the other members decided to go into hiding, uncertain what he was doing."

"So he wasn't acting on their orders?" Kendall asked.

"From what Nick has learned, he was not ordered to come after you. While you were initially a target, when it failed with the helicopter crash and you escaped they abandoned the plan and were going to focus on something else. Tariq disagreed and thought going after you by himself would win him a favorable status within the cell."

Shaking her head, she said, "I talked to my father and Fahdil is devastated. Even though it was Will, and not him, that was the traitor, he feels so responsible." Sighing heavily, she added, "He may be taken off certain projects." Throwing her hands up, she said, "And the whole group is stunned about Will. He was the last person anyone suspected."

"He was in debt up to his eyeballs several years ago and when Tariq approached him, the lure of money was too good to pass up," Charlie surmised.

The group fell into silence for a moment and Marc pulled Kendall's body back into his tightly.

"So," Faith asked, her smile landing on Kendall. "Have you decided what you're going to do?"

Grinning, she nodded as she felt Marc's arm squeeze her waist. "I've been to the University of Virginia and I've tentatively accepted their offer." Her grin broke into a wide smile as the cheers from all around hit her ears.

"And what about your job in Louisiana?" Sabrina asked. "Will that be a problem to leave?"

"Fortunately, I was working for Dad, who wants me to be happy, so it won't be hard. He's going to finish the latest round of research and then he might consider coming east as well. And," she shrugged, "my apartment was a rental, so it's no problem to leave."

Marc interjected, "We're going to fly back in a few days so that she can close everything out and we can arrange for movers to bring what she'd like to keep."

Blushing, Kendall observed the smiles and smirks from the group. "Yes, inquiring minds that want to know...I'm moving in with Marc."

Raised beers and iced teas toasted the new couple.

The next morning, Marc rolled over in bed, his hand finding the sheets cold where Kendall's body should have been. Smiling, he knew where she would be. Dressing quickly, he wandered to the kitchen where the coffee was already made and poured a cup. Stepping onto the front porch, he found her on the porch swing wrapped in blankets with the exception of one foot that stuck out, pushing against the plank floor to keep the swing in motion.

Bending to kiss her lips, he settled in next to her, pulling her close as she tucked her foot up underneath the covering, knowing he would now keep the swing going. Not speaking for a few moments, they watched the sun rise over the trees in the yard and the Blue Ridge Mountains in the distance. The peaceful quiet was broken only by the sounds of chattering birds and scampering squirrels.

Finally speaking, he said, "I remember my papaw telling me that I needed to find a good place to land when I was ready. He said that my mamaw was that place for him." He held her gaze as he continued with a smile, "Now that you're here with me, this is my place to land…"

Her smile rivaled the sunrise, capturing his heart.

Two Months Later

The setting sun slowly lowered in the sky as Angel and Monty said their vows in the gazebo at Bethany's Mountville Cabins. Kendall, sitting with Marc near the front, felt her heart would burst with happiness. Having completed the move, she was happily ensconced in her new job, her new home, and Marc's heart.

At the reception underneath a large tent, she held tightly to Marc as they swayed back and forth to the music. Unable to keep the smile from her face, she viewed her new friends, all huddled just as close on the dancefloor.

Marc lifted his gaze from her face, observing the other Saints as well. A sense of rightness filled his being…here with friends…here with Kendall. His gaze moved over the gathering, seeing Jack and Nick walk to the side of the large tent, deep in a private discussion. *Hmmmm, I wonder—*

Turning his attention back to the beautiful woman in his arms, he pulled her tighter against his chest, the warmth of her body fitting perfectly with his.

Looking up, she said, "Isn't it strange, the way our lives can turn so unexpectantly?"

"Like you and me?" he asked, nuzzling her ear.

Feeling his strong arms encircling her, she nodded. "Yeah…from a random meeting in an elevator to now. With all we went through, we survived."

"Thank God," he said, peering into her eyes. "Because I have to tell you…I love you, sweet girl."

Gasping, she sucked in her lips as tears threatened to fall. "I love you too," she breathed.

Bending down, he captured her lips like he captured her heart…completely.

Click here for the next Saint!
Celebrating Love

Don't miss any of my new releases! Sign up for my Newsletter

Cael

Jaxon

Jayden

Asher

Zeke

Cas

Lighthouse Security Investigations

Mace

Rank

Walker

Drew

Blake

Tate

Levi

Clay

Cobb

Hope City (romantic suspense series co-developed

with Kris Michaels

Brock book 1

Sean book 2

Carter book 3

Brody book 4

Kyle book 5

Ryker book 6

Rory book 7

Killian book 8

Torin book 9

Saints Protection & Investigations

(an elite group, assigned to the cases no one else wants…or can solve)

Serial Love

Healing Love

Revealing Love

Seeing Love

Honor Love

Sacrifice Love

Protecting Love

Remember Love

Discover Love

Surviving Love

Celebrating Love

Searching Love

Follow the exciting spin-off series:

Alvarez Security (military romantic suspense)

Gabe

Tony

Vinny

Jobe

SEALs

Thin Ice (Sleeper SEAL)

SEAL Together (Silver SEAL)

Undercover Groom (Hot SEAL)

Also for a Hope City Crossover Novel / Hot SEAL…

A Forever Dad by Maryann Jordan

Letters From Home (military romance)

Class of Love

Freedom of Love

Bond of Love

The Love's Series (detectives)

Love's Taming

Love's Tempting

Love's Trusting

The Fairfield Series (small town detectives)

Emma's Home

Laurie's Time

Carol's Image

Fireworks Over Fairfield

Please take the time to leave a review of this book. Feel free to contact me, especially if you enjoyed my book. I love to hear from readers!

Facebook

Email

Website

ABOUT THE AUTHOR

I am an avid reader of romance novels, often joking that I cut my teeth on the historical romances. I have been reading and reviewing for years. In 2013, I finally gave into the characters in my head, screaming for their story to be told. From these musings, my first novel, Emma's Home, The Fairfield Series was born.

I was a high school counselor having worked in education for thirty years. I live in Virginia, having also lived in four states and two foreign countries. I have been married to a wonderfully patient man for thirty-five years. When writing, my dog or one of my four cats can generally be found in the same room if not on my lap.

Please take the time to leave a review of this book. Feel free to contact me, especially if you enjoyed my book. I love to hear from readers!

Facebook
Email
Website

Made in the USA
Coppell, TX
21 January 2022

72059551R00218